THE LONG BLACK

J. M. ANJEWIERDEN

J M äj

To Leighton & Hamilton

enjoy!

THE LONG BLACK

BOOK ONE

OF

THE BLACK CHRONICLES

BY

J. M. ANJEWIERDEN

CJMA PRESS

Published by CJMA Press, Salt Lake City, UT.

Cover art from SelfPubBookCovers.com/Daniela

Editing by Christina Anjewierden

First Edition

FOR CHRISSY

PART 1
THE DEEP BLACK

CHAPTER 01

Many of my colleagues point to the loss of Sol as the catalyst for the descent of so many worlds into barbarism and cruelty. One only need to look to the history of the planet Hillman, and its graveyards masquerading as mines, to put that notion to rest.

- Professor Alfred Sagendorf, Royal University of Ena, Albion, Parlon System.

THE GROANING OF the corn stalks under their own weight was almost audible to Morgan. She could understand how they felt. The plants had not evolved to survive under twice standard gravity. Then again, neither had little girls.

Heavy gravity or no, Earth people had to eat Earth food, or near enough. Corn was one of the few crops that could grow at all in the alien soil of the planet Hillman, so corn it was.

One necessary thing lead to another, unintended consequences piled up, and here was Morgan, slaving away in the muggy summer air. There was no sun overhead, just the pale light that diffused through the thick cloud cover. For a close-orbiting planet like Hillman, those clouds made the difference between bursting into flames and tolerably hot. For some values of tolerable, at any rate.

Despite the oppressive heat, everyone kept their thick padded coveralls on. It was better to suffer the heat than get innumerable cuts from the sharp leaves of the corn. They still got cuts on their hands, of course. The children too young to work trudged back and forth along the rows bringing water to the workers. They were wearing little more than shoes and worn out coveralls cut into shorts. Many things were lacking on Hillman, but space outside the towns wasn't one of them, so the corn rows were widely separated. Not for the littles' sake, of course, but that of the guards, who had removed their shirts as they walked up and down the fields.

For once Morgan wasn't annoyed that despite 'becoming a woman,' as her momma put it, she hadn't developed enough to need a bandeau under her coveralls. She didn't want to imagine how much hotter that made the other women. Of course this also meant she'd have to leave it completely on once they headed back to town. By then the sun would have set, so it shouldn't be unbearable.

Presently, Morgan was trudging along behind the men sticking aluminum poles into the hard soil. Her job, as well as the job of all the boys and girls not yet full adults, was to tie the stalks to the poles. It was slightly more difficult than it sounded. She had to ensure that the weight of the stalk didn't tear the knot loose, nor lie in such a way that it would turn the tie into a dull saw blade.

It was boring, repetitive, and tedious. In other words, it was heaven compared to her normal duties.

All children twelve and older – by the Hillman local year – were expected to work. For the majority, this meant a year being taught how to maintain the mining equipment and portable generators. After that, they spent eight years of scrambling around the access tunnels on hands and

4

knees.

Those that survived were married and then assigned a job. For almost all of the men, this meant working the main shafts. Women ended up in the bakeries, factories, and other support jobs. At least, when they didn't have small children to care for.

"Look alive there," a guard said, prodding Morgan with one end of his heavy baton. It was one of the guards that worked Morgan's shift in shaft 3B. Six years in the shaft and she'd never learned his name. Officer Thirty-Four was all she ever called him to his face. 'Tin-Badged Tyrant' was how she always thought of him. She was hardly unique in thinking of the 'Tinnys' that way. Looking them in the eye tended to be taken as a challenge, so Morgan didn't look up as she finished on her current stalk.

This also meant most people learned to recognize the different guards by their stature and build, more than their faces, especially in the mines where everyone wore helmets. Right now what stood out most about Thirty-Four was the fact that his arms and chest were completely free of scars.

When she was little, she'd heard all the stories of the voracious predators that lived beyond the walls of Pari Passu and the other towns of the region, though she had yet to see one. Every time they came out to the fields, the town's 'Voice of the Comradery' would show them a holo of them, great ravening beasts with long teeth and longer claws. She then reminded the workers to be diligent and alert so they could finish work as quickly as possible and return to the safety of town. But more than that, she also went on and on about all the risks and dangers the brave guards took keeping their comrades safe, and how everyone was equal but extra risks required extra support.

The first time Morgan had come out to carry water, a year or so before starting in the mines, she'd been relieved that the guards were there. Then she noticed how they watched the people, rather than the edges of the field where it backed up against the thick forest.

She asked Daddy who the guards were watching, the workers or the animals. 'Yes,' was the only answer he gave, but Daddy was odd like that sometimes.

"You can go faster than that," Thirty-Four prodded her again in the ribs, hard enough this time that it hurt. Morgan turned and glared at him for a moment, careful to look at his mouth rather than his eyes, before moving on to the next corn stalk. He grunted at her, almost a growl. "Am I supposed to be scared? What your father does doesn't make any difference for you. A spoiled child like you needs to remember that you're no better than anyone else."

Tinnys hardly needed an excuse to come down hard on the workers, especially the mere tunnel rats, but Thirty-Four had taken a particular dislike to Morgan. She didn't think she had caused it in any way, especially since it had started almost the moment they met. No, he obviously had a problem with her daddy. Whatever it was, he was taking it out on her.

Her mood somewhat soured Morgan grimaced and got back to work. There was no way to know how much longer they would be out here, with neither the progress of the sun to watch or something as basic as clocks, but there was undoubtedly more ahead of her than behind.

✳✳✳

Thankfully the rest of the work went without incident. There hadn't even been any animal sightings. The lot of them stumbled and staggered back towards town, the guards making up the fore and rear of the ragged column, while the strongest men carefully carried the exhausted children.

At least their surroundings were moderately pleasant. To the north and south were the massive forests. Daddy had told Morgan that the trees had originated on Earth, introduced some three centuries before and aggressively supported with new imports up until contact had been lost with Sol. They were hearty oaks and pines for the most part, trees that were tough enough to push for the sky despite the gravity. Without any real competition or diseases, they had grown quickly, to the point that timber was now the planet's only export that wasn't tied to the mines. Hillman wood was apparently highly prized for its dense, durable nature.

The path was only marked with metal stakes painted white every few meters. Keeping it cleared was wasted effort as the path, along with the entirety of the plains below, was carpeted with the native analog of grass. It was closer to a moss than anything, a soft spongy plant that spread out like a two centimeter carpet across everything, rocks and dirt alike.

At the moment it was seed season and you couldn't go barefoot on it, thanks to the spikey winged spores the moss produced. But the rest of the year it was quite comfortable for walking and lying on. There wasn't much in the way of insect life on Hillman, at least not of any noticeable size. The few there were seemed to consider humans inedible, thankfully.

About a kilometer out from the town wall they passed under one of the wide supports for the elevated train tracks, connecting Pari Passu to the central shuttle launching facility. Craning her neck, Morgan followed the magnetic rails until they disappeared from sight at the base of the mountain. She liked watching the trains loaded with ore whirr past, a reminder that they weren't completely cut off from the rest of the universe.

He didn't talk about it much, but Morgan knew that Daddy had helped design and build the rails, modified from the systems used on friendlier planets. He was the only one in the town that had worked on the project. Now he repaired the equipment in the factories while the rest of the designers and engineers lived in the capital or, if they were really important, the space station above it.

The miners didn't talk to him much, but that just meant he had more time to talk with Morgan. He told her all kinds of things the miners didn't even guess at. His hours were longer than anyone's, the backlog of machines no one else knew how to fix never ending. In two days he'd even head up to the station to work on something or other, and he wouldn't be back for at least a week. Six whole days with no stories, no impromptu lessons about fixing things, Morgan frowned at the thought.

"You know we all hate it, right?" a feminine voice said from right behind Morgan.

Morgan lurched forward, startled, and then turned to glare at the speaker.

"Jane. I didn't see you there."

Jane was another of the workers on Morgan's shift, a year older or so, and probably the tallest tunnel rat on the whole planet, around 150 centimeters. She was also just about the only friend Morgan had.

"Yep. Too busy staring at the prison gate."

Morgan's brow furrowed.

"Huh?"

"Never heard it called that?"

Morgan shook her head.

"Before that thing, freighters had to land shuttles up here."

"And?"

"And I have a brother out there." She gestured heavenward in a general way. "He escaped on one of those shuttles. A lot of people did. They took that from us."

"I. . . "

Jane cut her off with another wave of her hand, "Oh, people don't blame *him*. He's down here suffering with us, isn't he? But every time we see that or hear it go by it's a reminder that we can't escape."

"No one talks about it."

"Why bother? 'Hey kids? There used to be a way out of here, but it's gone now. So sad.'"

"You knew."

"Mom talks about my brother sometimes."

"Do you miss him?"

Jane shrugged. "It was before I was born. I'm glad he got out, I guess. Makes me hate them more though."

"The Tinnys?"

"Well, sure, but everyone else up there too." She pitched her voice lower, though she had already been speaking quietly. "Comrade Father and the 'essential workers.'"

A heavy hand fell on Morgan's shoulder, its twin on Jane's shoulder a moment later.

"Stop gossiping and pick up the pace." It was Thirty-Four again, his deep voice practically growling.

The pair muttered the appropriate half-hearted agreements and started walking again, feeling lucky that he hadn't overheard what they were talking about. As he stalked off, Thirty-Four glared at Morgan before leering at Jane. Jane just turned her head and ignored him, but Morgan could see her face heat up, even in the dim light of dusk. Jane was so pale she was almost translucent and even a hint of a blush stood out markedly. Morgan did not have that problem with her decidedly duskier complexion.

As they trudged on, Jane zipped back up the top of her coverall, clasping her hands together so the too-long sleeves met, leaving only her neck and head visible.

It was just as well they had stopped talking, as it wasn't too long before they passed the oldest mine shaft on the planet. Everyone, Tinnys included, didn't want to linger too long there. The pace picked up noticeably.

The town's wall had been constructed with the rocks pulled from that mine in the first hardscrabble days, a ten meter tall construction of native stone and mortar. It was ugly, all odd angles and barely fit together rocks. Most people could forget where it had come from, or at least pretend they did, but it was harder to ignore when passing the actual mine. This mine, alone among all the shafts, had its own wall, fifteen meters tall and topped with razor wire.

It hadn't been a very productive or efficient mine, as the colonists essentially made their methods up as they went, lacking any training or experience in mining. Fortunately the planet had enough heavy and rare metals to keep the colony supplied via trade until it could get its feet under it. In that capacity the mine had literally saved the utopian colony that had fled Earth in the early days of the jump gates. Thanks to the quirks of space travel, it had actually been quicker to use a jump gate to come to Hillman than to make a round trip to Sol's asteroid belt. There were plenty of metals on Hillman usually only found in large quantities on asteroids.

History wasn't something The Voice encouraged anyone to learn or think about, however, so most of the town didn't know anything about it. No, everyone avoided Shaft One because of what it was currently used for.

Simply put, the mines of Hillman were dangerous at the best of times, and that was never truer than for that first haphazard shaft. It was too risky for normal workers, so it had been converted into a prison, with all of the scattered towns of Hillman sending their hardened criminals there to serve their sentences. 'Lengthy' was the best way to describe those sentences, but also the worst. Good behavior and above-quota production reduced these sentences, something even the most anti-social of prisoner was eager to do in a mine with such a high accident rate.

The planet as a whole had some millions of inhabitants, but there were no cities, no urban sprawls. People in a town knew almost everyone else, at least by reputation, and everyone knew someone who had ended up in S1. No one, in Pari Passu at least, knew anyone who had made it back out.

Just inside the gate was the large commissary where the town took its meals. Like almost all of the buildings, it was square with a flat roof. No windows, no frills, just poured concrete and metal doors with a row of chimneys along the back wall for the ovens.

As the long group of workers filed into the building the familiar smell of soup washed over Morgan. She smiled and breathed in deeply. This is where Momma worked, and the smell always reminded Morgan of her.

Jane smiled and waved goodbye as she darted off toward a group of tunnel rats loudly chatting at one of the closer tables. Her shift in the mine started four hours after Morgan's, so she wasn't in as much of a rush. Morgan just wanted to get some food and get home to her bed.

As small as the town was the mines were worked 28/6, all forty weeks of the year. There wasn't any sense of day or night in the mine of course, but even on the surface the difference between night and day was much less pronounced.

Morgan had never seen it, but Hillman had a massive moon that was just shy of being a twin planet. It was an airless white rock reflecting enough light onto Hillman to make the night only marginally dimmer than the already dim day.

The line moved forward quickly, easily accomplished when everyone got the same food in the same amounts.

Momma was at the end of the counter today, handing out bread.

"Well, there you are Morgan. How did working the fields go?"

Morgan shrugged. There wasn't exactly time for a conversation, after all.

Momma smiled, though it didn't quite reach her eyes. "A change of pace, at least." Her voice got more serious as she steadily ignored the other worker gesturing towards the line of people. "Your father had to go fix something in ore processing. I don't think he'll be home before morning.

Morgan's heart sank. It wasn't just that she wouldn't see Daddy until after her shift in the mines. This meant that there was no one at home. And that meant. . .

". . .You'll just need to stay there until I get out of here."

"It's summer time. It'll be roasting in there." Morgan tried to keep her tone level, but her voice rose in pitch in spite of her efforts.

"Morgan."

"I'll be careful. No one will know I'm there."

"No."

Morgan opened her mouth to argue, and then closed it again.

"Yes, Momma."

"We've had this talk. We can't have it again now. You can't act like you're a little girl anymore." Each point was emphasized with a wave of the loaf of bread momma held.

Out of the corner of her eye Morgan could see one of the Tinnys starting to walk over, probably wondering why the line wasn't moving. Hurriedly she snatched the bread from Momma's hand and walked off towards an empty table.

"Bye, Momma," she said quietly, her voice low.

If she had been asked at that point, Morgan wouldn't have been able to name a single good thing about growing up. It was so completely not worth it in her opinion. She couldn't be home alone, she had to be more careful where she went and who was around her, and on and on.

Not that she *felt* all that different, well, most of the time anyway. She didn't even think she looked all that different, certainly not when compared to Jane, at any rate. At the same time she had to deal with the apparent determination of boys near her age to be as stupid as possible. Morgan was almost convinced they were literally competing with each other to see who could take it the farthest.

Still, her parents were clearly worried, so Morgan didn't dare ignore them. There were times that she wondered if her parents really understood her at all, but she wasn't silly enough to think that there weren't things they did understand better than she did.

Since she was already eating into her sleep time Morgan just sat at the first empty table and dug into her food. It tasted fine, or at least did at the speed she was eating it.

Shoving the remains of her bread into a pocket, Morgan dumped the tray and utensils in the return chute and headed out, setting as brisk a pace as her aching legs permitted. That was another of the downsides to working the fields; she used different muscles walking about all day than she did crawling about in the tunnels.

The town was laid out with the homes opposite from the gate, tucked behind a smaller fence. Well, most of the homes. The Tinnys lived in small buildings scattered about the rest of the town. Officially, that was so they were near the factories and so on in case something happened, but even the kids younger than Morgan knew it was to keep them out of the reach of the miners when they weren't working.

The corollary to this was that it was illegal for anyone to hang around in town anywhere outside the living areas. Officially, this was because of the danger of bystanders being hurt in any potential work accident. Unofficially, it was just another way to control them.

The inner wall separating the homes from the rest of the town had a gate, not that Morgan had ever seen it closed. Given how much moss had grown up against it she wasn't sure it even could close at this point.

In front of the gate was the single biggest object in town, towering over the factories by ten meters or more and positively dwarfing the squat dwellings beyond. A single massive block of native stone had been carved over years into the likeness of Sam Hill, the founder of Hillman and the beloved Eternal Father.

Morgan had her doubts that he had really looked quite so. . . statuesque, but then again, living on a high gravity world certainly helped people stay in shape and build muscle, so maybe he had.

The statue was dressed in the same coveralls they all wore, though the statue's clothes fit rather better than they did on the actual miners. Morgan had heard a few of the miners grousing that the statue was the closest he'd ever gotten to the mines, but that was – for once – actually unfair to the man. However things were now, in the beginning everyone had worked equally. They wouldn't have survived otherwise.

As she passed, Morgan touched the small bit of stone jutting out from the base as she passed by. It had been left unworked intentionally, and was slowly being smoothed and rounded as the people touched it each day as they came and went.

When she had been little Morgan had asked Daddy why they had left that bit, and he'd explained that it was supposed to represent how everyone working together was what hat built the colony, not just the Eternal Father. Morgan thought it was actually a really nice touch, with the added benefit that it reminded Morgan that even something as broken as Hillman still had its good side.

A steady stream of other people headed home, some going faster than her, others slower, but they were all just as tired as Morgan, nothing but a bunch of individuals shuffling along looking at their feet. Tonight the unity the statue was supposed to represent was conspicuously absent.

The nearer buildings were the multi-family ones, big enough to fit three or four couples and all of their kids. These made up the majority of the structures, and helped the mothers take turns watching the children.

All the way to the back were the smaller huts for everyone else, those with grown children and those who didn't have any yet, widows, and the assorted others who didn't fit the mold. As far as she knew Morgan was the only one living in that part of town who wasn't an adult. Morgan didn't know why her parents weren't in a group home, but she suspected it had something to do with the reasons behind Morgan being their only child. She would have liked to know those reasons, but the pained look on Momma's face when she had finally asked had kept her from asking again.

As she turned onto the haphazard lane of moss that ran past the doors of that lane, including her own, Morgan heard voices chatting down the way.

Grumbling Morgan turned aside and headed around back of the line of huts. This rule was iridium-clad. No one was to see her coming and going when her parents weren't home. No matter that, as far as she could hear, it was just Betty and Valerie sitting in a doorway talking about bygone years.

For as long as she could remember a flock of hens had lived between her home and the adjacent house, nests patched together with torn up bits of moss and various bits of trash the birds had appropriated. While corn was grown because it could actually survive Hillman they kept chickens because they thrived.

The video record of the landing on Hillman – which they watched every year on Founder's Day – had included some footage of the animals Sam Hill had brought with them. The only ones Morgan recognized were the chickens, for the simple fact that they were the only animal still found in the towns. Even then, compared to the animals in the recording, the chickens milling about were gargantuan, bigger and stronger in every way. It certainly didn't hurt that they apparently found the local moss downright delicious, or at least parts of the plant.

A couple of the chickens wandered over as Morgan trudged past them, cocking their heads at her. Morgan smiled. It didn't matter how many times she'd seen them do that, the hens were silly things. Unfortunately, they were silly things who also had sharp beaks and claws. It was just as well Morgan didn't have the job of collecting the laid eggs.

Still, a small distraction was in order. Luckily, Morgan had planned ahead. Out of her pocket she grabbed the crumbs of her dinner along with whatever other bit of debris had been lurking in there, tossing it off towards their nests.

Losing interest in her completely, the hens went after the food, ruffling their feathers with some loud clucking for good measure. Morgan wondered if they kept coming over because they were territorial or because she fed them. As she approached the back window of her home she decided she'd rather not know than find out the hard way it was the former. Especially with the red one Morgan had mentally dubbed Bertha. That hen had been there for as long as she could remember, and was probably older than Morgan was.

From the outside, their family hut looked fairly spacious for only three people, especially when put up against the family homes that held upwards of a dozen or even twenty people, but this was somewhat deceptive. For one thing, the largest room was dedicated to the tools Daddy used in his work. Two small sleeping rooms, a bathing room, some small storage space and the large common room rounded out the building, and combined took up slightly more space than the tool room.

The tool room was also the only room of the house that had a locking mechanism. Indeed, it was the only room in any of the houses Morgan knew about that did. That was why Morgan didn't head for the back door, but to the small window next to it, after checking to make sure no one was around. It also locked, but Daddy had long since shown Morgan the trick to opening it. Once it was open Morgan pulled herself through the small opening onto the empty table pushed up against it. Securing the window behind her, Morgan hopped down from the table onto the floor. She sank a couple centimeters into the foam floor, the same padding that edged all of the rounded tables and chairs.

The first thing Morgan did was lean against the table and pull off her boots and socks. She plopped them on the floor under the table, right at home among the months and years of accumulated dirt and rocks dislodged from her boots day after day.

Padding over to the door in her bare feet, Morgan sat and listened for long seconds before unlocking it and peering into the rest of her home. The building's exterior reflected heat well enough, but it was still hot and humid in the house, the smell of the moss outside mingling with the oil and metal tang of the tools.

Moving purposefully, Morgan grabbed her improvised nightgown. It was a discarded pair of coveralls that Momma had cut the legs and most of the arms off of, as well as the inner layers of padding. It had been Daddy's, so it still hung down to her knees, and was patched and mended in many places. It smelled of Daddy rather than the mine though, which was comforting for Morgan.

Since she didn't have any scrapes or cuts serious enough to need tending, Morgan just took a quick shower. The water was welcome after the day's work, the persistent itch she'd been ignoring from the grime and dirt giving way to a dull numbness from the cold water.

The water was always cold, no matter how hot it got outside. In an effort to reduce evaporation and wasted water, the storage tanks were buried deep below the buildings. Chattering teeth and numb skin were viewed as acceptable losses to efficiency, if they were thought about at all. Of course the cold also dispelled much of her drowsiness, but it was still better than going to bed dirty.

Shoving her dirty clothes into the basin to soak, Morgan returned to the tool room, locking the door behind her.

Yawning she walked around the various benches and racks of tools, as well as a couple tables littered with dismantled bits of machinery Daddy was working on. She stopped when she reached the wall opposite from the window. It was dominated by a long row of larger tools in inset hooks, the tops of which were a half meter or so above her head.

Crouching down, Morgan pushed against the edge of the mounting which gave way after a few moments. Folding it down revealed a narrow compartment – perhaps two meters long and a bit less than a meter deep. Since the rack had been placed there after the room was finished, it still had the foam beneath. This was just as well, as it served tolerably well as a mattress. The pillow and sheet had been added later, as had the tiny doll made from scraps of clothing and stuffed with padding.

Morgan crawled in with a sigh, easily moving the mounting back in place with the help of small handles concealed on the inside surface. At her head and feet the sides of the tool rack had been modified to replace the original paneling with a tight mesh, vastly improving the airflow through the small space.

The airflow didn't help much with the heat, but the metal construction of the rack did, acting as an impromptu sink for Morgan's body heat. That helped less when the ambient temperature of the whole building was already high, as it was then, but it was still better than nothing.

Lying with her back to the wall, Morgan closed her eyes and tried to clear her mind, wishing she could fall asleep faster.

CHAPTER 02

It is true that many thieves do it to survive. They can be rehabilitated, certainly. Make no mistake though; there are 'people' out there who do it for no other reason than because they can. To them we're just as much things as the trinkets they'll harm others for.

- Police Chief Jacob Watanabe, Danan province, planet Trimbol.

IT TOOK A LOT to wake Morgan up when she slept in the hidden compartment. She wasn't a heavy sleeper. Not by any means. However, outside sounds simply didn't reach her in the enclosed hidey-hole.

So to say that she was startled to be woken by a loud banging noise coming from the other room was somewhat an understatement. Without any conscious thought she froze, barely breathing as she listened intently. It was hard to be sure, but it certainly sounded like someone was messing around with the tool room door. Morgan told herself that it was just Momma back from her shift, and maybe she'd dropped the key or something.

The banging came again, this time accompanied by the door rattling a bit on its hinges. The faint hope that it was Momma or Daddy vanished as whoever it was grunted, muttering something that sounded like a curse.

"Keep it down. Neighbors." The voice was muffled, of course, but

Morgan could at least tell it wasn't someone she knew.

"Must be valuable. Good lock."

The door rattled again, but without the banging this time. With everything else momentarily quiet she could hear something scratching at the handle, poking around in the workings.

They weren't in yet. If she could get to the window, run to the next house. . .

Panic welled up in Morgan's chest, her breathing quickening at the mere thought. She'd have to navigate the whole of the cluttered room first. They'd surely hear her, and the back door was a few steps from where they stood. Even if she got to the window she'd still have to grab her boots and get them on. She wouldn't make it a dozen steps barefoot across the moss, not in seeding season.

But if she stayed where she was there was nowhere to run, nothing to protect herself with. Daddy had designed it to be secret. Secret and quiet, but it had never been tested. What if they heard?

Morgan had expected to hear the click when they got the door unlocked, but she didn't. Her only warning was the door creaking while it swung inwards. Morgan could feel her body shaking, but she put all of her focus into breathing as quietly as she could. She was sure they were going to hear the pounding of her heart, but there was nothing she could do about that.

There was nothing she could do at all.

"What is all this stuff?" The voice wasn't muffled anymore. They were in the room with her.

"You idiot. You forget everything from being a tunnel rat? Tools."

"Oh. Yeah. Why lock that up?"

"Eh, just a front. There has to be something hidden."

"Where do we start?"

"Here, dummy."

Every moment they dug about in the chests and racks was unbearable, the noise ever so slowly getting closer to where Morgan lay.

What started as careful searching, clinks and thuds as tools were picked up and moved, was gradually replaced with wholesale clatter as the carefully organized instruments were shoved to the side or dumped onto the floor.

They were still meters away when Morgan could smell them, the musty dust of the mines mixed with the whiskey made with any excess corn each season. Wrinkling her nose Morgan tried to ignore it, but it felt like it was saturating the air, choking her. All she could do was bury her face in her pillow and hope they got frustrated enough to leave.

Morgan was trying to track them through the room, but the soft nature of the floor worked against her. They seemed to have no definite pattern to how they were ransacking the room. They were lurching from one spot to the next, bypassing areas Morgan would have thought obvious, only to go back to them halfway through whatever they were digging through.

And then they got to the rack above her.

"What are these massive pieces of junk?"

"Probably for the fabbers."

The rack vibrated, one of the tools moving in its mount.

"Valuable then?"

"Sure, but who would buy it?"

"Useless then." One of them kicked the rack. The rack as a whole didn't move much, but the false panel shifted on its mounting.

Afraid it would come loose, Morgan grabbed for the handles, her knuckles bouncing off the metal as she fumbled about for the straps.

"What was that?"

"What?"

"Is something loose in there?"

They kicked the rack again, but this time the panel didn't move as much with Morgan holding onto it.

"There's nothing here."

Something smashed into the opposite wall, thrown no doubt, hitting something else metal as it fell to the floor.

"Let's go. Running out of time anyway."

Running out of time or not, the pair didn't seem to be in a hurry. The noise they made as they retraced their footsteps out of the room was much more cacophonous than their searching had been in. It sounded like they were throwing about everything they could get their hands on, even tipping over tables and containers.

At last silence fell, announced with the almost quiet closing of the back door. Morgan slowly let go of the handles. She suppressed a wince as she realized just how badly they had been digging into her hands thanks to her death grip on them. She did not, however, try to open the compartment.

In fact she waited, as best as she could determine in the dark confines of her hiding place, a half hour or so before trying it.

Letting out her breath in one big worried *whuff*, shuddering from anticipation and paranoia, Morgan pushed out on the panel. . .

. . .only for it to budge a few centimeters at most. Shoving harder Morgan was rewarded with a lot of noise, metal and foam and wood banging against each other, but the panel didn't move any farther out.

Several more attempts yielded identical results. Something must have fallen against it, pinning the panel between the rack and whatever had fallen against it.

Morgan was quite strong, especially for her size, but then again pretty much everyone was when you lived on a world with twice Earth's gravity. Leverage, however, was another issue entirely.

Wiggling about in the narrow confines she braced her back against the panel. She then worked her feet up against the opposite side, just barely possible if she wedged her knees all the way up against her chest. Morgan took a few slow measured breaths then pushed. She started off modestly enough, slowly ramping up the force. More groaning from the metal, but there was still no give.

Or at least none in the panel. Morgan could feel her muscles straining, her vertebrae popping as she shifted a bit and threw more into the effort.

Abruptly the bottom half of the panel slid outwards, accompanied by a metallic grating sound of whatever was holding it in place shifting. The frame kept the top half from moving inwards, and the opening wasn't nearly big enough for Morgan to fit through.

It *was* big enough that Morgan's back slipped, throwing off her whole body. Her right ankle rolled inwards, exploding in pain.

Morgan screamed, biting her lip to stop herself, hard enough that her teeth cut into it. She could taste blood, but the pain of her torn lip didn't register above her screaming ankle. She froze, half expecting to hear the men coming back, to have heard her.

The ankle certainly felt sprained, but it was hard to be sure. Thankfully, it didn't feel like it was broken, but that was all she was willing to assume at the moment.

Turning about she propped her rapidly swelling ankle up on her other leg. In an attempt to distract herself and because she was still trapped, Morgan went back to work on the panel.

When the panel had shifted, whatever it was holding it in place had shifted as well. So, Morgan had more wiggle room to work with. She worked it back and forth, moving it in and out, coaxing the blockage to shift. At last it fell to the floor with a muted thump, letting Morgan see that it was one of the longer attachments for Daddy's largest power-spanner. Finally, she wasn't trapped. Morgan reached out the opening and shoved the tool out of the way. . . and promptly closed the panel again. There wasn't anywhere to go, after all. There were some bandages in the main room she could put on her ankle, but she didn't see any way to get to them without hurting her ankle worse. This was especially true with all the stuff littering the floor of the tool room, making even crawling out imprudent.

Gingerly, Morgan straightened herself out, tucking the pillow between her legs with the bulk under her injured ankle before balling up the sheet under her head. A few tears dropped onto it, and Morgan blinked furiously. There was nothing to do now but wait. Steadying her breathing she tried to tune out the pain. It took time, but at last she managed to get back to sleep.

***

The sound of the door opening and tools and furniture being shifted about didn't wake Morgan up this time. The hand on her shoulder did the job right quick though. She started awake, her body moving before her brain had even had a chance to understand the signals it was receiving. Luckily such a response had been expected. One hand kept Morgan from banging her head against the ceiling as the other kept a firm grip on her shoulder. Of course this left no hands to keep her ankle from hitting the back wall, even if they had noticed its swollenness. Morgan clenched her teeth tightly as the pain woke her up the rest of the way. The lingering drowsiness helped damper it somewhat, at least.

"Easy, Baby Girl. It's just me," Momma said, scooping Morgan into a hug. She had lain on the floor in front of the tool rack, her knees bent so she could fit in the cramped space. "Are you all right? What happened? Did they find you?"

"I'm all right," Morgan said. "I'm all right," she repeated the words, for emphasis.. She returned the hug tightly. Momma started pulling her out into the room. "Careful," Morgan amended as she was jostled about. Morgan didn't, however, loosen her grip. "My ankle."

"Oooh," Momma said as she released Morgan from the hug and moved so she could look at the ankle. "Sprained, maybe. Let's have a look at it." Standing up, Momma helped Morgan slide out into the room, then hoisted her up onto her back with Morgan's head resting against her shoulder and her legs dangling to either side of her.

It was Morgan's first chance to see everything that had happened. The room was in more disarray than she had expected. She couldn't see a single tool where it was supposed to be, and the floor was littered with the fallen instruments. It didn't look like Momma had bothered to pick any of them up, settling instead for scooting stuff out of the way to make a path from the door to the hidden hidey-hole.

Momma grunted. "You're getting big, Morgan. You grow any taller and I won't be able to do this anymore." Morgan didn't reply, content for the moment to hug Momma tightly, the smell of sweat and corn soup comforting as they slowly made their way out into the main room.

Carefully, Momma put Morgan down on the table in the main room, with the injured leg carefully placed so the ankle was just barely hanging off the edge. Out in the light of the main room it was easy to see that the ankle was not only swollen but had turned red. In a day or so it was going to be a spectacular bruise.

"Sit tight while I get the medicine," Momma said, ducking under the clothes and bits of cloth hanging from the ceiling next to the table.

"Can't you just wrap it?" Morgan asked, grimacing.

"Not if you want it to heal quickly, or for it to be stable enough to walk on in the morning." Momma pulled a small jar of Quicknit ointment from the back cabinet. There wasn't much there besides some vitamin D shots, bandages, and pads. Morgan added a wrinkled nose to the grimace. Most of her least favorite things, all in one cabinet.

Momma applied some of the ointment to her hands, resting them gingerly on Morgan's ankle. "At least it won't sting like it does with cuts," she said with a small half smile.

"I think moving my ankle will make up for that on its own."

"Deep breath," Momma told Morgan, giving her a bare two seconds before starting.

Morgan had learned the hard way not to bite her lip to keep from crying out for this part, clenching her teeth as the ointment was rubbed into her skin, each movement of her ankle a fresh stab of pain.

Her comments to the contrary, Morgan knew the pain was worth it. The ointment was one of the critical things traded for from other worlds, a real miracle drug designed to substantially speed up healing and prevent infections. It even – once given some time to work – dulled the pain. Every family was provided with some, though using it on unimportant things was a serious offense.

If the ointment had the rest of the night to work on her ankle, Morgan actually would be able to go to her job, as long as she was careful.

"All right, done," momma said, holding her sticky hands out so she wouldn't touch anything. "Now let's do the little things. No sense wasting it."

Morgan pushed up the sleeves of her nightgown the rest of the way up, pointing Momma to a few thin cuts on her arms. "Just some small ones from the corn leaves today," she said, pointing out a couple more on her legs once momma finished with her arms.

"Right, now your back," Momma said, rubbing the last of it in as Morgan pulled up the back of her nightgown. No cuts there, for the moment anyway, but the ointment would help her tense muscles at least a little bit, as well as her lungs.

With that done, Momma wrapped Morgan's ankle quickly and efficiently. They all had plenty of practice at it, after all.

"Okay, let's get you back to bed." Momma put the rest of the bandages back into the cabinet. As she closed the door Morgan could see her hands trembling, her shoulders slumping as she rested her forehead against the smooth plastic.

Instead of picking her up Momma helped Morgan onto her uninjured foot, the pair of them shambling over to the bed alcoves as Morgan hopped and leaned against her mother.

Instead of going all the way down to Morgan's room they stopped at her parents'.

"Your daddy won't be home anyway, so let's put you in here for tonight."

Morgan was starting to feel drowsy again, a side effect of the ointment, so she just nodded.

Morgan got settled on one edge. Momma leaned down, kissing her on the forehead.

"I'll be right back."

A few minutes later she returned, changed and cleaned up. She lay down next to Morgan.

"Come here, Baby Girl." She scooted over, pulling Morgan up against her, hugging her tight. "If you want to talk about it we can."

"I'm tired, Momma," Morgan said, shaking her head. "Just stay here, please."

"Of course," Momma said, kissing the top of Morgan's head, "I'll always be here for you."

Morgan drifted off just a minute or two later, listening to Momma's heart.

CHAPTER 03

Nano-fabrication may have freed society from most of its wants, but we can hardly 'cure' ourselves of the need for raw materials. The dangers of mining likewise. So do we prefer working in space where a single suit tear can kill, or underground where you're fighting gravity and cave-ins?
- Suhana Anand, owner of Khan mines, planet Shanti.

MORGAN COULDN'T SEE the sides of the tunnel around her, close as they were. The dim light of her helmet lamp barely showed her the tunnel floor right in front of her. The batteries were almost dead, but 'almost' meant nothing to the Tinny who worked as quartermaster for shaft 3B. Until the batteries were completely exhausted, she would receive no new ones.

If that meant she'd have to crawl through several kilometers of connecting tunnels with no light. . . well, it wasn't any concern of his. Still, at least it wasn't Thirty-Four in charge of supplies.

Failing batteries or not, right now time was her most precious resource. If she didn't get down to the field generator and fix it – and get back out – within four hours total she'd not get any food.

It was getting harder and harder to get around fast enough. It felt like the tunnels were getting smaller, but in truth it was her that was growing. For now she managed, though it did mean more cuts and scratches on her arms and legs where they stuck out of her already too-small coveralls. Of course, it was hard to tell the difference sometimes since she got so many *through* the coveralls too.

About the only good thing about her current task was that crawling in the smaller access tunnels meant she was off her still-tender ankle as much as possible. She could walk on it, albeit gingerly, but couldn't do so for long or put her full weight on it.

At last she reached the end of the tunnel, the wireless generator gleaming under the light of her lamp.

Looking it over, Morgan heaved a sigh of relief. A bit of the tunnel roof had fallen, knocking a couple of the arrays out of alignment. It was no wonder the workers in the shaft had lost power to their tools. This would be an easy fix, leaving her with plenty of time to get back out.

Morgan had done similar repairs more times than she could remember. Practiced hands nudged the components back into their precise alignments with hardly any conscious thought. Next was a gentle tightening of the connections to keep them that way. Finally a swift smack on the main housing got the whole thing going again. The generator was old, far older than her, and was grumpy in the best of times.

She had barely finished returning her tools to her belt when a blast wave hit, throwing her into the roof of the tunnel. The impact knocked the wind out of her. Morgan couldn't even begin to bring her hands up to brace her fall and she cracked her head on the floor.

Instantly she was plunged into darkness as her lamp broke.

"No. No, no nooo," she groaned. Her head was swimming, her thoughts scattered to the far corners of the tunnels. Frantically she blinked, wanting to believe that it was her eyes and not the light that had failed.

Closing her eyes Morgan forced her breathing to slow. She reminded herself that she had been here before, and gotten out safely. The blast had come from in front and below of her and not the way she had come. If the tunnel here hadn't collapsed, she could retrace her steps. Probably. She knew the forks to take to get out, even in the dark. She just needed to stay calm and take it slow.

Feeling about, Morgan found the generator. First she checked to make sure it was working and then used it to orient herself in the tunnel. Okay. The first turn would be to the right.

Before moving away from the generator Morgan felt to make sure her tools were still secured, her helmet's mask filter still sealed properly. Only then did she move down the tunnel, her right hand dragging along the wall. She inched along, her heart thudding in her chest almost drowning out her soft gasping sobs.

It wasn't long before she cracked her knee on a piece of debris on the tunnel floor. She stopped for a moment to rub the injured body part. Her hand felt sticky when she pulled it away. She didn't dare stop, nor take her other hand off of the wall. One turn taken. Then another. She stumbled into pieces of rock thrice more before she reached the third, and her whole body ached.

She was just past the sixth branch when a tiny pinprick of light appeared in front of her. She ignored it, concentrating on the wall passing by her hand, the floor under her. She had heard stories from the other tunnel rats that had gotten lost in the dark. Many of them talked of seeing lights that weren't there. Tricks born of fear, they said. She had only heard of one person who had followed the lights and gotten out. Morgan hadn't seen the lights herself before, but she wasn't about to let any hallucination distract her.

But the light got bigger, until she could tell it was another helmet light. Still Morgan kept on, ignoring pain and light and fear equally.

It wasn't until the light fell on her and she heard a voice call out her name that Morgan's determination waivered.

She stopped, wondering if she'd be able to start going again. "Jane?" she croaked out, recognizing the voice.

"Morgan! You're alive, I can't believe it." It was Jane, though Morgan couldn't see any of her past the still blinding light.

"Why?" Morgan managed to get out, knowing full well that the Tinnys wouldn't have bothered to send anyone to look for her.

"They wanted me to see if you'd fixed the generator before the accident."

Of course. The Tinnys wouldn't bother sending a rescue party for a worker, but they would send someone if they needed to check on the equipment. It was a dangerous duty but, given the slim chance of turning it into a rescue, they usually could get volunteers.

"I'm real sorry, Morgan, but I have to ask. Did you finish?"

"The explosion, or whatever, was right after I finished," Morgan answered, sagging against the side of the tunnel. She blinked, waiting for her eyes to adjust to the light.

Jane let out a big breath. "Oh thank the Father. Let's get you out of here then." Morgan could hear Jane pulling something off, then fiddling with some clasps and latches. "I grabbed a litter before I came down. I didn't dare hope I'd get to use it. . . " Jane trailed off.

"I can still move."

"Yeah? You don't look so good, Morgan. Let me pull you to the shaft.

Save your strength for the climb back up."

"The lift isn't working?"

"Not until they clear everything. The gossip is someone forgot to turn off one of their detonators when the generator went out, and when it started up again suddenly. . . "

"It's my fault?" Morgan asked. Given the timing she wasn't really surprised.

"No, of course not," Jane forcefully said. "I. . . think they know who left his stuff on, though. That's why they sent me in. To find out."

She had the litter folded out, helping Morgan roll onto it. It was a very basic design, essentially a tough pad big enough for a tunnel rat to lie down on, as long as they kept their arms folded across their chest. It attached to a loop of cord that clipped onto a ring on the back of the puller's coveralls. Not the smoothest ride, but it was better than nothing. "

Jane started crawling, forcing Morgan to repress a grunt as she jerked forward. Still, the chance to rest was nice.

"Was anyone hurt?"

"Besides you? I don't think so. They were waiting for the power to start up again before sending anyone back down." Jane was trying to keep her movements smooth, even succeeding a little bit. "Now be quiet. I'm not as good at remembering the turnings as you."

✳✳✳

Her arms and legs shaking terribly from exhaustion Morgan pulled herself off of the shaft's ladder and onto the main landing of the entryway. Her cuts had only stopped bleeding because they were stopped up with dust and dirt, and her helmet's filter had worn out some time previously.

While the hub was technically still part of the tunnel system it was a far larger chamber, with permanent lights hung on the support beams and even a few vertical shafts that connected to the surface for ventilation. The air still smelled of dust and metal, but at least it was fresh.

The bunker like building that served as the taskmaster's office had a prominently displayed shift clock. Right now it told her that she had been down there for six hours. Given how slow they'd gone getting out they had actually made very good time.

For the moment the majority of the workers were milling about, unable to work but unable to leave because of the Tinny guards sitting dourly by the mine cage that went rest of the way back up to the surface.

The shaft finished closing behind them, and Jane and Morgan pulled the masks off of their helmets, depositing them in the recycling chute next to the entrance. Morgan pulled off her broken light, clutching it in one battered hand.

Leaning on Jane the pair of them staggered over to the office window. No one moved to help the girls, not with every official eye on them. They pressed their thumbs against the scanner mounted to the wall, triggering the automated time keeper.

"Morgan 28431. Job complete."

"Jane 28445. Job complete."

"You are two hours late, 28431. Report to the foreman. 28445, you are early, report to the dispensary, extra food has been authorized. When you are done report back for your next assignment," the computer terminal droned at them. They removed their thumbs, a partial bloody print left behind by Morgan's. It wasn't the first.

"Thank you, Jane," Morgan said, stopping in front of the hermetically sealed door of the office.

"You'd have done the same for me. Good. . . good luck with the tin man." Jane walked away briskly. The computer tracked how long it took for them to eat and return for the next job.

Morgan knocked, and was surprised when it opened straight away.

"Well, shit," Officer Thirty-Four said as he looked down at her.

Morgan had far too much experience dealing with the petty tyrants to react. She just stood there, waiting for him to continue.

"I guess you win the pot," he called over his shoulder to one of his companions farther inside. "She didn't die." He turned back to her. "Stay there; I don't want you tracking your filth in here." He stepped down onto the entryway floor, crowding her to one side. "You finished your repairs?" Morgan nodded curtly. "Right before the explosion?" Again she nodded. "Anything else?"

"The blast broke my lamp, sir," Morgan said, opening her hand for him to see. He took it, looked it over, and then tossed it inside where his companion caught it. "Fine."

The companion reached over his shoulder for a fresh one, then tossed it to him. He slapped it on Morgan's helmet, clicking it on and off. "Get out of here then."

Morgan turned to leave when he spoke up, "Oh, one more thing." Morgan began to turn, but his backhand caught her in the side of the face before she was a quarter of the way around. She fell to the ground, her face stinging enough that she was pretty sure he'd broken the skin. "There are still penalties for being late. Don't forget that."

He had returned inside before she could scramble to her feet, the door sealing the dusty air of the mine out. Morgan did nothing, said nothing. She was already two hours into her off time, and if she was to be back here in the morning able to work, she needed to get home, get cleaned up, and get to bed. The guards let her into the cage, and she traveled up to the surface, alone.

At least tonight she *could* go straight home. For once her parents weren't working into the night. Hopefully they still had enough of the ointment, given the number of cuts and scrapes she'd gotten that shift and how much they'd used the day before.

✳✳✳

Morgan was tucked into bed, the drowsiness of exhaustion and medicine having finally won over the aches and stings of her cuts, when her parents' voices intruded, raised in heated discussion.

"Rachel, this is crazy. It'll never work. They'll catch us and make examples of us. *If* we're lucky."

"Sam, we're not going to get another chance like this. At least not before the comrades marry her off. You're the one who convinced me we needed to get her off-world. Can you think of any other way to do that, other than bribing one of the managers?"

"No."

"And do we have enough to bribe the manager?"

"From me? Of course not."

"We can do this, Sam. Think on what happens when we pull it off. Think about the life she'll be able to have."

"But what happens to her if we get caught?"

"What happens the next time there is an accident down there? I can't see her like that again, Sam. We were lucky this time. And all that a day after some thugs broke in here. *A day.*"

Footsteps sounded close to Morgan, and she shut her eyes more tightly, pretending to be asleep.

"Morgan, honey, you need to get up," her momma's hand gently touched Morgan's shoulder, unwittingly putting pressure on a couple of her bruises. Morgan suppressed a wince.

Morgan thought about asking why or protesting that she'd only just gone to bed, but only for a bare moment. She knew her parents would never hurt her, but some lessons about surviving the mines were too ingrained to be ignored.

Instead she climbed out from under the scratchy blanket and began stepping into her spare coveralls and shoes. Tossing her nightgown onto the bed she pulled her clothes the rest of the way on, with some difficulty. Her spare coveralls were spare because they were simply too small for her, even more so than her main pair. Of course, after the day she'd had the spare was probably in better shape overall. Hopefully the other could be fixed – she couldn't do up the spare all the way thanks to the too tight neck, and the sleeves and legs only reached just past her elbows and knees.

Clothes on, she ran her hands through her hair to at least get some of the tangles out and get it out of her eyes. It wasn't very long hair, by design, but it always seemed to get in the way anyway.

"Morgan, you remember us talking about how Daddy is going to go to the station to fix something?"

"Yeah."

"Well, you're going to go with him too. Only, I need you to trust me and do exactly what I say."

"I think there's enough space, Rachel." There was a crash from the main room, but Morgan couldn't see anything with the curtain separating it from the two small sleeping rooms down. Momma gestured forwards and they walked the few paces to join him. Daddy's big toolkit was on the table, the one with all his special tools no one else in town knew how to use. Well, officially. Morgan had been taught what almost all of them did over the last couple of years, not that she'd ever had a chance to use them.

Now most of the tools were scattered on the floor, the trays shoved on the table in a pile. He grimaced as he looked at the two of them. He heaved the mostly empty toolkit onto the floor, the wheels rattling as they struck a stay stone that had been missed the last time Morgan had swept.

He took Morgan's hand in his massive calloused hands, squeezing hers tightly.

"Morgan, I need you to get in the toolkit. If you pull your legs up to your chest and tuck your head down you should fit."

This was so odd a request that Morgan had to be sure she heard right. "You want me to get in there?"

"Yes Baby Girl, I want you to get in there. It's the only way to get you up to the station with me, and that's very important. Now," he paused unexpectedly, with a look on his face Morgan had never seen before. It sort of looked like he was in pain, but nothing hurt her daddy, he was too strong for that. "Now, you're going to be in there for a while, so go use the bathroom first, and then Momma will have some food for you. Take anything important to you with you, as long as it is small. You need to hurry though."

Morgan did as he asked, grabbing the small picture of the three of them from her tiny box of things; her bracelet was still on her wrist of course. The food was cold soup momma had brought back from work, but it was almost as good cold anyway. The bowl was almost overflowing it was so full; it had to be most of what she'd brought home.

"What about you?" She asked, looking at the food.

"We already ate," Momma said. Her voice sounded funny too, but Morgan didn't know why.

Food eaten, Morgan went over to the kit. She wasn't sure the best way to fit in there, so she just stood inside and went to crouch down.

"One moment, honey. Let me say goodbye." Momma grabbed Morgan in a big hug, squeezing her tight. With the thick bottom of the box beneath her feet, she was almost as tall as Momma. It felt weird. She kissed Morgan's cheeks, then rested her cheek against Morgan's forehead. "Now, you need to be brave, and stay quiet. Daddy will explain what he can while you travel on the train, but you're going away. We love you so much, but we can't give you what you deserve here."

"But no one leaves." Finally Morgan realized why they were putting her in the box. She would have realized it earlier if the mere idea hadn't been so unthinkable for her. "You're going to sneak me out? How? Why?"

Morgan's head began to swim. Actually get off Hillman? To get away from the mines and Tinnys and everything else? Sure, she'd just barely been talking about it with Jane. To actually do it, though? Her swimming head turned into a dizzying array of fevered imaginations, each more outlandish than the last as she tried to imagine even a glimmer of what life beyond the mines could be.

"We don't have time, honey; Daddy needs to get over there soon for his ride. There's a ship at the space station picking up ore right now. We're going to get you on it before they leave. Now," she paused for emphasis, "When they ask how old you are, you need to tell them you're twenty-six." Momma paused again; her fingers twitching as she mentally did some math. "Uh. . . seventeen. Tell them you're seventeen in Earth years. If they think you're almost grown, you can just find a job and live on your own. If they know you're still a child they'll want to put you in a home, and we can't know what kind of people they'll be. They could be nice, or not."

"Rachel, we're running out of time."

"Oh, Morgan. Be brave." She released Morgan from the hug, then went to step back. Before she could Morgan grabbed her in a hug of her own, burying her face against Momma's neck.

"I love you, Momma," she said, tears in her eyes.

"I know, baby. Don't you worry about us. We'll be fine. Every time we get lonely we'll think about all the amazing things you'll be doing, and we'll be happy too."

Momma helped Morgan cram into the box, her back against the side with her knees all the way up against her chest with her head resting on them. Daddy put some of the trays back in, covering Morgan up. Some of the tools went in next, and then he shut the lid.

"Get over there, Sam. I'll circle around and be ready to distract them when you get to the checkpoint. I'll move faster without the kit to pull."

"Be careful."

"Only for as long as I need to be."

With a grunt Daddy picked up the kit by the handle, tilting Morgan's world uncomfortably. Time was hard to gauge while slanted sideways in a dark box, but Morgan guessed it was something like a quarter hour before they got to the open field just outside of town where the train's loading station was. Having walked past it many times she knew there was a tall wire fence surrounding the field at a distance of some two hundred meters. It had a single large gate with a smaller person-sized one set inside that, guarded by at least two Tinnys with others walking the perimeter.

"Hey, think we could hurry this up? I'd like to be on the train before my wife catches up to me," Daddy said to the guards, the toolkit shaking as he did something with his hands that made the guards laugh.

"We'll try, but no promises."

"Get back here you bastard! Did you think I wouldn't find out about that two-bit whore you have stashed away across town?" Why was Momma saying this to Daddy? Morgan had never heard her sound this angry before.

"Oh like you care."

There was a thudding sound, and the toolkit dropped flat onto its side. Morgan stayed quiet, not an easy feat. What was going on? What were her parents up to?

"Step back," the guard said, any trace of emotion gone from his voice. "I don't care what he did, or you did, any of it. He's needed up top, and that's the end of it."

"He's not getting away from me that easily!" Momma was shouting, but she wasn't as close anymore.

"Buddy, just get me on board. She won't stick around once she can't get at me anymore."

"Yeah, better hurry up." The kit was picked up by the handle again, "Wow, this thing is heavier than it looks. Glad I don't need to carry it around."

"Thanks, I'll head straight in. Don't worry about the punch. She's just mad right now. I'm sure by the time I come back she'll be over it."

"Like I said, do your work and I don't care. Now get out of here."

***

The train ride was several hours long. Long, long, long. Definitely the right word for it. Morgan could hear two or three other people moving about in the car with Daddy. Her limbs ached from sitting so still in the cramped space, but there wasn't any way for him to get her out for a stretch. Morgan supposed he could have gone to the restroom, but taking his tools with him would have been suspicious.

"So where are you headed?" he asked them.

"We're being rotated to the station for guard duty. Reward for fewest problems on our shift."

"Congratulations," Daddy said warmly. It sounded like he was sliding down in his seat, getting comfortable. "I'm headed that way myself, some repair work."

"You're an engineer? I thought all of them lived up there?"

"Each town needs someone to keep the equipment running, don't they?" Morgan could practically hear him shrugging. He probably sounded just as friendly as before to the unfamiliar guards, but Morgan could tell most of his tone was an act.

"Oh. You're that guy." Morgan recognized *that* tone easily enough.

"That guy." Daddy sighed. "We all pay for our mistakes. Or other people's." Morgan doubted the guards had heard the second bit, muttered as it was. "Still, without me, more of you guards would be stuck out in the towns." There was sadness in his voice, enough that the other man noticed.

"So this is what? More punishment? Bring you up to the station to see what you've lost?"

Daddy didn't respond for long enough that Morgan thought he wasn't going to.

"No, they actually do need me to fix something. I helped design the train system down here, and they just duplicated it for the station. You see, magnetic suspension trains have been around for a long time, but we couldn't use them here, because of the high gravity. Anti-gravity plates can't fight a planet's gravity enough to work on their own, especially here, but they also don't work well near electromagnets powerful enough for something like a train system. So we needed shuttle pads pretty much everywhere."

"With guards."

"Exactly. What I did. . . well, me and a couple other engineers. . . was figure out a way to get the anti-gravity to work with the mag system, so the trains are light enough to actually move."

The third person, the guard Morgan hadn't heard speak yet, snorted.

"Whatever. I'm trying to sleep here man, just shut it."

"Sorry. I get restless easily, and I talk to help the time pass by."

"Well talk somewhere else then. I'm not wasting a chance to rest."

"Sure, no problem. I'll just move to the next car." Morgan's world tilted as he grabbed the tool kit by the handle. "Enjoy your nap."

It was a bumpy trip thanks to the metal grate floor, punctuated by a couple pauses as they moved through the doors separating the cars. At last the kit was brought back upright and the lid opened, the trays moved onto the bench beside them.

"Sorry that took so long, Morgan. I had to make it look it was their idea."

Morgan tried to unfold herself from the box, but found her muscles uncooperative. Her limbs felt like rubber where they weren't numb entirely. Daddy scooped her out of the box, propping her against his own body to help keep her upright. Feeling returning to her extremities as pins and needles first was not fun at all, but it still beat being in the box.

Not that there was much to see in the train car. Metal walls with no windows enclosed a narrow cabin bare except for some benches and a small bathroom. The doors at each end were more featureless metal save for the handle, and the floor was grating over the machinery below, dimly lit here and there by status lights and small displays.

"I hate to say it, but we can't risk you being out too long. I'll let you out again when we're almost to the launch pad so you can use the restroom and eat something, but there's no telling when the guards in the other room – or anyone else – might wander by." He looked down at Morgan and smiled. "I think we can risk it for at least a few minutes though."

"So why do we live in Pari?"

Daddy sighed, helping Morgan sit down. She rubbed her arms, trying to get feeling back a little quicker, and gestured for him to answer.

"It's not something I wanted to tell you about."

"There won't be another time."

"I'm afraid."

Morgan made an incredulous sound.

He laughed, though there was no mirth in it. "I know. Dads shouldn't be afraid of anything. At least not where the kids can see. The truth is I'm afraid of lots of things. The biggest one is losing your mother or you."

"Isn't that what is happening now?"

"Yes?" He drew out the sounds, turning the answer into a question. "We're sending you away so you can have a better life, but you're still our girl. This? I'm afraid that when you find out you'll never be able to forgive me. That is far worse than merely never seeing you again."

"Nothing could ever make me hate you, Daddy." She hugged him about the knees as tightly as she could with her still-tingling arms.

He laughed again, much more naturally. He put one calloused hand on her head, messing up her short hair.

"The faith of a little girl is a wonderful thing."

"I don't know that word," Morgan said, looking up at him with one raised eyebrow.

"No, you wouldn't. It's one of the forbidden words. So many things were hidden or destroyed to keep people from questioning the comrades."

"But we all question them."

"Yes, well, all too often the success or failure of a plan is not taken into account, especially by people like the comrades."

"And the word?"

"It's a religious word. It means. . . it means that you know something, but don't really have any solid evidence to back it up. You can't know the future, can't know what I'll do or have done, but you have *faith* that I wouldn't do anything to hurt you."

Morgan thought about asking what religious meant, but that question was just another distraction from what she wanted to know.

"So, what happened?"

He sighed and moved over to sit next to her.

"You know I didn't grow up in Pari Passu, that I never worked the mines as a child? Instead I went to school."

"To become an engineer?"

"Eventually, yes. My parents were both party members, but not like the Tinny brutes you know. They honestly believed in building a fair society, where everyone had what they needed and worked as they were able.

"It's a great feeling, Morgan. To be doing work that will help everyone. I thought the train project would be the start of improving everyone's life, a way to start making mining less labor intensive. Mag-lev married to antigravity could be used for so much more than the trains. They could have built drones and robots to take over much of the mining, and especially transporting the ore. The technology is quite old; we just needed better ways to adapt it to the high gravity of Hillman."

"Then why didn't they?"

"Control. Greed. I don't know, Morgan. Why do men do anything to each other? It's easy to keep the majority of the people from demanding too much if they're ignorant and exhausted. With drones and robots the workers wouldn't even need to be on the mountain. The workers could even live on the station and work from there. But of course there isn't room up there for everyone. The resources that the party members use to keep themselves as comfortable as anyone can be on this planet wouldn't stretch very far if it had to be distributed to everyone."

"And you were part of that?"

"I was. Oh, I had no idea how bad it was for the common miners. How could I? I'd never met one, much less seen them at work. But I knew that our vaunted equality was a lie. My mistake was thinking it was because of the necessity of mining, and not by design."

"I don't understand. What does this have to do with why you ended up in the mines?"

"It's simple really. After my work on the train was finished I started pushing for time to work on the drones. I was told we didn't have money for it, a thousand excuses really, and I got suspicious. I started digging, but I was sloppy. They were watching me, and eventually I was denounced as 'working against the people.'

"There was an 'accident' in the train yard, a few people even died. I was blamed, stripped of my position, and sent out here to fix machines, but never make new ones."

"And Momma?"

"We had just been married when this happened. They gave her a choice. Stay with me and be exiled too, or quietly get a new husband."

"What?" Morgan couldn't wrap her head around that at all. Marriages on Hillman lasted until death, and remarriage only happened if the surviving partner was still young enough to have more children.

"As far as the party was concerned, I was dead."

"But she chose to stay."

"She loved me, and I loved her. But I was selfish. I wish I'd been strong enough to let her go, to not ruin her life along with mine."

"How was that your fault?"

"If I had just left it alone we'd be living on the station, and you would have grown up learning things instead of crawling around in the dirt and adding to your collection of scars. Every injury you've had, every bit of abuse from the Tinnys, it's all *my* fault. It's my fault that you've barely had enough to eat, and that all you had to look forward to was getting married to someone you barely knew and watching your own children suffer in the mines."

Morgan didn't know how to respond to this. How could she even begin to imagine what her life would be like as the daughter of a party member living on Hill Station?

One question did make its way to the forefront of her mind forcefully. What would that girl think about the miners, the tunnel rats? Like the Tinnys did? Worse? Would she hate them as much as Morgan hated the 'essential workers' and the comrade managers?

"Am I right to hate the comrade managers?"

"What?"

"Everyone in town, some of the Tinnys even, hate the people hiding up on that station. Are they wrong to feel that way?"

Daddy was quiet for a minute, stroking his chin as he thought about how to answer.

"Some of them are good people. They just don't see how bad it is outside of their little circles. Others know what's going on and hate it, but are afraid of losing what they have. That said, no, the miners aren't wrong."

"Then why would I blame you for what they did? Would it really be better to be pampered on the backs of people like us, like Jane?"

"You only say that because you don't know what you lost out on. You've been doing hard labor for ten years already. On Hill Station you'd have another ten years of school before you'd even start to worry about marriage or a job."

"And what kind of job would I be looking forward to? An engineer like you?"

"Probably not." He shook his head. "No, definitely not."

"Why not?"

"Did you ever wonder why all the Tinnys are male? Any job with even the potential of contact with the common man is barred to women."

"What?"

"As much as they look down on the miners they're also afraid of them. Almost all of their stories deal with evil, lazy, or degenerate miners."

"Daddy, I think we're better off away from these people."

He sighed, resting his head on his hands as he ran his fingers through his hair.

"I don't deserve you, Baby Girl."

A metal rumble penetrated the car from the far end.

"That's the other car's door. Quick, back into the kit."

Morgan clambered back into the box. It helped that she'd already done it once, but her aching limbs made it harder, so it took just as long the second time as it did the first.

Getting the trays settled back in above her *was* easier this time, and it was a good thing too, as Morgan could hear their car's door opening as the lid snapped into place. Whoever it was didn't say anything, but just clomped along and sat down a ways back from them.

"Hello," Daddy said, his best amiable tone plastered on. "I don't know about you, but I'd forgotten how long this trip is. I think I'll follow your buddy's example and take a nap."

His words were as much for Morgan as the Tinny out there Morgan couldn't see. Sighing – quietly – she nestled her head the tiny bit more against her knees possible and closed her eyes.

CHAPTER 04

Altruism and selflessness is bred into us – literally coded for at the genetic level. This of course makes sense biologically, to perpetuate the species. It also makes sense theologically as an example and call to our higher selves, and to remind us that even as a father loves his children so does God love us.

- Presiding Bishop Alfonso Guzman, dean of Biological Sciences, Zion Institute of Technology (retired).

"YOU NEED TO STAY QUIET, Morgan. We're almost there."

Morgan had still been somewhere between simple sleep and the brutal unconsciousness resulting from the tremendous forces of the shuttle ride out of Hillman's heavy gravity well. As such she didn't register the words her daddy had said, but his voice was reassuring as she awoke. The box opened at last, letting in a wave of fresh air and light. Unfolding from the tight space, Morgan slumped against the wall. She waited for feeling to come back to her extremities, rubbing her arms and legs while her father's head darted back and forth keeping watch. She felt different, like a great weight had been taken off of her back. It was weird, but definitely a good kind of weird.

"We're not on the shuttle." Morgan was surprised the station was kept on lower gravity than the planet, but she supposed people from other places came here too. Anyone not born on Hillman would have a hard time just moving about, let alone working.

"No, this is the station. Too many cameras and eyes to risk letting you out until now. You slept the whole way up?"

"I must have." Morgan took a moment to look about, taking in the smooth metal walls and equally smooth metal floor beneath her thick soled boots. The room or hallway they were in was a few meters wide and curved gently in each direction. It was long enough that she couldn't see around the corners to where it ended. There were some square sections of wall next to her that looked like they could be removed, but they were too small to be doors.

"I don't see a ship," Morgan said, gesturing at the room. "Why did you open the box, is it close?"

"This is as close as I can get you. I managed to cut the primary circuits for the security in this section of the station while working on repairs." Daddy patted the small pair of wire cutters on his tool belt. "I told them I had shorted something out and graciously offered to fix the problem myself. That got us to this corridor."

Slipping his power spanner out of his tool belt, Daddy started removing the bolts on one of the small panels.

"And from here?"

"From here you can crawl through the service ducts to the tertiary docking bay where an independent freighter is offloading supplies in return for a cargo of heavy metals and local wood. They'll also be taking on some perishables – food and water.

"Will there be a lot of people? Won't they see me?"

"You can do this, Baby Girl." He had finished with the bolts, tugging the panel off to reveal the low passage beyond. The panel was larger than the passage it hid. For someone larger than Morgan it would be a tight fit. "It's right, left, straight three times, then a right. No different than in the mines. Once you're there, listen for a bit before opening the panel. There should be enough crates and containers to keep you hidden from view. If you can, just sneak onto the ship directly. If you can't, find a crate – one of the ones away from the wall – and get inside."

He handed her the spanner, then pulled his backup from his belt.

"Do you remember what turns to take?"

"Right, left, forward, forward, forward, right. What about the Tinnys?"

"They're watching the shuttle docks. They're not trusted to be near the departing ships any more than I am. We need to hurry, Baby Girl. Give me a hug goodbye."

Hugging him somehow was much more final than saying goodbye to Momma had been, and Morgan started crying. She blinked back the tears, trying to appear strong. Daddy grabbed her chin in his strong hand and pulled her eyes up to look into his, also glistening with tears.

"Don't be afraid to cry, Morgan. Where you're going they won't be looking for the slightest sign of weakness. Just be brave, and work hard and you'll have a good life." He kissed her forehead. He nudged her into the passage, giving her hand one final squeeze. As he released his grip he slipped a small bit of plastic into her hand.

Looking at it Morgan realized it was a data chip.

"What is this?"

"That is my life's work. The research that ended up causing my exile. I don't know if it will do you any good out there, but I want you to at least have it. Now you need to hurry, Morgan."

"I love you," Morgan said as he pushed the panel back into place.

Morgan heard the thump of his head against the metal, the panel slightly muffling his voice. "And I love you, Morgan, more than life itself."

Morgan forced herself to turn away from the panel as Daddy wasted no time replacing the bolts. It felt weird scooting and crawling along such a smooth surface, but Morgan hardly noticed it. The new sensation was lost amongst all the other strange new things she was experiencing.

Navigating the narrow passage was easier than the tunnels had been. For one thing, it was exactingly straight with no lower bits to bang her head on. It also had lighting at regular intervals on both walls. The light was dim compared to the room she'd come from, dimmer even than her helmet lamp in the mines back home. But unlike her helmet lamp, the light covered the whole passage and her eyes adjusted quickly.

Six intersections came and went quickly, and at last Morgan found herself in front of another panel. She stared at it for several seconds before the flaw in the plan really registered.

The bolts were on the other side.

It was even worse than that, the bolts were on the other side and the panel was larger than the opening of the passage, so she couldn't even get to the back end of the bolts.

Morgan willed herself to be calm. The urge to panic was tempting, an outlet for her frustration and all the aches and pains she was trying to ignore. Her poor body was still dealing with the mine explosion on top of spending so many hours crammed in a box.

Deep, regular breaths.

Okay.

What could she do?

Judging by the panel she had seen, the metal was about as two finger widths thick, so pretty sturdy. It'd have to be, given that she was on a space station and dealing with the vacuum of space was a real possibility.

Of course if she was going to try and force her way out, the question wasn't how strong the panel was, but how strong were the bolts?

Not that the answer to that question was likely to help her. The bolts had to resist the same forces as the panel, after all.

Morgan took a moment to shake her head. Who had designed this? What reason could they have had to make it so hard to get out of these passageways once in them? The answer probably came back to the same reasoning behind the train system – keep people from leaving – but at what point were placating these fears outweighed by problems the solutions caused?

There had to be a way out of here. What would workers do if they were cut off from where they had entered, or if someone closed the panel up thinking it left open by mistake?

She hadn't seen anything that would suggest the bolts were powered; Daddy had opened them with a hand tool, after all. But if there wasn't any physical access from the inside. . .

Morgan scooted back from the panel a bit and started feeling around the walls and ceiling directly adjacent to it. There wasn't anything immediately obvious, but these passages had to be used for something didn't they? In the mines they mostly just went from point A to point B, but the tunnels were surrounded by mostly solid rock. This was an artificial station; the interior spaces had to have machines and other things the station needed to work. Didn't they? The one constant of machines was they needed maintenance and repair, so there had to be a way to access them.

Several minutes of fruitless search later Morgan was wondering if panicking wouldn't be more useful after all.

She had seen the access spaces on the train. They'd been right beneath her feet, open and obvious under the grate floor. So why was everything hidden so thoroughly here? Even without the bolted close panels she couldn't imagine the party members ever stooping – literally – to use these passages. So why hide them?

Figuring out what parts could come off was easy. The walls, floor, and ceiling were all made up of square sections set flush with each other, designed to be removed. Figuring out how to unlatch them, that was hard. There wasn't any space between the panels for a lever or catch. The whole surface was patterned with rectangular markings, disguising whatever catches there were handily.

Reduced to just poking sections more or less at random, Morgan was finally rewarded with a quiet click as one of the rectangular sections slid in on the left side of a panel immediately adjacent to the hatch, on the left side. Poking it on the other side of the same panel yielded another click and the panel fell forward. Morgan yanked her feet back just in time, leaving nothing but the metal floor for the panel to land on, which it did with a loud dull clang.

Morgan sucked a breath in, pressing one ear to the closed hatch and listening. Did anyone hear her? If they did, would they be suspicious? She couldn't hear anything besides the pounding of her heart, and really, what were her options if they *had* heard her? She was quite stuck at the moment.

Turning back to the finally open section of wall Morgan grimaced. There were pipes and circuits all right, some of it far enough back that she wouldn't be able to even reach them, but none of it looked connected to the hatch right here, it all looked like it just went past here on its way somewhere else.

There was still one thing worth trying. Reaching in as far as she could with her left arm Morgan felt around the very edge of the space, flush against the sealed hatch. As with any task involving feeling around in the dark, it was frustratingly slow and haphazard. But then her fingers brushed up against a small mechanical box. Working her fingers around the edge, Morgan was rewarded with a rounded opening – and the back end of the hatch bolt. While this did tell her that there probably was some way to open the hatch from the inside – the bolt housing had some wires running from it, for one – this didn't help her much.

Having access to the actual bolt itself, even if only the backend? That Morgan could work with.

That wasn't to say it was going to be easy.

The common method for removing a bolt without a head was to drill a hole in the top then insert a bolt extractor. That wouldn't work here for several reasons, the important ones being she didn't want to leave evidence she'd been here if she could avoid it, and the slightly more pressing reason being she didn't have a bolt extractor.

But she did have her father's spanner. It was a much more sophisticated tool than the junk she'd used in the mines. One of the useful things it had was a powerful electromagnet on the extendible tip. Daddy hadn't used it when he'd opened the other hatch, but he'd had ready access to the bolts.

All Morgan had to do was get the spanner tip on the bolt, without touching the surrounding metal, and then turn on the magnet without jostling it. After that it would be a simple matter of putting the tool in reverse and pushing the bolt out.

Assuming this hatch was like the other one, it was eight sided with two bolts per side. And of course she wouldn't be able to actually see what she was doing, given the angle of the panels and the conduits.

Sixteen bolts by feel, each requiring precise positioning.

Nothing for it but to get to work.

Without taking her fingers off of the bolt she scooped the spanner off of the floor. Morgan looked back and forth between her arm, buried up to her shoulder in the cavity of the wall, and the hand holding the spanner.

Well, that wasn't going to work. Doing her best to memorize where the bolt was in the wall, Morgan pulled her arm out. This would be easier if she could use both hands, so first she tried getting her right arm in far enough to find the bolt again. She kept pushing farther in, until she'd actually gotten most of her head and shoulders stuck into the cavity, but she couldn't quite reach.

Sighing, she stuck her left hand through the carry loop of the spanner and reached back in. She found the bolt quicker this time, but lost it when she tried to get the spanner in position.

The second attempt didn't go any better, but the third time she got it on. The switch for the magnet was thankfully easy to get at.

Letting go of the spanner she checked on the alignment of the head on the bolt. It was close, but not close enough.

Adjusting it was painstakingly slow, as she thumbed off the magnet, nudged it ever so lightly, turned it back on, then checked again. Three times and it was close enough – not centered, but at least not touching anything but the bolt.

There was nothing left but to see if her desperate plan would work. Getting the spanner on in reverse was trivial, even by feel. At first it bucked in her hand, the bolt's grip on the metal stronger than her grip on the tool, but soon enough it started turning normally.

Morgan wasn't sure how she'd know when the bolt was all the way out; she was sort of hoping to just hear the sound of the bolt hitting the floor.

It took her ten seconds or so of the spanner turning without extending the tip any for her to realize that, no, she wouldn't hear the bolt falling, because it was still magnetically attached to the spanner.

Sighing Morgan thumbed the switch for the magnet. Now she faintly heard the tink of metal on metal as the bolt fell.

One down, fifteen to go. This should be easy enough.

***

Tired, sweaty, panting, and as scraped and cut up as she ever was after a normal day in the mines, Morgan had slogged her way through fourteen more bolts. She also had several painful burns to add to the list, an all-new kind of fun for her to experience. Some of the pipes were staggeringly hot, even through the thick insulation around them. Aside from burning her arms Morgan had even accidentally shorted out a couple wires when she incidentally pushed them too close to their heated neighbors. She hoped she hadn't done anything to draw attention to herself, but there was no way to know right up until and if someone came out here to fix whatever she had broken.

She was almost starting to hope for that eventuality, because fifteen bolts down and she was still stuck in here.

She could not reach the last bolt. It was the bottommost one on the right side, and no matter how she twisted and turned her arm she couldn't reach it. To buy herself time to think Morgan had replaced all the panel covers except for the bottom one on the right, but nothing had come to her.

The fact that it hadn't even budged with 15 bolts removed was maddening as well. She had tried just rotating it around so it was hanging from the one bolt, but the hatch was inset into the wall as well as bolted in place, so she couldn't get it out far enough to swing.

The chances of her being discovered grew by the moment. Even if she could find another hatch in the right area, she couldn't guarantee she wouldn't have the same problem. She'd still have to find her way back here to take care of the bolts lying on the floor below.

Morgan made one final effort to reach the bolt, wedging her shoulder against the floor as hard as she could, ignoring the pain as the edge pinched under her arm.

She had to be close, given where the others were.

Her fingertip brushed something that could have been the bolt. Excited she pushed even harder, trying to get just a little more reach, and her hand slipped. It snagged against something else, her arm jerking back as the pain hit, tearing her hand along the edge of whatever it was.

Morgan rolled onto her stomach, cradling the injured hand in the other one, blood already welling from what looked to be a fairly deep cut across her palm.

Sitting there trying to keep the blood off her clothes, while also trying to tear off a strip to stop the bleeding, used up the last bit of calm Morgan had left. In sheer frustration she kicked the hatch as hard as she could, not caring for the moment that someone might hear. At least then she could get out of this blasted tunnel.

The kick was unaimed, hitting around the middle of the hatch, but was delivered with a goodly percentage of her heavy-gravity-bred strength. The clang was louder than she had expected, but not by a wide margin. What was surprising was the grating of the hatch against its mounting as it moved forward a few millimeters.

She stared at it in incomprehension for a few seconds before she realized what had happened. Once she did she kicked it again, harder. This time, she kicked in the corner opposite the last bolt, and was rewarded with the hatch actually bending out a bit as the lone bolt buckled under the strain. The wave of air that rushed in to balance out the slight pressure difference between the room beyond and the crawl space was just as recycled and sterile as the air already inside, but to Morgan it tasted as good as breathing the surface air after a shift in the mines.

A third kick broke the bolt entirely, the hatch thumping down onto the floor below. Morgan was halfway out before she thought of the panel still open inside. Muttering to herself, she hastily replaced it. It was a sloppy job, but she couldn't bring herself to stay in there any longer.

There wasn't much to see beyond the hatch, luckily. A meter or so in front of the hatch was a row of crates, stacked nearly to the ceiling, easily three or four times Morgan's total height. The row extended nearly to corners of the room to her left and right, blocking out most of the light from whatever lights were mounted on the ceiling of the room.

Once out she took a moment to clasp her hands together before stretching her arms up, delighted to simply be upright again. That done, she shoved the hatch back on and replaced the bolts as quickly as she could. As a souvenir, and to avoid any evidence, she pocketed the now-broken sixteenth.

After a few last moments cleaning up any blood drops on the floor as best she could, she picked a direction – right – and slowly made her way towards the corner.

Peeking through showed Morgan only more crates, but this time they didn't extend all the way to the opposite wall. Creeping up to the edge, Morgan found herself looking at a busy loading operation, some ten or twelve people busily moving crates around by hand and with some small wheeled machines, as well as a couple people who seemed to be keeping track of what went and what came.

They clearly aren't from Hillman, given how tall they are, Morgan thought to herself. No, clearly they were the freighter crew, seemingly working unsupervised.

Once she'd processed the obvious height differences – she'd guess most of them were at least a third again as tall as she was, and even the shortest probably beat her by thirty centimeters or more – she paused to wonder at their clothing. They all wore the same thing, thick-looking white or grey fabric, a couple with different colors that clearly had been patched together piecemeal. It covered them from toes to the top of the neck, seemingly skin tight, with some buttons and monitors in a couple places. There was also what looked superficially like an air tank on the back. At least that was Morgan's guess, based on the bulky and heavy tanks she'd used before for especially long repair jobs in the mines. There weren't any hoses or anything that would confirm this, but she couldn't imagine what else it could be.

There was a helmet too, of course, with a clear faceplate that was divided into four horizontal sections. Morgan couldn't figure out why it was designed that way – surely the parts that overlapped and even the thin opaque edge around each section interfered with vision? More curious for

Morgan was the fact that she couldn't tell how the helmet attached to the rest, it seemed to link in seamlessly with the neck of the suit.

It was hard to tell with their odd suits, but they also seemed far too skinny to Morgan. No wonder the gravity of the station didn't match the gravity of the planet below, if the visitors were this spindly.

Slipping back from the edge Morgan moved her attention over to the large door leading to the other ship. There was movement back and forth, but not constantly. If she timed it well she should be able to slip onto the ship without being noticed.

Assuming, of course, that no one was watching on the other side. Not that there was anything she could do about that one way or the other.

Minutes went by as she watched. Efficient lot, but oddly quiet. Could the suits be connected? It would be hard to talk to each other with the helmets, otherwise, and she couldn't see how they could coordinate the loading without at least some chatter.

Morgan caught some movement in the corner of her eye and turned to look. One of the workers who seemed to be keeping track of everything was motioning for the worker closest to Morgan to come over. There was her opening. Morgan gave him a ten count to head over and then dashed forward, trying to stay as low as she could. Not hard really, given her background.

If she had dared glance back as she disappeared down the mostly dark corridor, she would have seen the worker who had gestured to the other looking directly at her before shaking her head and resuming her task. She didn't, however, and so missed it.

CHAPTER 05

Space is deadly. You've all learned this. There are many kinds of ways it can kill you. So you had better listen to me when I say that these dangers are miniscule compared to the dangers of someone wandering around a spaceship who doesn't know what they're doing. Watch them, carefully.

- Sergeant William Ted, Aegis Company, before assigning privates to escort duty.

HELGA

HELGA ALLRED had long-since adapted to the necessities of living and working in space. She didn't even remember a time when she wasn't a light sleeper. Within a couple seconds of her bedside intercom chiming she had woken, sat up, and answered the call.

"The cargo transfer?" She mumbled, already assuming something had gone wrong.

"No, that's going fine."

It was her sister, Mary. She was supposed to be working documentation in the station's cargo loading area. If there wasn't a problem why was she calling?

"You did have a reason for waking me?" Helga said when Mary didn't say anything further.

"Sorry, I was responding to one of the loaders. Multitasking is such a pain in my ass."

Helga snorted in amusement. "Careful Asad doesn't hear you talking like that."

"Yeah, yeah. My esteemed brother-in-law Captain can get in line to bite me," Mary said, chuckling herself. "I almost didn't believe my own eyes, but it looks like we got a potential stowaway here. She's trying to stay hidden, and doing a pretty good job of it. Without my helmet's built in low-light I wouldn't have seen her."

"A runner? Here? How in the galaxy did she get up to the station?" Helga didn't, of course, bother to ask why someone would be trying to escape Hillman. Just because they had to take jobs from anyone and everyone to keep the engines running didn't mean she liked what a lot of them did.

"No idea how she got up here. She didn't walk through the door, unless she did it before we got here. Definitely not from the station though. Her clothes are arguing whether they're mostly holes or patches. She doesn't quite look like the miners we've helped in the past though."

"Why do you say that?"

"You've seen them, practically albinos. She'd pass for Milatan, assuming her hair really is dark blonde and not just dirty. She's got enough scars for a miner though. Anyway, miner or not, what do you want me to do?"

"Don't spook her. Last thing we want is for her to run from us and get caught. Or worse, get us caught helping her. What's she doing?"

"She's just watching us. Probably waiting for a good chance to dart onboard without getting nicked."

"You want to give her a chance?"

"Of course I do. But can we afford another mouth to feed? Next stop is Breimley. No way could we offload anyone there, let alone a little girl. It's at least a month before we get to Parlon. Probably longer, given the bureaucracies of Breimley."

Helga blew her breath out as she thought. Could they handle at least a month feeding someone from a heavy gravity world? Growing kids needed plenty of food all on their own, even without the extra muscles to account for.

No. Helga knew she was asking herself the wrong question. As much as she tried to play it gruff and stern the question was a simple one. Could she sleep, knowing she'd sent a little girl back down *there*?

"Yeah, give her an opening. Just don't let on that you've see her. Pull whoever's close to the door over to 'talk' with you.

"And when she gets into our cargo bay? There's no one in there right now."

"Seriously? Where are they all?"

"Uh, in here with me? We're still unloading the third batch."

"We can't risk her wandering around the ship. Can you get someone back in there, make up some pretext."

"Yeah, I could, but it'll be hard to 'not see her' as they go past. Plus she might decide to wait until they come back, to keep us from catching her the moment she gets on Old Beamy."

Helga grumbled automatically at the hated nickname of her ship before responding. "Let me think," she said, running one hand through her sleep-messed hair. Not for the first time she wondered if she should give up and just cut it short like most of the women on board. "Everyone's either asleep, on duty, or working the cargo transfer right now, right?"

"Uh-huh."

"Okay. Go ahead and give her an opening. I'm going to head down there myself and snag her before she can get into trouble. Don't let the others know. They're good people, but, well, you've seen them play poker. Most of them couldn't lie their way out of a paper bag."

"It is one of their more endearing qualities."

"For you, maybe."

"Yeah, yeah. I'll start listening to you after I can stop buying spare parts with my poker money. Get down here quick. We're all risking trouble the longer she stays on the station side of the airlock."

Grumbling a bit at creaky joints and aching muscles Helga rolled out of bed. Tossing her robe aside she started shoving feet into her skinsuit where it lay unceremoniously on the floor.

She was getting old. Old and fat. It was becoming harder to get the suit on; she'd have to stop putting off getting it adjusted. Next time they were in a civilized system, she promised herself. And once she had the money, of course.

In the meantime, she'd been doing pretty well at avoiding the engineering parts of the ship where she needed the protection of the suit instead of her normal ship's jumpsuit, but something always seemed to come up. Like this latest wrinkle.

Years back they'd had a system in place for dealing with stowaways, even budgeted for extra food when they stopped at places like Hillman. She'd thought the centralization along with the station being finished had put a stop to the poor souls trying, but here they were.

Tight squeeze or no, Helga had the suit on in short order, another of the necessary skills when living in space. She'd never had to deal with a hull breach; much less one where she was caught outside her suit, but waiting until it did happen was a poor time to start practicing.

With practiced eyes she checked the indicator lights of her suit in the mirror before slapping her uplink unit onto the left wrist of the suit. It automatically tied into the suit's systems and was already tied into the ship's.

Heading for the door, Helga decided to leave her helmet retracted into the collar of the suit. She would probably frighten the girl less that way. If the girl was as pungent as some of the other stowaways they'd had years past, it might even help her find her.

The captain's quarters were close to the bridge, right near the center of the ship. The *Pale Moonlight* wasn't a large ship, as freighters went, but she still had several hundred meters of corridor to wind her way through to get to the cargo bays.

The corridors were, unsurprisingly, empty. Every crewman they could spare (and a couple they couldn't) was busting their butts getting the cargo unloaded so they could take on ore and get out of this utterly depressing system. There'd be some downtime once they hit subspace, but as the ancient saying went, time is money.

As she approached the main cargo bay she quietly triggered the voice commands for her uplink, connecting back to Mary.

"Is it done?"

"Yeah, she headed down the gantry tube a couple minutes ago. You aren't in there yet?"

Helga ignored the question and picked up her pace. A few simple whispered commands and she'd tied into the ship's controls, locking down the hatches into the cargo bay, starting with the hatch leading to the airlock.

Stopping at the end of the corridor Helga opened the hatch into the bay, closing it as soon as she was through. A quick glance around did not show her the stowaway, unsurprisingly.

"You might as well come out," she called out loudly. "We know you're in here, the ship has you on her sensors." This was a lie, the internal sensors were spotty at best, but the stowaway had no way of knowing that. Helga gave the girl a full minute to respond, the only movement the display on her uplink.

No response.

Helga waited a minute more, then called out again.

"You're safe now. We aren't going to give you back to them. Come out, please."

Still nothing.

Well, nothing for it. Time to flush her out.

Helga walked around the few crates still in the room, circling towards the airlock. As she moved she tapped the two buttons that controlled her suit's helmet. The segmented fabric slid up under its own power, sealed in less than two seconds. The equally segmented clear visor wasn't the easiest to look through, but having the helmet always at hand was well worth the drawbacks.

Plus it had features like low light amplification and infrared in addition to the heads up display. It was the later she triggered, bathing the room in shades of red and yellow, with some cooler blues and purples in places.

Helga turned about slowly. Hmm. Not good. She couldn't see the girl anywhere. Even if she was behind a crate she should have at least seen a slight spike in temperature levels. She looked around again – there was an odd heat patch against the wall opposite of her. Turning the infrared off she walked over.

It was an access panel into the service crawlways.

It was closed, and looked normal. Stooping down Helga looked closer at it, then switched infrared back on.

There was a faint heat increase around the edges, like someone had held onto it. Helga grabbed the edge of the panel and tugged. It came away easily in her hand.

Oh. That wasn't good.

"Mary," she said, linking back in to her sister.

"You get the girl?"

"That would be a no. How quickly can you finish up over there?"

"At least an hour, and then however long the ore loading takes."

"Try and hurry up."

"Sis?"

Helga closed her eyes and winced.

"You ever figure out how the girl got into the bay in the first place?"

"I hadn't thought about it. She couldn't have used the door. . . Oh. Are you saying?"

"It looks like the girl is in the *Pale Moonlight*'s crawlways."

"Well, shit."

For once Helga didn't remind her sister to watch her language.

***

She was going to kill her.

It was that simple. The choice made perfect sense.

They'd spent the last four hours tearing through the ship looking for one tiny girl. How she continued to elude the crew, the newest of which had lived onboard for several years, was as infuriating as it was baffling.

The girl did have a few things going for her, of course. The bulk of the crew was still handling the loading procedures, or the critical systems. Making the manpower issues even worse was the fact that she had to station a goodly number of the crew at key points, to make sure the girl didn't accidentally get into the really vital stuff. Modern, well-maintained ships would also have had motion and IR sensors in every compartment, but when you had to choose between fixing the internal sensors or the air scrubbers. . . well, priorities.

At least the sensors near the outer hull worked, since they were the first warning if something hit them hard enough to pierce the fairly thin armor the freighter had, but by luck or design the girl hadn't headed that way.

At the moment Helga was searching one of the less-used storage bays, making no attempt to be quiet. She doubted she was fast enough to actually catch the girl given their relative ages, so she was serving as a 'beater' to try and force the girl towards the waiting crew who were still young and quick on their feet.

Her helmet was retracted to keep from interfering with her hearing, and she'd pulled the earpiece attachment off her uplink so she could more easily keep abreast of what the crew was doing.

Presently the quiet squawk of the all crew circuit sounded, and Helga stopped to listen.

"She's been in the aft mess hall." It was Heather, the ship's medic. Cooped up in the tiny medical wing of the central crew quarters she probably knew the crawlways least of any of the crew, so she had taken it on herself to keep an eye on the common areas.

"You see her?" Helga asked, whispering into the tiny mic hanging off of the earpiece.

"Not as such. But she was definitely here. Last five, ten minutes maybe?"

"Right, she still has to be in the core somewhere. Seal off everything leading to the forward and rear sections, use the magnetic locks." Helga waited until everyone confirmed the orders, and then added, "How do you know, Heather?"

"Girl has a lot of moxie. Stole my blasted meal right off the table."

They really needed to find this girl, or at least get undocked. Something was going to blow up in their faces – probably literally, given the types of systems you could get at in the crawlways – and they'd find themselves explaining things to the station. Best case, the girl was turned over, and got whatever punishment attempted runaways got. Helga tried very hard not to speculate about what those would be. Worst case though? Worst case they assumed the crew was in on it and arrested some or all of them, or impounded the ship. Sure, eventually the crew's home port would investigate, but there was no guarantee they'd intervene, and it would take months at least.

Well, if the girl had been in the aft mess hall ten minutes ago, there was no way she was in this part of the ship. Helga took a moment to seal the scattered hatches in the room before exiting and sealing the door too.

It was really going to be a hassle to go back through and unseal every single one of these hatches and doors. By their very nature they couldn't be overridden remotely, nor all at once. Normally the mag locks were only used in cases of damage to a section required it be evacuated, especially when dealing with decompression.

They could also be used against boarders – or cheeky stowaways – which had bumped them up the maintenance queue enough that they all reliably worked, at least so far. They had never before been used in that capacity, thank the gods. As with so many defensive measures it was always better to have them and not need them, than need them and not have them.

"I think I saw something." The voice cut in suddenly, scattering Helga's thoughts. It sounded like Peter, where had she told him to look? Hadn't he been in the hydroponics bay? She was moving *fast*.

"John, Melly, you're closest. Seal your doors and get over there to help him."

"I've got a hold of her," Peter said after a moment, grunting with effort, "Stop fighting girl, we're not going to hurt you."

"Almost there," Melly chimed in, breathing heavily. Not the wisest thing to do, running through the corridors, given the number of low hanging conduits and patch jobs. They needed to get this over with, before someone got hurt.

A loud thud came through the line, accompanied by some grumbling.

"She's headed your way," Peter muttered after a moment, "I managed to get the crawlways sealed before she bolted."

"What happened?" Helga asked, "Are you hurt?"

"No, I'm fine. Just stumbled. I am also the proud new owner of one really ratty sleeve."

Despite herself, Helga snorted in amusement.

John laughed too, before adding in, "Really Peter, she's half your size."

"In height, almost. Not in weight. And she's stronger than she looks."

"Don't forget, everyone, she's from a heavy gravity world. Probably been doing a lot of manual labor to boot. Now stop yapping and nab her."

Helga sighed. She had made good time herself, and was almost to that section of the ship. It had been sealed off, of course, but she had the override codex in her uplink.

Mary's voice cut in as Helga entered the aft port crew section.

"We're all done here. You guys want to let us back in so we can shove off?"

Helga groaned internally. She had gotten so wrapped up in the search that she had forgotten to keep someone on hand to let the last of the loading crew back in.

"You can shove off; we're running ourselves ragged here." Helga couldn't tell who said it, the com line was open to everyone at the moment, and he had pitched his voice lower, probably as much from annoyance as a desire to keep out from under Helga's wrath.

"Enough." Helga said, her voice level and quiet.

"Gloria, you're closest to them. Get the door unsealed, quick. We don't want anyone wondering why our people are loitering around outside with the job done." She waited for Gloria's affirmative before continuing, "Captain, the ship will be ready to undock as soon as the last of the crew is on board. I would advise we do so posthaste. Most of the crew spaces are in lockdown, but the engineers aren't hindered in any way. We'll have at least three hours before we get to the planetary gate to catch her."

"Is that enough time?" The captain's voice didn't betray any emotion, but then it never did. After all this time Helga could read him easily enough regardless. That was as blunt a criticism as he would offer her in front of the crew, but it was still a criticism.

"With the crew section sealed off we could recheck every compartment twice in that time, especially once Mary gets over her with her team to help.

It's only a matter of time."

"Very well. All hands, be ready to undock."

Helga, meanwhile, rounded the corner and found herself looking at Peter, Melly, and John. . . and no girl. Calmly, slowly, Helga muted the pickup on her mic before talking.

"How could you have possibly lost her?" Her voice had raised at least ten decibels from sheer exasperation. "There isn't anywhere she could have gone without running into one of you."

"Are we sure she's not a gremlin sent to torment us?" Peter wasn't joking, at least not completely. "She got out of the compartment less than ten seconds ahead of me, and Melly and John weren't far off. The crawlways are sealed. We've got nothing."

"Just. . ." Helga paused, trying to figure out what they could even do. "Just retrace your steps back to the last sealed door, and then recheck everything. The door behind is sealed, and I'll wait here to make sure she doesn't try to get out of this section. Hurry." She turned her mic back on. "Everyone, stay alert. This girl is very determined to stay hidden. She's undoubtedly scared and isn't used to trusting anyone."

"We're good to go boss," Mary cut in, her yawn transmitting over the line for a moment before the program recognized the sound and cut out automatically. "Can we leave this dump, please?"

"Gladly," Asad said, mere moments later. He switched lines, calling up station control. Helga's unit patched her in to the new line automatically. Too many problems dealing with corrupt or criminal outfits had taught them the wisdom of having someone listening for subtle clues they were about to be swindled while the other talked. "We've finished our loading, Hill Station. We request permission to undock so we don't waste any of your valuable time."

The station had to have been expecting the call, but it was still half a minute before they responded.

"We show delivery in full on both ends, *Pale Moonlight*. Docking clamps will release in fifteen seconds."

Helga didn't think he sounded worried or harried at all. They couldn't have realized the girl had gotten on board the station, let alone her ship. The last time they suspected a stowaway they'd demanded to search the whole ship.

Twenty seconds later Helga felt the slight shudder as the clamps released, followed by the stronger nudge of the ship's thrusters pushing them away from the station.

"Main drive engaging in one minute," the chief engineer said, over the speaker system rather than the suit coms.

Once the speakers cut off Helga got back on the suit com. "Okay people. We're underway. We should be safe from Hillman, but we have to find the girl. It's unlikely, but if they discover her missing they may try and search us when we reach one of the gates. We have to have her in hand in case we need to hide her. Be thorough, be. . ." Helga paused to brace herself as the main drive kicked on. It wasn't a particularly powerful kick, but could be startling if you weren't expecting it. . .

. . .Which the stowaway apparently hadn't been, as she jolted off of the pipes snaking along the top of the corridor. The girl tried to correct her slide, but just ended up tumbling to the floor in an ungainly pile in front of Helga. She looked up, blue eyes wide in an incredibly dirty face.

"Um. . . hello?" the girl said, her Hillman accent thick and unmistakable. Helga thought she sounded young, maybe even ten or twelve.

The part of her brain analyzing that was quite small, however, overwhelmed by the part that wanted to cheerfully throttle this girl who'd been hiding right in front of her.

"Get over here!" Helga growled, not noticing the chorus of winces as her shouting transmitted to the entire crew. Her hand darted out, grabbing a big handful of the front of the girls' tattered outfit. She ignored the sounds of tearing fabric and the girl's surprised and probably terrified squeak as Helga pulled her upright with brute strength, assisted by the lighter gravity of the ship.

Before she could start chewing the girl out for wasting all of their time, and probably causing untold hours of maintenance and repairs, the speaker came back on, and this time it was Asad.

"Welcome onboard, young lady. You've been something of a bother, hiding from us like that. You will *not* be a problem any longer, or you *will* regret it. Now go with Helga, quietly. Everyone else, get us secured from lockdown. I want everything back to normal before we hit the first gate."

Helga dropped the girl, who slumped down into a sitting position.

"He sounds nice," the girl said hesitantly. Helga couldn't help laughing.

"Trust me. Of the two of us, I'm the nice one. Now get up. You're cutting into my beauty sleep."

CHAPTER 06

Everyone forgets that for every large freighter company, there are hundreds of single ships running the margins. Without them the galactic economy would collapse. For all the talk of taxing the profits of the large houses let us remember that it is the independents that will suffer the consequences the most.

- Senator Andy McGivin, addressing the Zion congress on the repeal of tariff measure 234b.

MORGAN FOUND HERSELF deposited in yet another sparsely-furnished metal room. There was a table in one corner, a bed in another, a couple chairs, a door leading to another room, and what looked to be storage space in the walls. The only decoration was a painted starmap marked with different colored lines on one wall and a portrait on the other wall of a smiling family. It was unsettling somehow to see such a large picture of a family, almost all the videos and images back home had been about Sam Hill or the world he had founded. They had especially been about the duties of the people to unite together and work hard for everyone's benefit.

Morgan's own sad little picture would have been confiscated and destroyed if a Tinny had ever found it, she only had it at all because Daddy had 'borrowed' the camera after using it to in his work.

Back home. Funny how Morgan was already thinking of it that way, never mind that she wouldn't ever go back there, even if she could have.

"Sit there," the rather frightening woman growled, pointing to a bare metal bench attached to a bare metal table. The woman didn't wait to see if Morgan complied, instead throwing herself into a cushioned chair opposite the table.

Morgan sat down straddling the bench so she could keep her back to the wall while also watching both the woman and the door. She absently ran her hands along the surface of the table. It was going to take some time to get used to everything being so smooth, and so clean.

And so sharp-edged, as well. Morgan frowned as she ran a finger along the edge of the table. She would hate to see what kind of damage a fall against the table would cause.

Morgan's attention was brought back to the woman, Helga, apparently, as she took several deep, rhythmic breaths, visibly trying to calm herself down.

"You aren't the first stowaway we've had from Hillman, so I won't bother asking why you wanted to leave. I do want to know why you tried so hard to stay away from us."

"That was my daddy's idea. You'd be less likely to turn me over if you didn't get me until after your ship left the space station."

"That's a lot of mistrust for people who haven't even met."

Morgan raised her eyebrows. "You just said you know why people leave my planet."

"Right, of course you don't trust anyone." The woman looked Morgan up and down. "Still, you could have easily gotten yourself killed, mucking about in the crawlways. You also needlessly annoyed the people whose goodwill you are relying on."

"They're not that different than the tunnels back home." Morgan knew she was right, that she *had* risked angering these people, but since she wasn't sure how best to apologize yet, she fixated on the other part of the woman's comment.

"A tunnel rat, then?" Helga must have seen the look on Morgan's face, as she added, "Oh, I know all about tunnel rats. They're the ones most likely to try and run, after all. The risk of death or capture is too high for most of the people in safer jobs to seriously consider.

"You need to realize that aside from basic shape, the crawlways and your tunnels are nothing alike. In the tunnels you're dealing with solid rock. Here you have all kinds of machines and computers running through the walls, plus things like the power lines, coolant pipes, and so forth. We're flying through empty space in a metal wrapped bubble of air. Dangerous doesn't *begin* to describe it."

Morgan knew she was right. Hadn't she taken advantage of that very fact to get the panel off in the, what had she called them? Crawlways? She had firsthand experience of what the woman was saying.

"You're right. We didn't think of that. Daddy wouldn't want me to harm anyone, especially the people he was counting on to help. I'm sorry."

"Keep this in mind, girl. I'm helping you because I wouldn't want to leave anyone on that awful planet, and I like being able to sleep at night. You have not made a good first impression. Make sure your second impression is better."

It was odd. For all her anger and raised voice, Helga reminded Morgan of the few elderly women in town that had helped care for the little children, though she looked both older and younger than them. She was round and rosy skinned, with hair that was almost pure white. Despite the white hair, she wasn't nearly as wrinkled as the town grandmothers. The way she talked, and the look in her eye, suggested to her that this woman was quite old indeed. She did have the same sternness as the town grandmothers, though.

Before either could resume the conversation, the door opened and a woman stepped in. Morgan couldn't see anything about her beyond gender, since she was in the head to toe skintight outfit she'd observed in the loading bay with the helmet up. She was carrying a box in both hands. She stepped over to Helga, her helmet folding up over her head and into the collar. "I found the box you were talking about, sis. It was near the back of the storage space."

"Ah, good," Helga said, gesturing for the crewwoman to put it onto the table next to Morgan.

"Rude or not to say, girl, but it is a fact you stink to high heaven. Best empty your pockets of anything you wish to keep. Those clothes are going into the fire as soon as we can get you cleaned up and changed."

The new woman turned from Morgan and opened the box, which apparently held clothes of various types and sizes. "You are pretty small, even for someone from a heavy world. I don't suppose you know what standard size you are?"

"I'm still small enough that the child outfit fits me, mostly. The factory clothing fits a bit better, but the fabric isn't as durable," Morgan said, carefully pulling the small folded portrait from her pocket, the data storage device tucked inside. Then she tugged off the handmade bracelet on her left wrist. Finally she pulled her daddy's spanner from its belt loop. The woman held out her hand for them, taking them gently and placing them on the table.

"That's what I was afraid of. Mass produced in just a couple sizes then? Don't worry, we'll get you sorted out. We can hardly send you back to that sh. . . nasty place, can we? I'm Mary, Mary Tempest, by the way. You've met my big sister Helga. The voice on the speakers earlier was her husband, Captain Asad Allred. Are you ready to tell us your name?"

No one had actually asked her name yet, but Morgan didn't mind.

"I'm Morgan. I only have the one name. So. . . what are you going to do with me?"

Mary opened her mouth to answer, but closed it when Helga cleared her throat noisily.

"We'll talk more after you get cleaned up. Mary here will show you to the bathroom and where everything is," Helga answered instead, "We're headed out-system now, which will take some hours. But first things first. Get cleaned up, and then Mary will get you some food."

"Some more food, you mean," Mary said with a crooked smile.

"Sorry," Morgan said again, feeling her face heat up. "I wasn't sure if it would be hours or days before you left."

"Be sure you don't steal any more food while you're onboard my ship," Helga said, her voice taking on a bit more sternness for a moment. "Space is always at a premium on a spaceship. We don't have extra food just lying around."

There was an awkward silence for a moment, and Morgan considered apologizing again.

"Well, I like your spirit," Mary said, pointedly ignoring Helga's glare.

"What's a spirit?" Morgan asked, the word unfamiliar to her.

"A long conversation we don't have time for," Mary said, glancing at her sister's impatient face. Instead she changed the topic. "Is that all you have?" Mary asked, putting Morgan's handful of belongings into a small box she had pulled from under the clothes.

"I don't have anything else," Morgan said, glancing around the room and seeing again how little she had had, even before leaving home.

"Well, don't worry. Once you get settled in a new home you'll be able to get anything you need to keep," Mary said, smiling at Morgan. "Sis, any of it look like it'll fit?"

"Just the one." Helga held up a garment that was a pale yellow, with patterns that looked a bit like the flower Morgan had seen once growing in one of the few patches of bare dirt near the mines. It was the prettiest thing Morgan had ever seen. "Now, it's a dress, so be careful if you go through any of the areas of the ship that don't have gravity."

"What's a dress?" Morgan asked.

"This is a dress," Helga said, exasperated, holding the garment up so Morgan could get a better look at it. The neck hole was bigger than she was used to, and the sleeves much shorter, and it only had one opening for legs, much wider than any pant leg. Morgan supposed it would be something like the improvised nightgown she'd worn back home. It would be horrible for crawling around in, and hard to keep in place on any of the windy days Pari Passu was known for. . . not that she needed to worry about either of those now. Though given the warning about wearing it around the ship, Morgan supposed they didn't consider it especially practical wear either. Thinking about it, she supposed keeping the lower part of the dress from flying up in her face would be hard without gravity. Then she wondered if she'd get to see what no gravity felt like. So far she was certainly enjoying having less than on Hillman.

Her mind now wandering Morgan thought about the offhand comment about burning her current clothes, and how rich the ship captain and his wife must be. The clothes were barely five years old and her arms and legs were only a little bit too long for them. Sure, one sleeve had been torn off, but that was easily fixed.

Once she started comparing the two garments she realized that on top of the impracticality of moving around in the dress, it also looked like the fabric didn't have padding of any kind. While they were patched and dirty, at least her current clothes were thick enough that she wasn't likely to break anything if she tripped. This dress looked far, far too thin.

"I guess it isn't surprising they don't have anything but work clothes down there," Mary said, looking Morgan's outfit over, "And dresses certainly aren't practical for mining. Not for space travel either, for that matter. I wonder where it came from?"

Helga waved her hand dismissively, "Oh, I'm sure some foolish passenger or other left it behind, years ago if the style is any indication."

Mary took the dress from Helga, deftly folding it into a small bundle she was able to put into a hip pocket.

Morgan was nodding like she understood this, but really she was so overwhelmed with all the new words and things that she only knew which way was up because her feet stuck to the floor. Then it hit her. She was on a ship, flying through space to other planets, so even 'up' was probably wrong. Or could it even *be* right in space? Perhaps that was why everything felt so light, so flimsy. She felt lighter here than she had even on the station. Then again, the gravity here and on the station was artificial, so it could be set higher or lower as the person in charge wanted.

"Mary can help you if you have any trouble. Go on and get cleaned up, and try not to bother me or the captain." Helga said, and Mary nodded in agreement. She gestured back out to the hallway, and Morgan followed her out.

"That was a very brave thing to do, stowing away, leaving behind everything you've ever known," Mary said as they got into an elevator near the captain's room. A crewman looked like he wanted to get on too, but Mary waved him off. "Especially since you couldn't know how we'd react. The captain would have been well within his rights to send you straight back to Hillman."

Morgan thought about that for a moment, thought about leaving her parents behind, and the life they had led. She also thought about what would have happened if she'd been caught and returned. If that had happened, she wouldn't have been around long to regret it in any case.

"I thought it worth the risk."

The doors closed and they began to move. Mary leaned against one of the walls, her arms resting on the hand railing. Morgan stood in the center of the elevator, shifting her weight from one foot to the other, crouching down on her haunches on pure reflex.

"Are you all right?'

"I don't trust elevators much."

"Because they're enclosed?"

Morgan shook her head. "Because they are held up by little more than cables. My main job was tunnel maintenance, places the grown miners couldn't get to. That and checking the damage after accidents."

"Not rescue?"

"The Tinnys wouldn't complain if we found survivors."

"That must have been horrible."

"It isn't always bad. Most days I just did my job and went home. The Tinnys didn't care if we lived or died, but the managers got after them if the work slowed too much."

"Honey, that *is* horrible. People's lives matter a lot more than how much ore a stupid mine puts out." The elevator stopped. "We're just one floor down from the skipper's quarters. This is the rank and file's spaces."

Morgan could see that. There were a dozen men and women milling about, with room for four times that, most of them in the skin tight outfit Mary wore. There were others in coveralls not too different from what the miners' back home wore, though of much higher quality. Fewer holes too. They didn't appear to be nearly as thickly padded.

"Right," Mary called out in a loud voice. "Everyone, this is Morgan. She's the spunky girl who snuck on board. Don't crowd her, kindly. Cap'n is going to let her stay till we get to Parlon. Heather, would you please clear everyone out of the women's shower?"

"Sure thing, Mary," the woman who Morgan assumed was Heather replied, disappearing into the doorway on the other side of the room. What was Parlon, Morgan wondered, but didn't ask. A planet? A system?

"This will be a moment," Mary said, shaking the dress out. "Come here for a sec; let's see if this will fit." Mary held the dress up, careful not to let it touch Morgan's dirty clothes. "Yep, she has a good eye. This should fit you okay. I think it was meant for someone shorter than you, if you can imagine someone that small. Luckily the sleeves are a loose design, or they'd be tight too. You've certainly got a lot of muscle on you.

"It's too bad we don't have any shoes. Just stay away from places like engineering, okay? We will have to figure something out for underwear."

Mary put the dress down on the table sitting down next to it. She turned to one of the other ladies.

"See what you can do there, would you Gloria? Maybe one of the smaller ladies has something?" Gloria nodded and headed off down the hallway as Mary called out, "New is better, but at least clean, for Pete's sake."

Morgan looked at her in puzzlement. Under where? What did that mean? From context it was clothing of some kind. Noticing her confusion Mary threw up her hands. "Oh for the love of. . . Those assholes really kept you all in piss poor conditions didn't they? Underwear is meant to be worn under your clothes, partly for comfort, partly hygiene, and partly modesty." Mary flushed a bit. "Oh, sorry about the swearing. Not one of my better habits, especially in front of kids. How old are you anyway?"

"I'm not sure, exactly," Morgan said slowly. At least that wasn't a lie. She *didn't* know when her birthday was. "The only date that is important on Hillman is the anniversary of the first ship landing. I'm twenty-six or twenty-seven, I think."

"Uh, that would make you. . . " Mary looked up, twiddling the fingers on one hand as she did the math. "Eh, screw it." She hit a button on the screen that was clamped onto the back of her left arm, just above the wrist. Morgan had wondered about it. It obviously wasn't part of the suit (which had its own screens and buttons) but beyond that she had no idea what it did. Whatever it was made a chiming noise as Mary activated it, and she brought it up closer to her mouth.

"Compute, twenty-six local years, planet Hillman, in e-standard."

No sooner had she finished talking than the device answered in a pleasant feminine voice that sounded a lot more lifelike than the computers in the mines.

"Seventeen years, four months, Earth standard."

Morgan felt a little bad about lying to Mary, but her parents were right. Better they thought her old enough to support herself. Morgan wasn't about to trust her future to anyone ever again, especially not another government, and it was very doubtful any of them would trust a thirteen-year-old to live on her own

"Wow, you look a lot younger, even assuming you don't have anti-aging treatments." Mary held up a hand, palm up. "That's another long conversation we don't have time for now, but trust me, you don't. The short version is that, once we get you to a doctor with the proper equipment, you're likely to live a *lot* longer than anyone from that shithole of a planet." Mary blushed again. "Sorry. Please don't pick up my bad language, and uh, please don't tell the captain about it either."

Heather reappeared in the doorway, giving Mary a thumbs up signal, holding a large fluffy piece of fabric that she tossed to Mary, along with a couple of bottles of something Morgan couldn't identify immediately.

"Right," Mary said, pointing to the door while holding out the bundle, tucking the dress amongst the folds. "I'm willing to bet a lot of things are going to be nice surprises out here in the civilized galaxy, but I don't think many will compete with a long hot bath, *especially* with bubbles."

***

More than three hours later Morgan sat in a very soft, very comfortable chair in the captain's office. Sit was almost the wrong word. She felt so relaxed that she felt more like a liquid that had been poured into the chair. If only the ship hadn't been so cold. It had been easy to ignore when she'd been running about trying not to get caught, but after the hot bath the cold had settled into her bones.

There had actually been two baths, the first just to get most of the dirt and grime off, the second to soak in. Mary had been right, the dress only came down most of the way to her knees and elbows, but she didn't care. It was the softest piece of clothing she had ever worn, softer than she had even imagined possible. And her hair! She hadn't even noticed how itchy and messy it had been until she'd finished washing it with the shampoos and whatever all else there had been. If only. . .

. . . If only her parents could have been here too. With that sad thought Morgan sat up in the chair, hugging her knees to her chest.

She knew there was no way they all could have gotten off planet. Just getting *her* off very nearly got her killed. She knew her parents would rather she be here than them. Repeating that to herself helped, but only a little. Hillman had been a horrible place, but it was *home*. Now she didn't know what would happen to her in an hour, let alone the coming weeks and months.

"How you doing, kiddo?" Mary said as she walked in the room, closing the door behind her.

"I'm a lot more relaxed than I was," Morgan said, "Thank you for all your help."

"Don't worry about it. You just needed to be shown how things worked. Easier than giving my nieces baths, that's for sure.

"I should warn you, that's the last bath you'll get while onboard." Morgan's face darkened and Mary quickly added, "Oh, no, it's not anything bad. It's just that there isn't a ton of space on this rust bucket, so we do what we can to conserve water. A quick shower has nothing on a good soak, but it does the job and uses a lot less clean water."

Morgan nodded. Rationing she could understand. Really, it was almost a relief to find out that they didn't have an endless supply of everything.

Morgan noticed Mary staring at her arms, her mouth pressed into an unhappy line.

"What?"

"I talked with Heather about your checkup."

That had been an interesting part of the bathing process. Heather had insisted in checking every part of Morgan, both physically and with a device of some kind held a few inches off the skin. She had made a lot of clucking noises that sounded disapproving, but hadn't explained herself. She had asked Morgan all kinds of questions, seemingly at random, along with questions that were obviously relevant to her health.

"What about it?"

"You're healthy, for the most part. Obvious signs of old broken bones, a couple healed concussions, a bit of malnutrition, stuff we'd expect to see in mine workers. Then there's your collection of bruises, it's quite impressive, you almost look like a rainbow with the different colors blending together."

"What's a rainbow?"

"It's. . . not important. Were you being beat on?"

Morgan looked down at her arms, tucking her legs under her and hiding those bruises as she turned her arms over and looked at the patchwork of purples and greens.

"Working the mine is dangerous. Just yesterday there was an explosion in one of the shafts, threw me around a bit."

"Why weren't you treated properly though? And then there are your scars. I tried not to, but I noticed a lot of them while you were in the bath. Skin like yours, they stand out."

"Of course they were treated," Morgan said tersely, "My parents might not have had much, but they always did their best for me."

"If they did, why all the scars? In places it looks like a roadmap."

"You're not making any sense. What does getting my cuts treated have to do with them scarring?"

Mary stopped her response and closed her eyes, her eyebrows knitting together as she thought.

"What were they using?"

"Quicknit. They provided it to all the workers, proof of their 'love for us,' imported at 'great expense' to keep us healthy. Mostly they just didn't want us missing work while we healed."

Mary covered her face with her hands, slowly dragging them downwards.

"Quicknit is just about the cheapest medicine anywhere, just above slapping a bandage on a cut. It's only meant for bruises and muscle problems, as well as helping bones heal. It's not used for cuts because it doesn't prevent scarring like Quickheal does. Quickheal isn't even *that* much more expensive. We just delivered ten gross of both to the station. Its cost maybe accounts for a cubic meter of ore we took on. Probably not even that."

"Is that a lot?"

"The main ore hold is two-hundred meters cubed."

"So one out of two-hundred? That sounds like a lot."

"No, honey, two-hundred meters to a *side*, not two-hundred cubic meters. It holds eight million cubic meters."

Morgan leaned back, her mind reeling. All those scars, simply because the leaders could save a little bit of money by buying a cheaper medicine? She wasn't sure if she wanted to strangle someone or vomit. Both perhaps, with tears thrown in for good measure.

Mary noticed how uncomfortable she was making Morgan, changing the topic abruptly. "Sorry, I am here for a reason. Our first jump was delayed as the. . . jerks didn't want us leaving because of some problem down on the station.

"They actually were hinting that someone had snuck on board. Imagine that. We're finally cleared, and I thought you might want to watch."

Mary pushed some buttons on the control panel next to the door, and most of the wall opposite the two of them turned on with a faint buzzing noise. At first it was pure black, but then the picture resolved itself into the star-field and the round grey-green orb Morgan realized was Hillman.

She had known, in a general way, what her home had been like and the rudiments of space, but that is a far different thing than seeing it for the first time. The effect was compounded by the fact that Morgan had never before been more than a few miles away from the spot she was born on.

Mary was saying something about how it was a pity they couldn't afford to update the ship's screens to holographic displays, but Morgan didn't hear her. Every ounce of her attention was on the picture before her.

"It's beautiful," Morgan whispered, to herself or no one. "From space, even Hillman is." She didn't notice the tears running down her cheeks as she said goodbye to her home world, hopefully for the last time.

Mary sat down in the chair next to her, slowly reaching out a hand to put it on her shoulder.

"Obviously you've never jumped before, but do you at least know the basics of how it works?"

Morgan shook her head, forcing herself to look away from the screen and at Mary's face. Mary pointed back at the screen. She hit a button and the view changed, showing instead what Morgan assumed was the gate. It didn't look like much from this far away, a dull grey ring of metal with lights winking here and there, forming an empty circle.

"Well, I don't understand the physics of it, but I can give you the simple version. Basically the gate opens a hole in normal space, letting the ship go, well, somewhere else, where the laws of physics are different. Ships can go immensely fast there, and things are closer together. A heavy mass – like a planet or star – forces a ship back into normal space.

"Instead of weeks or months to get from planet to planet we can do it in hours. And instead of years or decades between star systems we can travel it in weeks.

"We almost never saw the night sky. Too much cloud cover. Every glimpse of the stars was another reminder that there were other places out there, better places."

"Most of us don't even really see the stars anymore. You see something often enough you start recognizing it and not really seeing it anymore." Mary gestured to the display. "Like that behemoth out there. You're in for a real light show when we go into that thing. Me, though, I never have time to stop and just take it in.

"It's seven jumps to get from here to where the system gate is. After that it's a week or so in subspace before we arrive at the Breimley system. We have a couple stops there, and then it's on to the Parlon system."

"And you'll be leaving me there?"

"Yes. Asad and Helga, along with myself, we own the ship, which is a great, but profits are thin. We can't afford to have anyone on board who doesn't pull their weight. Besides, you need to get an education, medical treatment, and a thousand other things we can't give you here. You should probably start thinking about what you want to do, since you are nearly of adult age." Something in her tone made Morgan think Mary didn't really believe that she was seventeen, but as long as she didn't call her on it Morgan would be fine.

Morgan could only shrug. She was starting to realize that having infinite options open to her was in its way almost as bad as having no options.

"There are lots of jobs that will always be in demand, whatever planet you end up on. Technicians, mechanics, repairwomen. Everyone seems to want the flashy or fun jobs, but those are rarely as stable as something like fixing things."

"I like fixing things. What about jobs in space?"

Mary laughed. "Those are always in demand. Nearly six hundred years since we left Earth, and people are getting complacent. Hundreds of worlds to choose from, why take the risks of working in space? Sure, new exploration isn't happening much, but you always need to haul junk from one end to the other. It's not glamorous so most folks consider it beneath them."

No one spoke for several minutes until Mary stood up. "I'm needed on the bridge, I'm afraid. Be sure to watch the jump. There is only one first time. Later we can talk about how you're going to be helping us during the journey, earn your keep." As she walked over to the door Mary grabbed a blanket off of the other chair, draping it over Morgan. "You were shivering. Don't worry, you'll adjust eventually. Most planets aren't as hot as yours, but we humans can adapt to just about anything."

As the ship got close the space inside the great ring began to ripple, a wavering in the light of the stars beyond. Then the stars disappeared from view all at once. The fabric of space became so black it seemed to leech the light out of the silvery metal of the gate's struts. The gate took up the entire screen now, the edges just outside of the frame. There was a flash of light and the absolute black of the gateway became a dizzying array of every color Morgan had ever seen, and a few she had no words for. She was never sure how long the moment lasted. She would have believed a second or a minute equally, but either way it was too quick. Then they were through, surrounded not by the brilliant colors of the gateway, but a dimly lit grey expanse with a star-field of its own, but here the stars were all a sullen red color. Subspace, Morgan had heard it called. The word meant nothing to Morgan, beyond that it somehow allowed ships to travel much faster than in normal space.

It felt fitting to Morgan, for all its strangeness. Fitting that something completely unknowable would be the thing to take her to the unknown. Take her to where her future wasn't planned out in advance by the comrade managers and their Tinnys who ran the planet.

PART 2:
THE BLUE ISLE

CHAPTER 07

For all the talk of the importance of education, why is the public not flocking to trade schools? We don't have a shortage of schools that are churning out philosophers and theorists, or even doctors and lawyers. What we do need are more trained mechanics, pilots, and electricians. Prices go up because there aren't enough hands for the jobs. While I'm sure my graduates appreciate the higher wages, I'd imagine they'd like vacation time too.

- Nick Oar, President of Keldar Integrated Trade Schools, planet Keldar

A FEW ZION/EARTH MONTHS LATER

"YOU'RE MORGAN, RIGHT?"

The sudden break in silence startled Morgan, but she forced herself to look up slowly. After the twentieth time she'd been told she looked like 'a caged animal' she'd started pretending to be less observant than she was. She didn't even try to appear quite as oblivious as her fellow students though. How they had survived to twice or thrice her own age blundering through the world was beyond her understanding.

Sitting with her back to the door was a good way she had found to seem more normal, though she could only bring herself to do it in places like her school, which had access restricted to students.

It still resulted in unpleasant surprises from time to time, unfortunately.

There was a woman standing in the classroom's doorway, smiling in a fairly maternal fashion. Her age could have been anywhere from mid-twenties to sixty. Everyone looked young to Morgan. She was still used to the mine wearing people out early. Once the universal anti-aging treatments were factored in, tripling lifespans and slowing aging considerably. . . well, Morgan had simply given up trying.

Morgan thought the woman was one of the other students in her repair and maintenance classes, but she wasn't sure. In class most of them wore plain and sturdy clothing – like Morgan's own tan coveralls – but right now the woman was wearing an ornate robe/dress thing Morgan had seen a couple of times on the street, her hair done up in fancy style that Morgan suspected took far too long to achieve.

Right. She needed to say something.

"I'm Morgan. I'm surprised I'm not the only one here."

The woman smiled wider and stepped forward a bit. As she did so, Morgan caught sight of a little girl hiding behind the woman, clutching at her skirts. She had short jet-black straight hair, compared to the woman's longer and wavy light brown. Their eyes were also different shapes, but clearly, the woman was her mother.

"Well, you were almost right Morgan. I'm only here to grab something I forgot. I'm Gertrude, by the way, and this," she motioned to the child behind her, "is Haruhi." The little girl waved shyly, one eye poking out from behind the woman to look at Morgan. Morgan smiled at the little girl. After all the changes in her life, she'd been relieved to discover that children were children, whether on Hillman or Zion.

Gertrude sat down across from Morgan, grabbing the edge of the large tablet Morgan had been studying. She spun it around so she could see the schematics and text.

"I'm surprised you're still studying this," Gertrude said, tracing a finger along the schematic. "I watched you make this repair last week, faster than most of the class."

"I still need to understand the principles behind the machine," Morgan replied, turning the tablet back around.

Gertrude looked at Morgan, her eyes narrowing as she scrutinized her. "Do you have trouble with the reading?"

Morgan felt her mouth open in shock, but couldn't think of anything to say for a moment. "I thought you Zionites tried to always be polite," she finally got out.

"Oh, I'm too blunt, I know. But you have to understand, you've piqued the curiosity of our entire class just by being here. You don't talk in class or answer questions, yet you act like you've been fixing things your whole life. No one can figure out where your accent is from. Most of all you're in an evening tech class designed for working adults, but you look like you should be in junior high."

"What does that have to do with reading?" Morgan asked. She wanted to ask what junior high was, but she'd learned those kind of questions only drew more attention to herself. She'd just have to look it up later.

"My guess is you're a refugee," Gertrude said, very confidently. Morgan scowled, her lips pressing into a thin line. Gertrude just waved one hand at her, "Oh, there isn't anything wrong with that. Really, it's commendable that you're trying to make something of yourself, wherever you're from. It's just – I've seen some of my nephews struggle with reading, and watching you in class reminded me of them. There are a lot of places out there that don't encourage reading, after all."

"Say you're right. Why are you wasting my time instead of letting me get back to studying?"

Gertrude laughed. "With this little one here I've rather gotten used to worrying, so it isn't any extra trouble for me to worry about you too. Besides, you look like you could use a friend."

"And why would I need one of those?"

"You're sitting in here struggling through classwork while the rest of the city is either at home enjoying the holiday or actually at the Obon Festival. Besides, I can help you."

"Really?"

"I've done it before, with my nephews. My brother and his wife are great parents, but not very good teachers."

"Lady, I don't know you," Morgan started.

"She's not a Lady. She's Mom," Haruhi piped up out of nowhere, grasping the edge of the table and looking over it to peer at Morgan with her big dark eyes.

Morgan couldn't help but smile at that. The little girl was just so earnest. It was cute.

"Oh she is, is she?" Morgan suppressed a small laugh as Haruhi nodded vigorously. "And what kind of mom is she?"

Haruhi didn't answer, her shyness having gotten the upper hand again. She dropped back from the table and gave Gertrude a fierce hug.

"Look, come with us to the festival. It's very public, and you can decide for yourself if you like me. Plus, it'll be *fun*."

Haruhi bounced in place a little bit, nodding again.

Morgan smothered another small smile. "What is this. . . bon thing?"

"It's a memorial. The Obon Festival. We're honoring our ancestors. Especially those we've lost recently. But it's also a big carnival, with games and rides. Later there will be fireworks. You've missed the first two days already, but at least they save the best for last."

Morgan gestured to the robe thing Gertrude and Haruhi were wearing, "And is there a. . . dress code?" She stumbled a bit over the unfamiliar term.

Gertrude looked down at her outfit. "The kimono? It is traditional, but don't worry about it. The festival welcomes everyone, especially those who aren't Buddhist or Shintoist. By now, you should have learned that Zion's national pastime is proselytizing. Besides, there isn't really time for you to go home and change."

"You seem sure I'm coming with you." Proselytizing wasn't a word Morgan had heard before coming to the Parlon system, but she had learned it quickly – Gertrude wasn't exaggerating, it really was the planetary pastime, if polite and courteous to a fault.

Gertrude shrugged, then carefully scooped up Haruhi into her arms. "Of course I am. Can you really say no to this face?" She gestured to Haruhi, who nodded furiously.

"Come have fun," the little girl happily said. "I made a paper 'tern for otou-sama."

Morgan looked at Gertrude for a translation.

"That's right, Haruhi," Gertrude said gently, "We made a paper lantern to put in the river for your father."

She was smiling, but her eyes looked sad. Morgan was about to ask about him when she realized the likely reason for having something for a family member in a *memorial* festival.

"Well, okay," Morgan said instead, offering her hand solemnly to the little girl, "But only because you asked."

Since Morgan hadn't been tinkering with any physical parts, all she had to do to clean up was put the tablet back in its holder. As they left Gertrude stopped at her locker and pulled out the paper lantern, a tall white rectangular affair with some markings on it. They looked a lot like some of the signs she had seen in parts of town, so she guessed they were writing. She didn't ask what it said.

The three of them left the tech school on foot. Or rather, two of them on foot and the third carried as they walked towards the center of town and the large park that straddled the Mossbank River. The day was clear enough that Morgan could see the towering structures of Ein city, some fifty miles away. The ground under the suburb of Isa couldn't support the massive weight of a single two hundred story tower, let alone the dozens of interlinked towers that made up most modern cities. As such, Isa was much more spread out, giving it the feel of the old pre-space cities on Earth.

Or so the government employee had said back when Morgan had first arrived on Zion. It had been the employee's task to help Morgan find a school, a job, and place to stay. She'd recommended Isa for that very reason, since Morgan didn't have any experience living among the massive crowds of a modern city. There were downsides, of course. The rent was higher than in a tower, since you couldn't fit even remotely the same number of people in the same space. The only reason it wasn't much higher was because demand was low. Most people *had* grown up in the dense cities, and for them not being a short elevator ride away from practically all of life's necessities was an unpleasant and foreign experience.

That Isa had one of the better tech schools, particularly if you wanted to study the maintenance and repair of space ships, had been a welcome bonus as well.

Several blocks before the park Gertrude turned onto a side street.

"I hope you don't mind, there is a brief stop we need to make before we join the festivities, part of the original festival."

"I don't mind," Morgan said. She hadn't been in this particular neighborhood before, not being one to explore the city without a set destination in mind. Presently they came to a graveyard, surrounded by a well-maintained brick wall. Gertrude led them to an un-weathered marble slab with recesses in front of it, one holding flowers, the other a lit stick of incense.

It had more of the writing Morgan couldn't decipher in three vertical lines, one of which was painted red.

After standing there silently for a minute Gertrude started talking, without turning to face Morgan. "We buried my husband not quite a year ago. A training accident. His family lives in the Makor system, so it's pretty much just Haru and me, at least since my brother got a job on Albion."

"It's difficult, being away from your family."

Gertrude put Haruhi down, and the little girl walked up to the stone, running her fingers along the carved writing.

"His unit stops in pretty regularly, and their spouses help with stuff like babysitting while I'm at school. I could have moved to be closer to his family, or mine, but that would have meant leaving home behind."

"I don't understand," Morgan said slowly, "It's just a building, they can be replaced."

"A home is more than just a house," Gertrude said slowly, "It holds memories, hopes, and dreams. Every time I look out my window, I can see the fence that Naru built one weekend with half his unit. I think of all the time they spent joking around and drinking beer, covered in white paint and sawdust. They spent as much time at that as they did actually working. Every time I put Haruhi to bed, I can hear him singing lullabies to her. There are a thousand memories, just like that.

"My home reminds me of Naru. Sometimes that's hard. Sometimes it helps. No matter what I do I will always miss him, but at least this way it feels like he isn't as far."

"I'll have to think on that," Morgan said.

They stood in silence for several minutes, worlds apart in experiences, yet thinking the same kind of thoughts.

"Come on little one, time to get to the games," Gertrude said, holding out her hand for Haruhi to take, which she was only too happy to do.

The sounds of the carnival reached them several blocks before they got a look at it. Morgan took her time taking it in as they walked, this massive jumble of lights and sounds and voices. It certainly wasn't like anything she had seen back home.

There were booths scattered about, some selling food, others with what she guessed were the games. The food wasn't anything she recognized, since the part of town she lived in was predominantly settled by people whose ancestors had come from someplace called Texas. It was at least easier to identify them as food than to guess what the games were. Well, except the small cylinders of what looked like rice wrapped in something. Morgan had no idea what those were. Several others had bunches of useless looking items, soft fabric things made up to look like animals, that sort of thing.

Toys, that was the word. She'd never even imagined such a thing before coming to Zion. On Hillman, only the youngest children ever had time to play. Even then, it was done with stuff they cobbled together from rocks or sticks or trash. Throw in the possibility of injury or death from simply tripping, even with their denser bones and muscles, and it wasn't hard to see why play was discouraged on Hillman. That was even before you factored in their leaders and strict laws.

"What, you never have anything like this where you're from?" Gertrude asked, ignoring Haruhi's attempts at tugging her towards the games.

"No, not really," Morgan said over her shoulder, taking in the larger festival. One large corner was filled with people dancing, nearly all of them dressed in kimonos, while the general crowd was about fifty-fifty. In the center of that area was a small tower with a band on top, a trio of women singing in a language Morgan didn't recognize. She assumed it was the same language as the writing she's seen elsewhere.

There were mechanical contraptions too, small vehicles whose whole function seemed to be going fast or spinning about. They reminded her of the carts they had used to get about in certain parts of the mines, though she doubted these had any practical purpose.

"Momma, look!" Haruhi said, pointing excitedly at one of the booths. "Penguin!"

Morgan had never heard of a penguin before, but it wasn't hard to figure out that the little girl was pointing at the biggest of the toys hanging above a cluster of games. It looked sort of like a bird to Morgan, but far too fat to actually fly. It was hard to tell. Humanity had brought a lot of species with them to the stars, but birds hadn't been among them on Hillman. Or at least none that had survived to the present day. Most of the birds on Zion

Morgan had seen were small colorful things that flitted about singing, but didn't seem to do much else.

Gertrude looked like she wanted to say no, but Haruhi had started bouncing up and down.

"All right, I'll try and win one sweetie, but the game looks hard."

Morgan just watched as Gertrude gave it a try. The point of the game was to throw small balls through holographic hoops, without touching the holograms. It seemed simple enough, but Gertrude only managed it with a single one of the balls, evidently not enough for a prize, let along the large one.

After trying and failing twice more Gertrude turned to Morgan. "Do you want to give it a try? Much more of this and it would be cheaper to just go out and buy one of them."

"I really don't think that's a good idea," Morgan said, grimacing, "We never really played games with balls."

"You can hardly do worse than I did."

"You want to bet?" Morgan sighed as Gertrude handed her the first ball. It was even lighter than she had expected.

Morgan eyed the hoops carefully. They weren't too far away, but the holes were barely bigger than the ball.

She drew back her arm and let the ball loose. . . and it sailed right past the table entirely, bouncing off the back of the tent.

The second did better, if only missing the table by centimeters instead of meters could be considered a worthwhile improvement.

She could feel her face reddening, heating up.

"You don't need to throw it *quite* so hard," Gertrude said, chuckling.

"It's falling slower than it should be," Morgan muttered. Then she remembered. It *was* falling slower than it should, if they were on Hillman. Different gravity, different falling rates. She *knew* that, but it was so easy to forget. "I'm not going to make it, you take the last throw," she added louder.

"Game rules little lady, one person per go around," the tall lady manning the booth said quickly.

"Why," Gertrude started asking, but cut herself off, shaking her head. "Never mind. Just try then. Who knows, you might get lucky."

"Is there maybe another game I could try for the same prize?" Morgan asked, rolling the ball around in her hands.

"Just the mallet," the lady replied, pointing to a small pedestal with a target on top and large mallet lying next to it. A holodisplay stretched upwards a meter or so past the top of the tent, numbers dully flashing interspaced along it next to helpful labels like "weakling" and "strong man."

"What? I just hit the target with the mallet? That's it?"

"If you want the penguin you'd have to max out the meter," the lady said, "but yes, that's 'all.'"

"Just try the ball, Morgan. I can try again after that," Gertrude said, glancing down at Haruhi who was still intently looking at the penguin. She seemed to have realized they weren't likely to get it, as she had stopped bouncing, her smile drooping.

"I think I can do that," Morgan said, eying the mallet carefully. It was nearly as long as she was tall, but lifting it here would be fairly easy.

"Tell you what, little lady," the lady said to Morgan. "I'll even let you trade your last throw for two swings." Clearly she didn't think Morgan could do it.

Morgan shrugged. "Sounds good to me." She walked over to it, carefully hefting it in both arms. She had guessed right, it wasn't heavy, but the bulk would still be an issue. "What's the best way to swing it?" she asked Gertrude quietly. Not quietly enough, as a couple of the people standing around waiting their turn snickered a little bit. Morgan didn't think they were being mean about it. She imagined she did make a funny sight.

"Swinging it from behind your back over your head gives you the most force," Gertrude answered. "Though I don't think I'm strong enough to pull that off." Left unspoken was *and neither are you.*

Morgan tried it, hefting the mallet above her head. Nope. As she brought it up perpendicular to her body her coveralls started pinching and digging into her shoulders and upper arms. They were simply too tight for her to swing it that way without tearing something. She'd already ruined one pair by accidently getting an acid based cleaner on it. That incident had been a whole lot of fun for her too, come to mention it. She'd ruined another that had gotten caught on a machinery edge. It had torn so badly it was easier and cheaper to just replace rather than repair. She couldn't afford to lose a third over a game.

So she settled for raising it up as far as she could, then bringing it down as hard as she could, the flat head hitting with a resounding gong against the pedestal's sensor.

The hologram sprang to life, lighting up in vibrant red as it measured the force of the blow. Up it climbed, slowing down a bit, then stopping a couple meters from the top.

"Wow," Gertrude said as the meter fell back down, the lights dimming, except for the flashing word "Strong Man."

"That's not quite enough for the penguin," the lady said, not sounding particularly sorry, "but it is enough for the monkey." She did seem mildly impressed that Morgan had done even that well.

"How about a nice monkey, Haruhi?" Gertrude asked sweetly, bending down to bring her head closer to the little girl.

"Penguin's better," she replied sadly.

When she had woken up that morning, Morgan would not have believed she would be willing to put so much effort into winning something so useless for someone she had barely met. But she couldn't just disappoint the girl if there was some way to avoid it.

"All right, I got one more try, I'd better make it count," she said, putting the mallet back down. Hesitating for a moment she undid the top couple of buttons of her overalls. Luckily she had bothered with an undershirt today, she didn't as often as not.

"What are you doing?" Gertrude asked.

"It's too tight, I can't swing properly," Morgan answered, finishing unbuttoning it down to her navel. Peeling it back she bunched it up around her waist, tucking the sleeves in so they wouldn't stick out. She glanced about, self-conscious about her scars, but no one seemed to notice. Or if they did, they didn't care.

Gertrude did seem to notice, frowning slightly, but saying nothing. Morgan ignored her for the moment too. The lady running the game, however, seemed more interested in the size of Morgan's arms, a dawning realization that Morgan could have a chance at winning.

Picking the mallet back up, Morgan swung it up over her head easily.

"Much better," she said, readying herself for a moment before bringing it down on the target with all the force she could muster. The reverberation of the gong was even louder this time, as the holographic display climbed upward quickly. Just as it seemed to have stopped it passed the last line, and the 'Super Man' sign began flashing, so fast that it almost hurt to look at.

"The penguin, please," Morgan said to the lady.

"You're from a heavy gravity world. That's cheating."

"You can't know that," Gertrude cut in. "And even if she is, that little rule isn't displayed anywhere. Besides, it looks like she earned those muscles the hard way." She smiled broadly, the effect decidedly not warm and soothing. "I'm sure you've already made money off us." Gertrude leaned in and added, "And how many of the young men who saw that little display are now going to be eager to prove that they're just as strong as this 'little girl?'"

The booth lady chuckled, acknowledging defeat. "Fair is fair. One penguin." She reached up with a small stick and snagged one of the large black and white toys off of the display. "Have a nice day."

Gertrude handed the penguin to Morgan, who just looked at it. It was cute, she supposed.

"Here you go, Haruhi," she said, squatting down and handing it to the girl. The toy was almost a meter tall, which was as tall as the girl and decidedly wider. She hugged it tight, somehow managing to remember to add in a 'thank you' to Morgan.

Morgan just laughed and shook her head.

"Sweetie, maybe mommy can carry it so it doesn't get dirty on the ground?" Gertrude said, holding out her arms for the toy.

Haruhi's nose scrunched up as she thought about it. "Okay," she said at last, "You can carry Penny. Who will carry me?"

Well, at least she'd gotten the naming part decided quickly. "I can carry you, if you want," Morgan said. She wasn't sure Haruhi would agree, she had seemed rather shy so far. . .

But then she nodded enthusiastically and jumped into Morgan's arms. Well, Morgan supposed a giant toy was a good way to get a child on your side.

"I think we should get some food. I don't know about you but I don't have a lot of money to spare for the games. The lantern ceremony isn't for a couple hours, and we need to try and get there early to get a spot where we can reach the river and still see the fireworks. Have you ever seen fireworks, Morgan?" Gertrude said.

Morgan shook her head. "I don't think so. What are they?"

Gertrude laughed. "Well, you are in for a treat then."

As they walked away from the booth Morgan could hear the lady calling out to the crowd. "Try the Strong Man challenge. So easy a tiny girl just won top prize! Surely you strapping young men can do better?"

CHAPTER 08

There were many attempts in the early days to automate spaceships; to reduce the crew down to a bare handful, even a single person. Technologically the method was sound, but the egineers forgot the first lesson of humans. We're pack animals. The need to belong to a group is so strong that sailors named their ships and give them a personality so she could belong to the pack with them. That impulse remains, for all that an ocean was traded for the stars.

- Ralph Baksis, Head Shipwright, LaForce Shipyards

MORGAN HELD THE STUFFED PENGUIN against her shoulder, not too unlike how Gertrude carried the dozing Haruhi. She felt nearly as stuffed as the toy, having tried literally dozens of different foods that, as of this morning, she hadn't even imagined existed.

She still wasn't sure how she felt about eating uncooked fish, but she had to admit it had been tasty. Luckily it had also been free, or Morgan would probably have had to skip meals for several weeks to stay on budget. As for the games, well, those she *had* skipped entirely after her success with the hammer. It was just as well, most of them appeared nearly impossible to win in any case.

Gertrude had explained that the food was either donated by local restaurants – these were easily identifiable by the advertising prominently displayed on the booth – or made by the local temples and their members as gifts to each other and any visitors. This meant that the same dish could easily be available in a dozen different varieties and recipes, and Morgan had found it all too tempting to try everything.

And the fireworks! So many patterns and colors mixing in the inky sky, she had never imagined something so splendid, if loud. She supposed a similar display wouldn't have worked on Hillman, thanks to the cloud cover, even assuming they would have wasted money on something so frivolous.

Well, they probably would have for Founder's Day.

Morgan put aside thoughts of home as she struggled to keep up with the taller woman. For all its light, fluffy, construction the toy was more than half as tall as Morgan herself was, and she was trying to be careful not to let it drag on the ground.

"What did you think of the lantern ceremony, Morgan?" Gertrude asked over her shoulder as they passed the graveyard again. It looked different at night, dark save for the candles here and there along with the scattered red glow of incense sticks. It was a stark contrast to the dim but consistently lit streets and their walkways.

"It was," Morgan paused to find the right word, "peaceful. The lanterns twinkling and reflecting on the river were quite beautiful. A good way to remember your family, I think."

"Do they have anything similar where you come from?"

"Back home? Not really. There was a graveyard, but markers were little more than a name and a date stamped in discarded metal ore. The wall was sturdy though."

"What about a funeral?"

"I'm. . . not familiar with that word." Morgan supposed she was blushing, but stopped herself from looking away. Gertrude couldn't really see her anyway, and the night was dark.

"The lanterns are part of a memorial ceremony in the years after a death; the funeral is the ceremony when we bury the deceased."

"Oh. We don't do anything like that. The family might gather as they can in one of their homes, but the only people who go out to the graveyard are those who draw the lots to dig the grave, and then again those who draw lots to bury the body."

"They aren't done at the same time?"

"Most of the deaths, where I come from, are mining accidents. It might be weeks before the body can be recovered, especially if the collapse was a large one."

"That seems callous."

"It takes a lot of time to clear a collapse safely. At least. . ." Morgan cut herself off. She'd been about to say 'at least they let us have a graveyard,' but she didn't want this woman's – or anyone's – pity. It also felt wrong, talking ill of her former home, now that she wasn't there anymore.

"At least?"

"Nothing. It doesn't matter."

They walked in silence for a moment before Gertrude changed the topic.

"Do you have a large family?"

"I only ever knew my parents. I think they had family in the capital, but that was very far away from where we lived."

"No siblings?"

"No. Most families in town were large, but my parents couldn't have

119

any after me."

"That must have been lonely."

"There wasn't time to be. There was always work to do. At home daddy would talk with me, teach me."

"You miss them."

Morgan thought for a moment before answering. What kind of question was that?

"Of course I do."

"Oh, that wasn't a question. It's always hard being away from family, even if you don't get along with them. We also feel the absence keener, being in a strange city on our own."

There didn't seem to be any proper response to that, so Morgan let the conversation lapse.

As they got near to the part of town where Morgan's studio apartment was, she spoke up again.

"Is your home far? I wouldn't want you have to carry the both of them very far."

"Another ten minutes or so. Not too bad."

Haruhi stirred, nuzzling against her mother's shoulder, whispering something Morgan couldn't quite hear.

"Okay honey, we'll find a bathroom, just try and be patient."

"My place is just a few blocks that way," Morgan said, pointing out towards the outskirts of town.

"I wouldn't want to be a bother."

"How would it be?" Morgan started down the street, stopping for a moment to heft the toy up higher. Glancing back Morgan saw Gertrude frown slightly before following. With her longer legs she caught up to

Morgan before they'd gone half a block. Morgan noticed Gertrude's free hand had opened the top of her small bag, resting inside.

Gertrude was looking back and forth, her eyes lingering on the faded facades of the buildings, the alleys lit only by slivers of light spilling out of windows here and there.

"You live out here?"

"It's quite cheap 'out here.' The neighbors can be a bit loud, but I'm usually either at my jobs or school anyway, all of which are in walking distance."

"And you aren't worried about crime?"

"There is always crime. I learned that long ago. Try not to look like a target and you'll be fine, most of the time."

"Most is not all," Gertrude said, glancing down at Haruhi.

Morgan shrugged.

"Something could fall and kill me twenty seconds from now. Most is the best we get."

Morgan motioned Gertrude over as she stopped in front of her building. Gertrude started up the steps towards the main entrance, but Morgan shook her head.

"No, down here."

Half hidden by the stonework of the building there was a staircase leading down just forward of the front of the building. A dirty metal door was barely visible at the bottom from the light spilling down from above – there was no light in the stair. Morgan fished her identification card from one of her coverall pockets and tapped it on the sensor, unlocking the door. The hallway beyond was lit, barely, by a red light back from the doorway. Doors lined either side of the hall, spaced a few meters apart. The third one on the left was Morgan's, which also opened with her ID.

"The bathroom is straight through to the back," Morgan said, stepping aside to let the other woman in first.

Gertrude let Haruhi down, the girl trailing behind, rubbing her eyes with one small hand.

Morgan didn't bother pointing the way, given that it was scarcely ten steps from the front door to the bathroom door. There also wasn't anything between the two besides a small chair and table to one side, a cot on the other. Throw in a sink, cabinet, and kitchen work space in one corner, a closet in the other, and that comprised the whole of Morgan's living space. The cot was the only thing in the room with anything beyond the bare minimum, as it had a snug canopy over it that closed with Velcro straps.

There were no windows, which lowered the rent somewhat. That suited Morgan just fine. Morgan put the penguin on the chair, while Gertrude put her purse on the table, taking a moment to straighten and tighten her kimono.

"This is where you live?" Gertrude said as Haruhi closed the door to the bathroom. Morgan could tell she was trying not to be judgmental, but it was hard to keep out of the tone of speech, especially for Morgan, who had been studying the local speech in an attempt to erase her own accent.

"I don't need anything more right now."

"I suppose."

"Listen, Gertrude,"

"Yes?"

"Thanks for inviting me."

"Of course. Work and school are important, don't get me wrong, but having fun and relaxing from time to time is as well."

The bathroom door opened.

"All done." Haruhi said loudly.

"Really?" Gertrude asked. "Did you remember everything?"

Haruhi stopped, tilting her head as she thought.

"Oh, hands!" She said, heading back in. With the door closed Morgan couldn't hear if the water was running or not.

"How did you know?"

"No water, besides the toilet."

"The door was closed."

"Parenting requires superpowers. One of the many things they don't tell you beforehand."

"Who's they?"

Gertrude just smiled.

The door opened again and Haruhi came out, proudly showing her palms.

"Good job, Haru. Can you walk for a bit so I can carry Penny?"

Haruhi nodded.

"You sure you don't want me to walk with you to your place?"

"I'm sure. You're already home, it's late, and my home really isn't that far."

"It wouldn't be a problem."

"Don't worry about it. Thank you for coming, Morgan. It's been fun getting to know you a bit. You certainly seem to have Haruhi's vote, which isn't easy to get."

Morgan opened the door to let them out, surprised when Haruhi hugged one of her legs tightly before bouncing out the door.

Cute kid.

Morgan watched them walk down the hallway until they had started up the stairs, the door closing behind them and locking automatically. The small clock perched on the head board of her cot proclaimed the time as 22:05. As tired as she was Morgan had to pause and work out what that meant. Day and night on Hillman might have been nearly interchangeable, but it was still noticeable, and people needed a regular rhythm. Long before Hillman had been settled the intergalactic community agreed to keep using the same seconds, minutes, hours, and weeks from Earth – one of the few things they actually did agree on. As it happened Hillman's day was just about 23 hours, which was close enough to Earth to not cause too much of a problem. What's one less hour for sleep for the perpetually sleep deprived anyway?

Morgan much preferred the day on Zion. Twenty six hours, without extra work or school time to go with it. People here were much more likely to actually get eight hours of sleep than the busy people on most planets.

Except for tonight, it seemed. Sure, it was still four hours until midnight, but Morgan needed to be up and getting ready by quarter to three for her janitorial shift at the trade school at three-thirty. That job ended at eight thirty, giving her barely enough time for a meal before her other job started at ten, assisting a mechanic who owned his own vehicle repair shop a few blocks over. Finish up there by four, then school at five.

At least she had already eaten. A quick shower and she could get to bed. Only. . .

. . .Morgan didn't quite feel right, letting Gertrude and her little girl walk home the rest of the way alone. She couldn't identify what was bothering her, just that something was.

Morgan stood there, stock still, for long seconds before shaking her head and heading for the bathroom, idly working on the buttons to her coveralls as she kicked off her shoes. Paranoia was fairly useful on Hillman, but Zion was a vastly safer place. The people were friendly and productive, and the police were efficient and dedicated.

Morgan had closed the door behind her, half out of the coveralls when the feeling returned again, worse.

What had she told Gertrude? Try not to look like a target? What would a woman in the movement constricting kimono with a child in one hand and a large toy in the other look like?

The bad feeling increased twofold, and Morgan made up her mind.

Better to waste the half hour walking them home than try to sleep wondering.

Decision made the sense of urgency and dread she felt only grew. Morgan stepped back into her shoes hastily. She was halfway down the hallway before she remembered to make sure her ID was still in her pocket, the normal process of checking tricky as she simultaneously tried to shove her arms back into the sleeves of the coveralls.

Morgan headed back out towards the main road they'd turned off of to get to her apartment, hoping that Gertrude had retraced her steps rather than try a winding path through the neighborhood. She needn't have worried; Morgan began to hear loud voices less than a block from her own apartment.

Three boys, or men perhaps, Morgan wasn't wasting time guessing, had gathered around Gertrude and Haruhi. They didn't seem especially threatening to Morgan, but plainly Gertrude thought them such. If Morgan had seen them in the street while she was out walking she would have kept an eye on them, at the very least.

They had their backs to Morgan, and Gertrude was too intent on them to have noticed Morgan approaching.

"This isn't hard, lady. You pay the toll, and we go away."

Well, that settled that. Morgan had been warned about this kind of scam within days of moving into the neighborhood. Most of the people doing it were counting on intimidation to get their way more than violence, but telling the genuinely dangerous from the bravado filled was nearly impossible short of violence actually breaking out.

As such, Morgan didn't feel the least bit sorry for rushing in and sucker punching the closest one in the kidney, followed by a swift kick to the groin. The kick she pulled her strength on, she was trying to incapacitate him, not do permanent damage.

If these were punks 'hustling the tourists' they wouldn't be interested in sticking around for a fight, and if they weren't Morgan's only shot was distracting them long enough to get Gertrude and Haruhi and then running. She was strong, sure, but there were three of them.

As the first guy went down the other two turned to her, giving her an excellent opportunity to hit number two in the jaw. Morgan had never hit anyone in the jaw before. She was surprised how much it hurt, but Morgan forced herself to ignore it and dodge to the side as the third guy kicked at her.

His timing was off and the kick unbalanced him enough that he staggered forward, actually tripping over the fallen first punk.

Shaking her aching fist Morgan turned to face the second guy, stepping a little bit closer to negate some of his advantage in reach.

Meanwhile Gertrude had fished something out of her bag with one hand while pushing Haruhi behind her with the other.

Morgan had no idea what it was, beyond the obvious – black, cylindrical, easily fit into the palm. Gertrude held it out towards the second guy and depressed the top. A stream of some kind of orange liquid hissed out, hitting the second guy squarely in the face. A lot of it splashed off, as well as misting in the air around him.

Then the splashing liquid hit Morgan too, part of it in her eyes.

She was almost instantly blinded, her eyes stinging and watering so bad that they involuntarily squeezed shut.

"Ahh! Lady, lay off the spray!" He yelled. Morgan could hear him stumbling back, crashing into a garbage can that was standing at the edge of the sidewalk.

Morgan tried blinking, easier said than done, but she managed it. It didn't help, nor did the tears streaming down her face.

Luckily her being able to see didn't seem to be vitally important. She could hear the injured punks stumbling off.

"Are you okay, Haruhi?" Gertrude asked, her voice shaking.

"What's going on Gertrude? I can't see."

"Don't rub your eyes, Morgan. That will only make it worse."

Not exactly an answer, but Morgan supposed the information was at least useful.

"I'm sorry you got hit with it too. I've never had to use it before, I had no idea it would splash that much." Morgan could hear Gertrude moving around a bit, but couldn't make out where the men were, or Haruhi. "Where did you come from, I've never seen anyone move so fast."

"Heavy worlder. They are gone, right?"

"Oh, yes. They've run off. I don't know what would have happened if you hadn't of been here."

"My eyes?"

"Do you have any medical supplies at your place? It isn't just pepper spray; it will take a bit more than water to get it off."

"I don't."

"Give me your hand, Morgan."

Morgan heard the chime of an uplink being activated.

"Where is the nearest open medical center?"

Morgan couldn't see the holographic display projected into the air above them, but she could dimly hear the machine working.

"My home is closer than any of these. Let's get you there."

"This hurts quite a lot," Morgan agreed.

"Is it okay?" Haruhi asked in a very small voice.

"Everything's fine, Haru. Morgan just got something in her eyes. We're going to take her home and make it better."

"Who were the men? They seemed angry."

"They were angry, but they've gone. We didn't have what they wanted."

Walking the blocks to Gertrude's home blind proved quite problematic. Gertrude had to guide Morgan and keep hold of Haruhi's hand. Penny the penguin, forgotten during the brief fight, was picked up and dusted off as best as possible, then given to Morgan to hold.

Morgan couldn't decide if it was all unbearably embarrassing or unbearably funny. Her stinging eyes negated much of the humor, though at least that subsided a bit after a couple minutes.

"There are some steps ahead. Haruhi, can you open the door?"

"Okay!"

Morgan was amazed that the child was so awake at this time of night, as well as seemingly oblivious to what had happened, but it was just as well.

"Door. Open!"

"Voice print recognized. Three heat signatures recorded. Please identify."

"Me, Momma, and Morgan!"

The door swung itself open, and Gertrude helped Morgan up the steps inside.

"Just drop the toy. There's a couch just over here." Gertrude guided her a few steps forward, then to the left. Morgan's shins bumped into something soft. She put Penny down and reached forward with her now free hand, feeling the edges of the couch before turning around and sitting.

"I'll be right back with the medical kit. Haruhi, go to your room. It's time for bed."

Haruhi grumbled something Morgan didn't quite make out, and she heard Gertrude's steps as she walked out of the room. The room felt large, and the floors sounded like wood, but she couldn't tell much else. The stinging wasn't too bad, but she didn't dare open her eyes just yet.

Morgan heard Gertrude's steps approach after less than a minute.

"Can you stand up and lean your head back. I need to wash your eyes out."

Morgan complied, taking a step away from the couch.

"Keep your mouth closed. This stuff isn't toxic, but I doubt it tastes very good."

Slowly Gertrude started pouring a liquid on Morgan's eyes, it wasn't pleasant, but it did take the stinging away almost immediately.

"Now open your eyes so I can get the rest out."

Morgan complied, though the urge to close them again against the pouring was strong.

Blinking in relief Morgan looked around. She was standing in a very large room with three large couches arranged around a low table in the middle with a large holotank taking up the fourth wall.

This room alone was at least twice the size of Morgan's whole apartment, and she could see two doors in the hallway they'd walked in from, besides the door leading outside.

No wonder Gertrude had been shocked at how small her place had been.

"Careful you don't touch your clothes," Gertrude said, bringing Morgan's attention back to her. The spray is still potent, and there is a fair bit on your coveralls.

"Let me help you clean up," Morgan said, gesturing to the puddle on the floor and the liquid still dripping off of her shoulders.

"Nonsense. You need to take a shower to get the rest of the spray off of you, and so we can clean your clothes. I can handle this. If you head back out to the hallway the bathroom is the third door to the left. There are towels and a robe in there you can use. Use the shampoo and soap in the blue bottles. It's what I use after coming back from class and is definitely strong enough to get any of it left off safely. Leave your clothes on the floor so you don't get it on anything. My washing machine can have them clean in less than an hour."

"This really isn't necessary," Morgan said, faintly embarrassed at the amount of attention Gertrude was giving her.

"Morgan, you attacked three grown men to help me. More importantly, you helped my daughter. How could I ever repay that? Cleaning your clothes and letting you use my shower is nothing compared to that. Now get moving before you manage to get some on your face again."

Morgan complied, leaving the older woman busy putting away a bottle she'd evidently pulled from the medical kit, sitting on the table next to a large pitcher of water, now mostly empty.

The bathroom was actually smaller than Morgan had expected, given the size of the other rooms she passed. She supposed there was only so much space you needed for a bathroom, especially one meant to be used by a single person at a time. The towels were readily apparent, as well as the robe once she closed the door behind her. The shower had a door instead of the curtains Morgan had expected, glass that was mostly opaque. Carefully shedding her clothes, leaving them in a pile on the floor, Morgan walked into the shower. She was relieved to see the controls were basically the same as in her apartment – both were quite different than anything she'd seen on Hillman or on the *Pale Moonlight*, after all.

There was a knock at the door a few minutes later.

"Morgan, do you mind if I reach in and grab your clothes so I can get them washing?"

Morgan thought about it. Having the woman in the room with her would be a little awkward, but Morgan was short enough that none of her was visible above the opaque part of the glass door, and she really needed to get home and get to bed.

"Go ahead," she called out.

The door opened and shut in the space of a few minutes. Satisfied that there was no chance of any of the nasty spray lingering Morgan got out of the shower a couple minutes later.

Hurriedly drying off, Morgan slipped into the robe. It was too big, of course, dropping almost to her ankles and covering her hands even after she pushed the sleeves back.

Not knowing what else to do Morgan headed back to the front room with the couches.

"Gertrude?" she called out, quietly. Hopefully Haruhi was asleep by this point, even before the excitement it had been a long day for all of them.

She found Gertrude sitting on one of the couches; her kimono replaced by another bathrobe like the one Morgan wore. She was rocking back and forth and Morgan could see she had been crying.

"Are you okay?"

"No. Yes? I was so scared, more for Haruhi than for me. I'd never been in a situation like that before, especially not without Naru there to protect me. Us. What if you hadn't have come?"

"You'd have sprayed them all in the face instead of just one."

"Would I? I don't know that I would have been able to get it out without you distracting them."

"Does worrying about what could have happened differently help?"

Gertrude shook her head.

"Then don't worry about it. Haruhi is safe. You're safe. Those three won't be so keen to rob people in the future."

"I'm sorry, Morgan, I didn't give you enough credit."

"What do you mean?"

"When they first came up to us in the street, my first thought was to wonder if you had sent them."

Morgan had no idea how to react to this. To have someone assume she was a criminal was insulting, but so out of the blue that she had to wonder why she could even conceive of that.

"Because of the timing?"

"That, and because you don't wear an uplink."

Morgan shook her head, trying to parse what Gertrude was saying. No, it still made no sense.

"I don't understand."

"Did you notice that the thugs didn't have uplinks on?"

Morgan shook her head again, this time to answer Gertrude.

"Most criminals don't. It's easy for the police to track, and most uplinks are set to electronically handshake with any other nearby units automatically, making figuring out who was nearby when a crime is committed easy."

"I suppose that makes sense. Why are you telling me this?"

"Because I owe you. Because I don't want to leave anything I should apologize for between us."

"Do you need to apologize for something the other person doesn't even know about?"

"Yes. Especially then. What we do when no one is looking is more important than what we do when they are. Tell me, Morgan, why did you come out to find us?"

"I got to thinking that you and Haruhi, with the silly toy, would be a tempting target."

"And what started you thinking that?"

"I don't know. A bad feeling?"

"One you acted on."

"Yeah, so?"

"No one was watching. You could have just gone to bed. You offered, and I said no. No one would think less of you."

"I don't quite follow what you're saying."

"Never mind. This probably isn't the best time to be having heavy philosophical discussions. Probably not a good time to have any serious discussion, but there is one thing I want to ask you."

"What's that?"

"How much is your rent?"

"Your thought process is really hard to follow. Anyone ever tell you that?"

"Naru, all the time," Gertrude said with a sad smile. "How much?"

"Five hundred a month."

Gertrude winced.

"That's more than I expected for something that size."

"I couldn't find anything cheaper than that in the whole city."

"I guess I haven't looked at rent prices in a long time. Anyway, what would you say to renting a room from me, for three hundred a month?"

"Why would you offer?"

"It's the right thing to do. Plus it actually would help me out. With Naru gone making ends meet until I finish school has been hard. Especially since I can't get a part time job and leave Haruhi alone."

"I'll have to think about it," Morgan said. She was pretty sure she liked Gertrude, but this was a sudden offer, and not one to be decided lightly.

"Good. Why don't you lie down on a couch there for a bit? The throw pillow's pretty comfortable, and there is a blanket folded up on the shelf beneath the table top. I'll check on your clothes. Is there anywhere you need to be in the morning? Church or something?"

"I have to be up at two forty-five to get ready for work."

"Where do you work?"

"I actually work cleaning the school," Morgan stammered.

"It's probably a bit closer from here than from your current place."

Gertrude said as she left. "And isn't tomorrow a holiday anyway?"

"Oh. You're right. I *don't* have work tomorrow."

It wasn't until Morgan had laid there for a minute that she realized that at some point it had been assumed that Morgan was just going to stay the night in Gertrude's home. Crafty woman.

No sense arguing it now. She really did need sleep, even if she didn't have to be up super early.

With the blanket pulled up over her head she was able to at least pretend she wasn't exposed in the cavernous room, sheer exhaustion did the rest.

CHAPTER 09

With civilization spread across the unfathomably vast light years many think the time of tribes and fire-forged friendship are over, that our connections to each other as humans don't matter. These people, of course, never served in the military or on a starship.

- Major Jamie O'Neill, (retired) professor of psychology, 1st Ena University

TO SAY MORGAN took pride in being a light sleeper wasn't quite accurate. It was more that she took comfort in it, given her background and upbringing. Living in Isa, Morgan routinely found herself woken by a strange sound six or even seven times a night. They were always false alarms, but one day it might not be, and besides she usually fell back asleep within a few minutes.

That night Morgan slept without waking, and she couldn't be sure why. Had she been exhausted? An effect of her body dealing with the damage to her eyes perhaps? The result of the earlier adrenaline rush of the fight?

These things she wondered later, however. The first thing she was aware of after falling asleep initially was waking up and finding Haruhi staring straight at her face from less than ten centimeters away.

Morgan sat bolt upright, gasping in surprise.

"Hi!" the little girl giggled, bouncing on the balls of her feet.

Morgan took a moment to tighten her robe and to compose herself.

"It's not polite to wake people up like that."

"Umm, Mom said breakfast and is Morgan up?"

"And did she tell you how to wake me up?"

Haruhi shook her head.

Morgan snorted in amusement. "She probably meant calling out my name or tapping me on the shoulder."

"Oh. Okay!"

And off the little girl went.

Morgan could see sunlight streaming in through the gaps in the curtains on the far wall. It was at least eight in the morning, possibly later.

Well, first things first. Morgan stood up, stretched, and headed for the bathroom. Her clothes were folded neatly on the counter next to the sink, so she dressed gratefully after doing her business and a quick shower. As she was pulling on the coveralls she noticed a newly repaired rip along one of the seams of the right arm. She must have torn it during the fight. Clearly, Gertrude did nothing by halves.

Including breakfast. Morgan found the dining room and kitchen by following the smell of bacon to the other end of the hallway. The table was already full with piles of eggs, bacon, sausage, stacks of some flat bready-looking circles she didn't immediately recognize, pitchers of juice in five different colors, smaller thin necked bottles of thick looking brown liquids, several plates of sectioned fruits, bowls of oatmeal, rice, several plates with assorted muffins, and even several pitchers of steaming coffee and what smelled like hot chocolate on a side table.

One thing there wasn't on the table was anywhere to put a plate to eat from, nor even silverware to eat with.

Was cooking how Gertrude dealt with stress? Could she still be shaken up about the attack? Morgan needed to talk with her. She just hoped Gertrude wasn't planning on the three of them eating even a fraction of that food.

Between the dining room and the kitchen there was a half wall topped with a counter running most of the length, a pair of swinging doors next to it. Morgan couldn't see Gertrude, but the sounds coming from the kitchen suggested where she was.

"Gertrude?"

"In here, Morgan."

Walking into the kitchen presented Morgan with a scene of utter chaos. There were dirty dishes piled on any surface not actively being used for food preparation, and most of the cabinets and drawers were open, things scattered haphazardly. Gertrude and another woman Morgan did not know were busy cooking at least three things each, including more eggs and bacon.

Both were wearing flour dusted and food stained aprons, but the similarities ended there. The strange woman was quite tall, probably fifty centimeters more than Morgan, fifteen or so more than Gertrude. She was wearing a high collared, long sleeved dress that was cut very sharply, faintly reminding Morgan of the military uniforms she had seen at the spaceport in Ein city. She was slim with a sharp face and hard eyes, the same jet black color as her neatly braided hair.

"Are you going to have enough food?" Morgan asked.

The other woman laughed.

"Oh, I hope so. Last I heard at least a dozen were going to make it today," Gertrude answered.

"Make it to what?"

"Oh, right, I didn't tell you last night. I guess I didn't expect you to sleep in quite that long. Not that you didn't have good reason to, the day we had yesterday."

Morgan motioned for Gertrude to continue.

"It's a memorial holiday. As many of Naru's squad that can get together for the holiday along with their spouses. My house is the best suited to hosting, at least on Zion, so we do it here."

The woman cleared her throat.

"Right. Let me introduce you." Gertrude made a grand pause to twirl her hand in a theatrical flourish. "This is Lady Dame Colonel Emily Davenport, DCB, thirteenth Baroness of Novan. She was Naru's commanding officer."

Emily glared at Gertrude for a moment. "Just Emily, if you please. We're hardly at court here. And I'm retired in any case."

"Which is why all the guys still call you colonel on reflex?"

"Those are titles then?" Morgan interjected.

"Not from around here, huh?" Emily asked.

"Lady Novan," Gertrude started, pointedly ignoring the injunction to call her Emily, "is part of the nobility of Albion, with her holdings being the area called Ena Crossing. Dame is the title for women who have been knighted, and the DCB tells you which order. Colonel is a rank of officer in the military, Marines in this case."

"And Gertrude loves tweaking my nose with them every chance she gets."

Morgan regarded Lady Emily, and then motioned to the food.

"I don't have much experience with nobility, but do many of them spend time cooking?"

Emily laughed.

"Not many. So who are you, that you don't have such experience?"

"This is Morgan," Gertrude said, "Though I can't rightly tell you much more than that. She's in my mechanical class."

Emily looked Morgan up and down, pursing her lips as she considered her.

"Gertrude isn't one to make friends easily. She must see something special in you." Morgan squirmed a bit under Emily's gaze, but stood her ground. "So, who are you?"

"Gertrude already told you, I'm Morgan."

Emily waved her hands dismissively.

"That's your name, or part of it at any rate. I want to know who you are."

"Actually it is my whole name," Morgan replied, straightening up to her whole hundred and forty centimeters. She wasn't lying, saying she had little experience with nobility, but that didn't mean she didn't recognize the type. The Voice of the Comradery carried herself a lot like this woman did, as had the few visitors from the capital they'd had in Pari Passu. Morgan wasn't going to let herself be intimidated by this woman's titles, nor let her have power over her. "Not that it is any of your business, but I am from Hillman. I worked in the mines for years before my parents got me off planet. Now I'm here, preparing to work in starship maintenance. I take care of myself, and keep to myself, mostly. So, who are you?"

Emily responded by laughing again, surprising Morgan.

"You've got spirit, kid. I like that. Too many people refuse to stand up to me, seeing the titles rather than the person."

"Morgan has certainly shown that."

Something about the way Gertrude said that caught Emily's attention, and she turned her intense gaze on Gertrude.

"You've been a little quiet today. What happened that you aren't telling me?"

"It's nothing," Gertrude started to say, before Emily cut her off with another wave of her hand.

"When I came in this morning you looked like you hadn't slept at all, there was a strange girl sleeping on the couch wearing one of your robes, and you've been distracted the whole time. Not to mention the fact that as I came inside, I thought I smelled pepper spray."

"Are all your friends this observant?" Morgan asked.

Gertrude sighed, turning back to the stove to check the sausages.

"I was almost mugged, okay? I'd taken Morgan to the Obon Festival, and three guys attacked me after I dropped her off at her apartment."

"Haruhi seemed okay this morning. She *is* okay, right?" Emily's bearing went from stern to worried in half a moment, showing Morgan a slightly less prickly side of the strange woman.

"She's fine, she's fine," Gertrude seemed to wave away Emily's concern. "I don't think she really understood what was going on. They didn't have long to threaten me before Morgan showed up out of nowhere and took one of them out."

"And the pepper spray?"

"With Morgan's distraction I was able to get it out of my bag and spray one of the muggers. Morgan was standing close enough that she got hit too."

"You were lucky, in other words." Emily turned to Morgan. "What prompted you to go back outside? Did you see them following her?"

"There aren't any windows in my apartment. I just had a bad feeling about letting Gertrude go alone. I thought she'd look like a tempting target."

"*Deo gratias*," Emily muttered, though Morgan could have been hearing it wrong. It wasn't a language she recognized, let alone understood.

"What was that?"

"Oh, nothing. Old habit. Giving thanks is all."

"Emily, I think your pancakes are burning," Gertrude said suddenly, reaching across the other woman to pull the large frying pan over to a different part of the stovetop.

"We should finish talking later, perhaps," Emily said, taking the handle of the pan from Gertrude. "The others should be arriving any time now."

"Right." Gertrude grabbed a plate off of a pile near the counter, a clean pile. "Obviously we won't be eating in the dining room. The other door in there leads to the patio, which is already set for the meal. We'll be eating buffet style, so go ahead and fill your plate with whatever you want to start with and go find a seat. We're almost done here and will join you once as the others arrive."

"Sure," Morgan said, taking the offered plate. She hoped Gertrude would be out soon, she didn't enjoy the thought of meeting the rest of the guests without any sort of introduction. So far her experiences with military men and women hadn't been especially pleasant.

With so much food to choose from, Morgan didn't even try to get some of everything. Not even a good sampling. She did grab a few of what Gertrude had called pancakes, which she topped with some fruit, as well as eggs and bacon. Heading outside, she snagged the spot farthest from the door to one side. There were two empty glasses to each place setting so she went back in for some juice and hot chocolate. Having now been introduced to chocolate it was never to be passed up, hot or not. She had years of deprivation to make up for, after all.

The following hour or hour and a half passed by in one big blur of unfamiliar faces and confusing stories and recollections.

In the end there was closer to twenty people crowded out on Gertrude's patio than a dozen, all loudly talking and laughing about old times and absent comrades. Morgan did her best to stay out of the way and only answer direct questions, aided by the fact that the wives tended to clump together in one corner, the smattering of husbands in another, the veterans in the middle. Gertrude moved about from one table to the next, hardly seeming to slow down long enough to eat or drink anything herself. She certainly didn't have time to talk to Morgan, not that Morgan blamed her for the lack of attention.

Emily, interestingly enough, mostly stayed in the corner opposite Morgan, smiling at the jokes and stories, answering the various questions put her, but not volunteering much information herself. Clearly the men and women who had served with her respected her immensely, but it was more formal and stiff. Morgan gave up after a while trying to figure it out, instead choosing to concentrate on the surprisingly good food.

Even with the dining table practically groaning under the weight of all the food on it, several varieties ran out in short order, first being the bacon, unsurprisingly.

At last something seemed to shift in the gathering and couples started leaving. Within another twenty minutes there was only four people left besides Morgan, Gertrude, and Emily. Morgan stood, placing her plate and utensils in the plastic box with all the other dirty dishes.

"I think it's about. . ." she started saying when a man she had not seen previously walked out onto the patio and somehow managed to clear his throat loud enough to be heard and yet remain unobtrusive.

"Is the child-wrangling proceeding apace, Boris?" Emily asked with a faint smile. The man stepped closer and Morgan noticed that he had several food stains on his otherwise immaculate black vest and pants, and there were a few damp spots on his white dress shirt.

"Lady Novan, while I am sure you jest, I fear wrangling may indeed be the best verb for it. These children seem to believe that any picosecond spent not exuberantly engaged in horseplay is wasted. They didn't waste the food, at least," Morgan noticed his hand twitch, as if he was stopping himself from pointing "For the most part."

"Thank you Boris. I had the utmost faith in your abilities, wrangling or otherwise. Was there anything you needed?"

"Indeed, Lady Novan. Young mistress Haruhi was asking for her mother. Since the gathering is beginning to disperse I thought it an appropriate time to relay the request."

Gertrude quickly slipped out of the room, followed a few step back by Boris. Morgan frowned slightly. It was time she left, but she didn't feel right leaving without at least thanking Gertrude. Not wanting to talk to the two remaining couples Morgan busied herself picking up discarded dishes and fallen pieces of food. As she bent low to grab a bit of bacon from under a table Morgan sensed someone standing behind her.

Morgan straightened up before turning about, unsurprisingly finding Emily standing there.

"Persistent. And nosy as well," Morgan said.

"Guilty, though I suppose it's a bit silly to plead guilty to something you don't feel is wrong."

"Oh, why is that?"

"My job – any of them, pick one – basically revolves around knowing what is going on and making decisions based on that to make things run well. If I miss something important people could die on the one hand, or people could lose their livelihoods on the other. Such decisions weigh much more heavily on me than 'being polite' ever will, especially when I have to put on such a façade for my political interactions."

"I suppose I should add wordy to the list."

That got a quick laugh out of Emily.

"Also guilty. Give me one second," she said, turning back to the door where the other couples were leaving. "You keep your husbands out of trouble. I'm not around to babysit them anymore." The departing women laughed, while the men saluted smartly.

"So why do you care about me? I'm not a soldier and I don't live wherever Novan is. I'm not even on the same *planet*."

"I am in your debt, and I pay my debts."

"I've never even seen you before this morning. How could you owe me anything?"

"Do you know what the core of nobility is?"

"I'm not even sure what that means."

"At its most basic, a government with nobility is based around duty. To some people more is given, but of them more is also expected."

Now it was Morgan's turn to laugh, but not out of amusement.

"Oh, *that*. I know of that. Where I grew up they phrased it 'Everyone is equal but extra risks required extra support.' Funny how it was never the guards dying in the shafts. Funny how we never even saw any of the essential workers or the party leaders, except the one lady who came to give us speeches. Her and her perfectly smooth hands, and that impossibly wide, white smile."

Morgan had let more venom creep into her voice than she had intended, but Emily didn't even blink.

"That is what happens when the people in charge ignore their duty."

Morgan bit off her retort, instead taking a deep breath in.

"I'm sorry. I really must be going. Would you please tell Gertrude thank you for her hospitality. I will think on her offer and let her know in a few days at school."

Emily didn't move, so Morgan stepped around her and darted through the door. She actually caught up to the other departing guests, who had stopped to finish some bit of conversation Morgan didn't care about in the entryway, so she edged around them and got out to the street.

That Emily was an odd one, and unsettling. Gertrude was nice enough, but despite what she had said Morgan wasn't planning on taking her up on the offer. The money saved would be nice, there was no point in denying that, but it also meant giving up a lot of her freedom, *and* being tied to someone else. Morgan wasn't about to rely on anyone she didn't have to.

CHAPTER 10

When faced with a dedicated criminal class, the police are often at a disadvantage. They don't want to hurt anyone, but the old adage about it taking two to tango but only one to brawl should be remembered. There is also the matter of reputation on the streets – it is literally considered a good thing for these criminals if it takes multiple cops to subdue them, and reputation can be lost if they lose to someone viewed as weaker.

- Captain Leslie Kraft, Precinct 35, Ein city

INSTEAD OF GOING back to her tiny apartment Morgan walked over to the trade school. It was closer to Gertrude's house, Morgan grudgingly admitted. There was still plenty of studying to do, and precious little of it she could do at her own place. None of it really, without a device of her own that could connect to the city's network of computers and uplinks.

The building was locked up for the holiday, of course, but Morgan was on file as both a student and employee, so the system let her in without any fuss.

Taking apart one of the practice air circulation systems made her feel better, though the grease and oil did get everywhere.

Putting it back together took longer than Morgan would have liked. It was all going smoothly at first, but she got one of the innumerable small details wrong, and she had gone half a dozen steps farther before realizing it. Undoing those steps was made much harder by the mistake – it was designed to smoothly assemble and disassemble a certain way after all, and the tiny error was enough that things weren't fitting right. Between finishing that, cleaning up as best she could, and slogging through the reading she needed to do, it was well into the early evening by the time Morgan had finished and put everything away. Time to go home, it seemed.

Thinking that word, 'home,' still had an interesting effect on Morgan. Her apartment was far smaller than her parents' home, even if you took out the tool storage spaces, but it was hers.

Putting those thoughts aside Morgan started contemplating dinner. Breakfast at Gertrude's had been large enough that she hadn't stopped for lunch, not intentionally, but because she simply hadn't been hungry.

Mentally going through what she still had in the refrigerator and cupboard, Morgan decided she'd best get some supplies on the way home.

She made it all of four blocks before she ran into the first missionaries of the day.

"Have you heard the good word, my child?" the woman of the pair asked. Morgan was pretty sure their clothing – a loose sleeveless robe that showed off a lot more skin than was normal for the preachers she typically ran into – was an indication of which religion they were from, not that she knew enough to guess.

"I've heard five good words just this week," Morgan replied with a smile. It was hard to get too annoyed at the preachers – they believed they were helping her by trying to convert her, after all.

"Not surprising, in a city like this. But surely you can spare a few moments to learn more about our creators?"

"I need to get home," Morgan said, gesturing towards Bo district and her apartment."

"There is no need to inconvenience yourself, my child," the man said, "We would be happy to walk along with you partway."

Morgan would have said no, politely, but she was feeling a little on edge out in the open. The attack the day before had rattled her a bit more than she had realized. They preaching wouldn't hurt her, and most of the criminals seemed to leave the preachy types alone. . .

"Sure, for a few blocks."

The pair actually bowed to Morgan. She was able to wipe the smile off of her face at the silliness of it before they straightened up, thankfully.

"We belong to the Order of the Shepherding Stars," the male said by way of introduction as they walked. "Are you familiar with the tenants of our faith?"

"You worship the stars, right?"

"Yes. The vibrant stars are the source of all life, both in their continued sustenance given freely to all as well as the very particles that make up our beings, created by stars that sacrificed themselves to scatter more complex materials through the universe."

It actually made a kind of sense. Even Morgan had learned enough science to know that all but the most basic types of matter had originated in the furnaces of the stars. She still didn't see how that made the star a god, though.

"And what does your god ask of you?"

"They ask little of us, child, but that we be happy and fruitful, and guard the precious lives they give us," the woman answered.

"We show our devotion to the creators by basking in their glow as much as possible, as well, reminding ourselves of the live they give," the male added.

Well, that explains the clothing, Morgan thought to herself.

"So killing is a sin, then?" Morgan asked, more to keep the conversation going than from any doubt as to the answer. She didn't think she could belong to any religion that banned bacon.

"Murder is a sin," the woman clarified. "Nothing can live without taking from another, even if it is from the stars themselves. Nothing lives forever, but that does not mean we can be wasteful or cruel."

"Did you never wonder about your place in the universe, staring up at the stars in the sky each night?"

"Sort of," Morgan admitted, "Though we couldn't usually see the stars."

"You lived on a station, perhaps?"

"No, just a really cloudy planet."

"How sad, to be blocked from contemplating the creators."

"It was," Morgan agreed, though for slightly different reasons than the missionary meant.

Morgan was able to get away from them gracefully as they passed the store she liked a few blocks from her apartment. Thanking them for their time, and reluctantly accepting the small data chip with their literature, she ducked into the store.

It was the work of only a few minutes to grab the essentials for dinner. In this case that would consist of meat, bread, and cheese. Mustard she had already. Throw in some chocolate milk, some local juice, and a bunch of apples for breakfast and she was good to go. Having planned ahead – or more accurately having left the folded bag in a pocket on a regular basis – Morgan shoved it all in a cloth backpack and headed home. Despite having lagged at the school it was even still early, and Morgan was looking forward to getting some extra sleep before her early morning shift.

Her good feelings lasted right up until the brick hit her squarely in the back.

The force of the impact sent Morgan to her knees, the right one cracking against the curb of the road painfully. Her hurt knee ground against the rough pavement as she fell the rest of the way.

Rolling over onto her back Morgan saw the brick that had hit her and was frankly surprised she wasn't injured more seriously. Then she noticed her hand was sticky. Looking down presented her with the sight of a brown liquid pooling out around her.

The luck that had guided the brick to hit the jug of chocolate milk in her pack ran out, as the men who had thrown it reached her before she had time to even try standing up.

One of the three of them – and clearly these were the same men from the previous day – kicked her before pressing his boot down on her chest.

"You'll stay down if you know what's good for you."

Morgan was fairly sure his idea of 'good for her' and her own were not exactly the same, so instead of listening she rolled as hard as she could to the left into his other leg. This, having the desired effect, sent him toppling. Unfortunately, it sent him toppling directly onto Morgan, eliciting grunts from both of them. He tried to grab her hair but it was too short to get a good handle on and she wrenched her head from his grasp. Kneeing or elbowing him seemed a good plan, but Morgan couldn't get the leverage or angles she needed to pull it off.

The other two, meanwhile, pulled their mate off of Morgan, hauling him bodily upright. The moment he was clear Morgan started scooting back as fast as she could to try and get clear to stand up and run.

They had anticipated this and a boot came down hard on Morgan's left arm. It caught her arm on the edge of the curb. There was a loud snapping noise but Morgan didn't hear it. All she was aware of was pain.

Morgan wasn't unfamiliar with broken bones, but this one was felt a lot worse than most of those had. She forced herself to look at it. Her lower arm was bent sharply, a bone jutting out of the torn skin. There was blood everywhere. It probably should have hurt more than it did

"Well, that quieted you down some," one of them said, before kicking her arm. This had the positive benefit of being so painful that Morgan passed out.

It *also* had the negative consequence of being so painful that Morgan passed out, leaving her to the dubious mercy of the men attacking her.

***

The next few events were blessedly hazy for Morgan. Movement, the sound of something tearing, more pain from her arm and most of the rest of her body, muffled words she couldn't understand.

She next completely woke up in an unfamiliar bed. Unfamiliar place, really. White walls, bare white tile, off-blue curtains on rails that would have looked less horrible had they been white, and a bed that might, at one time, have had white blankets and sheets.

The first thing she checked was her arm. It was resting on top of the blankets, encased in what had to be this place's favorite color, a white cast. She couldn't move it much, or feel it yet, but it at least was pointed the right way. The cast was quite different than the ones she'd had the misfortune to use before. Those were bulky, itchy things made of wrapped cloth and plaster. This was hard plastic that looked like it had been made especially for her arm, exactly fitting its contours and barely a centimeter thick. It was as comfortable a cast as she supposed possible.

She felt too weak to move much, but Morgan checked the rest of herself over as best she could. Her clothes were gone and she was wearing a thin, short gown that felt like it wasn't closed in the back. Nothing else seemed broken, but a lot of the bits that weren't covered were turning a rather stunning shade of purple.

The pain was quite fuzzy, and Morgan found it hard to concentrate on anything. She really had expected the pain to be much worse. Gradually her thought process caught up with the fact that she was on Zion, not Hillman, and painkillers were not a scarce treasure.

Thirsty, she was thirsty though. There was a table on her right side, white of course, near the bed. There was a pitcher of water on it and a cup already filled, helpfully.

Focusing she slowly raised her arm to grab the cup, but stopped once she realized that her wrist was fastened to the railing of the bed with a metal bracelet, connected by a short chain. She hadn't realized it at first because the bracelet on her wrist was buffered with a soft cuff beneath it, keeping the metal from biting into her skin.

What?

Nothing made sense. Where was she? Why was she alone in a room, chained to the bed?

Her thirst reminded her of the immediate priority and she returned to getting the cup. Her hand was shaking, and she got more of it on herself than in her mouth, but even those few swallows helped.

There was a tapping sound, getting louder. It took Morgan long seconds process that they were footsteps and that someone was approaching her little curtained off room.

Pushing the curtain aside a man with a long white coat and a rather ugly green shirt and matching pants walked up to the bed, pausing to look at something Morgan hadn't noticed above her head. Craning her neck, she saw there were some displays full of squiggly lines and numbers that presumably meant something to doctors.

"I want this," she held up her hand, as best she could anyway, "off."

"I'm afraid I can't do that."

"Bullshit." Morgan had picked up some colorful words from Mary, despite her absent friend's best efforts, though Morgan tended to reserve them for appropriate times. Being chained to a bed without cause seemed one of those times. "No reason for them. Take. Them. Off." Morgan was fighting through the mental fuzziness, and she was slurring her words a bit, but the anger helped her focus a little bit better.

"We have learned from painful experience that without these regrettable restraints too many people in your circumstances run off," here he paused, so briefly Morgan wasn't sure she had imagined it, given her current state of mind, "before they are well."

"My arm's in a cast. Doesn't require bedrest."

"Perhaps not. You did nearly die though. Lot of blood loss from a compound fracture. You nearly bled out before the paramedics got to you. If someone had called the police even a minute later you wouldn't be here. Now, we could send you home, if you'd give us your parents' names?"

"My parents? Different planet. I live alone." Morgan pushed aside thoughts of dying, and focusing on what she could answer helped.

"At your age? You expect me to believe that?"

Had Morgan not already been as pale as she got from pain and injury the color surely would have drained from her face. How did they know her real age? She had identification on her, official, that listed her as a refugee and her 'birthdate' as the first day of the first month twelve years ago by the Zion calendar, which was five hundred twenty-six hour days long, making her legally an adult.

"I'm twelve."

"Earth years? That I might believe."

"No, Zion years. I had an ID card on me. Where are my things?"

The pain medication seemed to be wearing off. Morgan could think more clearly, but the pain was more noticeable as well.

"All you had when you were brought in was one of the more noticeably fake IDs I've seen in a while, with a door chip attached. Your clothes weren't even worth saving, as torn and bloodstained as they were."

"Not fake."

"I'll admit most of it looks pretty good. Next time you might want to make sure there's a fake last name to go with the first, 'Morgan.' A birthday of 1/1 isn't very clever either."

The doctor, or whatever he was, had dropped the feigned concern pretty quickly.

"It isn't fake. Contact. . ." Morgan hesitated, still unwilling to rely on anything from a government, a hesitation that her current interactions with an employee of what was most likely a government hospital reinforced," Contact the refugee office here in Isa. They'll have me on file."

"Sure they will, Cupcake. Anyway I'm just here to check that you haven't fled or died on us. This close to your neighborhood we're always pretty busy. I've wasted too much time here already. I'm sure an officer will be along eventually to talk to you. I suggest you don't lie to him."

He walked off, shaking his head.

"Wait," Morgan called out a few seconds after the curtain stopped swishing back and forth. "What do I do when I need to use the bathroom?"

***

It was some hours later before anyone else entered Morgan's room. Meanwhile, Morgan had used the privacy to get to the small bathroom attached to her small room and back. She had to sit with the door hanging open and her arm stretched out towards the bed, but she managed. She was only able to do this at all because the bed had wheels. They worked poorly, but they did work. They had probably intended her to use the odd shaped container tucked against one corner of the bed, but to say Morgan didn't care for that option was an understatement.

Getting back into bed had proven more difficult, and then turning over so she was lying on her back harder still. She had only persevered in the end because she refused to let anyone catch her in such an undignified position.

Morgan was idly examining the locking mechanism of the bracelet on her wrist when a uniformed police officer shoved the curtain door aside roughly.

"I suppose you're wondering how much trouble you're in, and plotting on how you can avoid it?" He said without preamble or introduction.

"No. Wondering how long it will take you to do your job and verify my identification. I'm also debating on whether or not you'll apologize. It is unlikely."

"You think I haven't seen this bravado before? I've lost count of people who think they're smarter or tougher than I am, that can get away with anything because the law can't touch you. I've even seen it in punks younger than you."

"You treat everyone who is attacked in the street this way?"

He shrugged noncommittally.

"You live in Little Kamagasaki town. How often do you really think I run into victims of a crime that weren't doing something illegal themselves, in *Kamatown*?" He ducked outside the curtain again, pulling a chair into the room which he sat in heavily. "So, what's your story about the arm? Who did you cross?"

"I don't live in Kamagasaki Town, little or otherwise. My apartment is in the Bo District."

"What possible advantage do you think it gives you to pretend you don't know that nickname?"

"I'm new here. Or do you not notice the accent?"

"So you say. I do notice you haven't answered my question. The arm?"

Morgan sighed. "Yesterday. . . or was it the day before? How long was I unconscious?"

"Today is the 4th."

"The day before yesterday then. I went to the Obon Festival with a friend I met at school. She walked me home then headed back to her place. I decided to walk her home, given the neighborhood, and went to catch up. When I got there she was being robbed by three men. I helped her get away from them. Yesterday after I was returning from school the same three men attacked me from behind. I tried to get away and one of them stomped on my arm. Next thing I knew I was waking up here, chained to my bed."

"Where do you go to school?"

"The Isa Mechanical College."

"That's a school for working adults. Yesterday was also a holiday. Try again."

Morgan grunted. "I *am* a working adult. I work there as a janitor. Assuming they haven't fired me for not showing up today. I also do my studying there because I don't have access to the network from my apartment."

"Okay then. What is the name of your friend?"

"Gertrude. Gertrude. . . Something?"

"You do seem to have a problem with last names, don't you?"

"I've only known her a short while. The festival was the first time we'd gone anywhere together." Morgan chuckled. "I did meet another of her friends while I was there. Hard to forget. Emily Davenport. She's in charge of some place called Novan."

Morgan could have anticipated several responses to this statement. The policeman laughing uproariously was not one of them.

"You're claiming to have met the Iron Colonel?" He finally said once he had stopped laughing. "The most decorated officer in Albion's military? The woman who held back twenty thousand rebels for three days with a single battalion? *That* Emily Davenport?"

"I didn't realize she's famous. Yes, I did meet her, yesterday morning at a gathering at Gertrude's house. It was for the holiday. Gertrude's husband served with her."

"Okay fine. I'll humor you. It's so farfetched to be entertaining at least. Where did you say you meet her?"

"At Gertrude's home."

"And where is that?"

Morgan thought for a moment. She'd been a bit riled up when she left and not paying attention to her surroundings. It was also close enough to the school that she hadn't needed to check where she was to get there, navigating automatically.

"I don't have the exact address. It is close to the school. A bit southwest."

"You don't remember. Color me surprised. How did you get there then?"

"Gertrude led me."

"Led you? What, blindfolded?"

"Sort of. Before we got away from the robbers she used something on one of them. Pepper spray I think she called it. I was standing close enough to him that I got splashed with it. Until she got it off my face and eyes at her home I couldn't see anything."

"Funny that you didn't mention that before."

"It didn't matter before."

"So you say."

"Look. Just contact the refugee center and verify my identity. Or contact the school and check to see if I work there. Then you can check my classmates and ask the only Gertrude there. She can verify all of this."

"I'm not in the habit of wasting other people's time. I know from experience," he paused to give Morgan a hard look, "how aggravating it is to have others waste your own.

"So three guys attacked you. I'll assume – for the moment – that that is true. What did they look like?"

Morgan described them as best as she was able, their style of dress, and so on.

"And what did you do to them?"

"I told you already, I stopped them robbing my friend."

"So you said. Attacking someone in retaliation over a lost score is rather disproportionate. Especially in the open like that, even in Kamatown. You claimed one got hit with pepper spray. What else happened when you 'got away?'"

"I came up behind them. I hit one in the kidneys and the groin, then punched another in the face. Before they could hit me back, Gertrude got the spray out."

This seemed to actually get his attention. He sat up a bit more in the chair.

"You're telling me you attacked three Kamatown thugs, and got away, without them laying a finger on you?"

"Yes."

"Either you're stupid or you think I am."

"At this point I'm starting to wonder."

"Where are you from then, if not around here? You aren't high class, but if you aren't lying you are way too naïve for the likes of Kamatown. Especially if the list of old injuries I saw is accurate." As he said this he looked at Morgan's bare arms and the scars visible there.

"I don't suppose you'll take 'none of your business' as an answer?"

"It rather is. Besides, you suggested I call the refugee center, didn't you? You don't think they won't tell me? Assuming, of course, you're not lying to me."

Morgan grunted again. "I'm from Hillman. A little mining town, with long shifts crawling through the tunnels fixing things, since I was eight Earth years old. The local cops would have fit right in here; from what I've seen. They were a bunch of bullies too."

The cop just sat there for a minute, looking at her.

"You know. I *might* believe you."

"So how about you take this off?" Morgan held up her left arm, much steadier this time.

"Let's not get ahead of ourselves. The doctors here are positive you're at most ten years old, local. Certainly not a legal adult. So either you are lying to me and you've run away from home or something, in which case you should fess up, there are laws protecting abuse victims, or you lied on your refugee forms, and you're stuck here until someone from the foster system gets here."

"Absolutely not. I have a life. School. Jobs. Jobs I might lose because you bunch of Tinnys are keeping me here against my will. My birthdate is clearly labeled on my identification, which is not fake."

The cop shrugged. "That isn't something that is my problem, one way or the other. Catching the men who nearly killed you? That is my job."

"Great. Sure. Catch them. Just go verify my story so I can get out of here."

"Whatever. I'll be back later with some pictures to go through with you. Local thugs we've arrested before. Your description will narrow it down a bunch. Don't go anywhere in the meantime." He chuckled at his crass joke. "If you decide to stop lying to me and tell me the whole truth, ask the nurse to contact Detective MacGregor."

Morgan said nothing as he left, not wanting to antagonize him further. She did, however, employ a few of the ruder hand gestures she'd learned since arriving on Zion.

Morgan lay there, pondering her options.

Two options. Try and escape, or not.

She was pretty sure she could get the bracelet off. The inner locking mechanism wasn't especially complicated. She could repurpose some of the medical equipment within reach to finesse the lock, but then what?

She didn't have clothes, and she didn't have her identification. She could leave without her things, but then she couldn't even get back into her apartment, and tracking her down afterwards would be exceedingly simple.

So she'd have to escape *and* sneak about until she could find her things. Of course, that would tremendously increase her chances of getting caught, but that brought her back to the option of doing nothing.

If she just stayed here eventually they would shuffle her off to some family or government institution.

At the moment they hadn't proven anything. That was Morgan's best chance. Legally she was still twelve, still an adult registered for classes with jobs and money, however little. The longer she stayed the more likely that status would be changed, especially if the official from the foster system showed first.

Okay. If she tried to escape and was caught, was she any worse off? Not really. If she escaped and they came after her, what would happen then? A fine maybe? Accuse her of trying to get out of paying the hospital bill? She could counter that by saying they intentionally made the bill larger by not letting her go, when clearly a broken limb didn't require actually staying in the hospital. It was flimsy, but better than nothing.

If she escaped and managed to avoid them, she could get on with it. She had slightly just under two years of classes left before graduation, and then she could get a job and be safely off planet.

There was no risk free option, so Morgan picked the one she had the most control over and started trying to pick the lock.

✳✳✳

Morgan may have been overly optimistic about the ease of opening the bracelet. Morgan had assumed it was something the hospital used on dangerous patients, but she was starting to think it was a police tool primarily, given how resistant it was to her fiddling. Then again, she was trying to work on the lock holding a makeshift tool in the arm that was immobilized by a cast. The cast extended partway down her hand, so she couldn't rotate her wrist, and only sort of move her fingers.

It had been hours since the policeman had left. Aside from another adventure in getting to the bathroom she had done nothing but pick at the lock, with no visible results.

Well, besides the scratches on the metal around the keyhole, anyway.

Occasionally people walked by past the curtain, giving Morgan a frantic few moments as she hid her makeshift tool, but neglect seemed the norm in this hospital.

Given the fact that Morgan hadn't eaten since the previous morning at Gertrude's, she would have welcomed an interruption if meant she could get some food.

That had been the most surprising thing about living among people who lived under 'normal' gravity; they simply didn't need as much food as someone from Hillman did. Logically it made sense; they had less muscle mass on average and used less energy for everything from breathing to walking.

Of course Morgan needed less food here than she had before, but she still needed noticeably more than most, especially for her size.

Which was all a roundabout way of saying she was starving in addition to being sore over most of her body, itchy under the cast on her arm, and generally angry at the government here acting like a bunch of Tinnys.

Grunting in frustration Morgan gave her makeshift tool a rougher shove into the keyhole, which, given her general luck over the last day or two, of course snapped off in the hole. . . and clicked the lock open.

Good luck and bad, that was all she seemed to be having. She quite thoroughly wished she could have *no* luck, at least for a while.

Shaking her head, Morgan pulled the bracelet off her wrist along with the cuff beneath it. Idly rubbing her wrist, she realized she now actually had to figure out how to find her things – and clothes – instead of just planning on doing it.

Her deliberations were cut short by the sound of approaching steps and raised voices.

Quickly Morgan put the cuff and bracelet back on, tucking her arm against the side of her blanket covered leg so the bracelet hanging open wouldn't be visible.

As the steps got closer Morgan was able to make out some of the words.

"You . . . come back . . .," someone said. It wasn't the policeman or the hospital staff she'd talked to, which didn't really narrow it down much. If she was in the hospital just outside the Bo district it had to have hundreds of staff, after all.

"You . . . . . . stop us? Try." Wait. That sounded almost like Emily. It was hard to be sure, she hadn't talked with her all that much. . .

"Shall we. . . . . . false imprisonment?" That one was definitely Gertrude. That they were here for anything besides Morgan strained credulity, but so did them being here *for* her.

Despite Morgan's skepticism the curtain was pulled back and it was indeed Gertrude and Emily in the hallway, dressed similarly to what they had worn the day before, along with some unknown woman in the same white coat ugly green getup the earlier man had been in.

"You don't look so bad for someone who 'couldn't possibly be moved.'" Gertrude said with a sad smile as they walked in. As happened so often when talking with Gertrude, Morgan had no idea what she meant.

"Was that supposed to make sense?" was about the most coherent thing Morgan could think to ask, given the circumstances.

"She also sounds quite lucid, for someone on a massive dose of painkillers," Emily added, arching one eyebrow up and somehow making the simple expression menacing.

"I'm not on any painkillers. What are you talking about and why are you here?"

"We're here to bust you out, dear," Gertrude replied with a bit happier smile. "It wasn't easy finding you; you're listed as 'Jane Doe' in the database."

"How could you possibly get Jane Doe from Morgan?"

"Oh, you can't. They seem to think you're not who you say you are," Emily answered, glancing at the hospital woman. "Why they think that, and why they think it advisable to lie to *me*, well, that I can't say."

"Jane Doe is customary in cases where we do not know someone's legal name. The only identification she had was obviously forged, poorly at that as it lacked even a last name. This child is not to leave until the Bureau of Child Development can verify the facts of her case. That is standard procedure."

"Child?" Emily stepped closer to the other woman, uncomfortably close in Morgan's opinion, though the doctor didn't back up or otherwise visibly react. "Because you made it so *difficult* to locate this young woman I had to make substantial inquiries into her background in my efforts to find her. Whatever you might think you know, this woman is an adult, legally, morally, and emotionally. She also, *legally*, has no last name, because the planet she comes from doesn't use them, instead assigning their *slaves* numbers. We are leaving immediately, *with* Morgan. If you wish to do anything about it you can take it up with the Albion Consulate in Ein. Now, where are her things?"

By this point Emily's nose was practically bumping into the shorter woman's forehead.

"You can't intimidate me. My duty is to ensure the wellbeing of my patients, and this *child* should not be living on her own."

"Who are you, exactly?" Morgan interjected.

"I am Doctor Emar. Your doctor, in fact."

"Really? I've never seen you before. In fact, I haven't seen anyone besides a pushy police officer in quite a few hours." Morgan's statement was lent further credence by her stomach choosing that moment to rumble quite loudly. "No one has told me what is going on, given me any food or medicine since I woke up, and certainly no one has bothered to listen to me and actually check my identification."

"Doctor," Emily put a lot of venom into the word. "You have three choices. My recommendation is for you get Morgan's things, without further argument. The second thing you could do is explain why you have handcuffed the victim of a crime to her bed like a criminal. The third starts with you trying to do anything else, then quickly turns into me forcing you to take me to Morgan's things."

"I can call security."

Emily sighed. "You can, but that brings us back to option three, followed by a diplomatic incident. Do try to keep up."

"You and what army?" Emar said, actually managing a small smirk. The way she said made Morgan think it was some sort of old saying, though not one Morgan had heard before. Emily's initial response was another smile, one so cold Morgan felt a momentary need to flinch back, even though it wasn't directed at her.

"Why, *my* army. Surely you've heard of it? The Novan Nomads?"

"They're on Albion." Emar was less sure of herself now, backing up a half step.

"Oh, most of them, to be sure. All of the active duty ones, as well. Do you really think I need more than a handful of them to take care of you. . . and this place?" The 'this place' was nearly an afterthought of the question, an unstated threat about who Emily would hold principally responsible.

"I will lodge a protest over this," Emar said, but she was beat and she knew it. She was already stepping towards the door, her shoulders slumping.

"Boris," Emily called out into the hallway.

"Yes, Lady Novan?"

"Go with the good doctor and retrieve Morgan's things. If she gives you any grief or tries to involve security be so kind as to let the others know."

"Of course milady."

Morgan went to speak once Emar had left, a thousand questions to ask, but Emily held up her hand.

"We'll talk once we're out of here. Hopefully the doctor thinks I *forgot* to make her unchain you first, and she'll be planning on getting security here before they return." Emily pulled a small key from the cuff of her sleeve. "Hold out your hand and I'll have this off of you momentarily."

Morgan allowed herself a laugh, tossing off the bracelet, pausing to pull out the broken tool she'd used on it. Looking it over for a moment Morgan tucked it into the top part of her cast. It was a good memento, and would leave fewer clues for them to figure out how she got out.

"Well done," Emily said, slipping the key back into its hiding place. "We'd best be going."

Gertrude assisted Morgan hop off of the bed, then helped her stay steady as a wave of dizziness hit her.

"Given how pale you are, you're probably still suffering from blood loss. I suppose they didn't want to give you a larger transfusion than absolutely necessary. I can't say that I really blame them for that. Supplies are tight in a place like this." Despite her words Emily was frowning slightly. "Though not feeding you is another matter."

Gertrude enveloped Morgan in a hug, forcing a small squeak from Morgan as the larger woman's arms tightened around her.

"You're certainly a worrying one to have as a friend," she said with a broad smile.

They must have looked an odd sight walking through the corridors, Emily in her severe militaristic dress, Gertrude in her casual blouse and skirt, and Morgan, well, Morgan was barefoot with one hand on Gertrude's arm for support, her cast-clad arm holding the hospital gown closed in the back.

"How are we going to get past whoever is watching the doors?" Morgan asked, unable to hold off asking that rather pressing question.

"Walk out like we own the place. Lady Novan can pull that much off in her sleep. The air car is waiting for us right outside. We'll be away before they can do more than complain."

"Besides," Emily added, "By the time we get there, Doctor Emar should have called much of the security to your room.

There were actually several patients seated near the exit to the building, talking with what Morgan assumed was friends and family. They had robes on over their gowns, and slippers on their feet, but weren't otherwise noticeably different than she was.

There was still a call from the front desk as they approached the doors.

"Ma'am? You need to sign out before you can leave."

Gertrude kept on walking with Morgan while Emily turned back to the desk.

"I'm sorry, I didn't know how you do things here," she said, suddenly having a much thicker accent, her vowels elongated and the ends of words slightly cut off.

"They need to be. . ." the man at the desk was saying as Morgan and Gertrude walked out the automated doors, his words cut off.

As promised, there was black air car waiting right there, a couple other vehicles behind it with rather cross looking drivers.

There was a man standing next to the door, dressed like Boris had been, only with an added long black coat, who opened it for the two of them, offering a hand to help Morgan step into the car. Once they were inside the quite roomy vehicle he shrugged his coat off and offered it to Gertrude without a word.

"Thank you," Morgan said as Gertrude helped her slip it on. He bowed and closed the door, entering the vehicle in the front next to the driver. As soon as his door was closed the vehicle started moving, quickly climbing into the air. Amazing what you could do with antigravity tech with only .89g to deal with. Seeing the sky and sun for the first time since she'd been attacked Morgan realized it was evening again, nearly a full day later.

"We're not waiting for Emily and Boris?" Morgan asked Gertrude quietly.

"There is another car waiting for them. They can't do anything to her, and this gets you out of their reach quickest."

Opening a small hatch in-between the seats Gertrude pulled out a bottle of water and what looked to be some food wrapped in foil. "You should eat."

Nodding Morgan started eating. After six or seven bites she paused to wonder if it really was that bland, or if she was so hungry and tired that she simply wasn't noticing the flavor. In either case it wasn't long before she started eating slower, leaning back farther into the very comfortable chair.

She was asleep before she even thought to ask where they were taking her.

CHAPTER 11

One of the most difficult lessons of adulthood is learning the difference between relying on others and living like a parasite, and leaning on others for mutual benefit. Like so many things there isn't a fine line dividing them, but a nebula of uncertainty.

- Second Minister Jaron, Nerrul System

MORGAN WAS GETTING REALLY TIRED of waking up in strange places.

The pale purple paint on the walls was the same shade she'd seen at Gertrude's, so she was probably there, but this was a room she hadn't seen before.

She was lying on a very large bed, too soft for her tastes but comfortable nonetheless.

Gertrude's room, perhaps? There was something that looked like a desk along one wall, full of drawers and a large mirror. There were pictures tucked into the border of the mirror, from her somewhat distant vantage on the bed many of them looked to be pictures of Haruhi, so it was likely.

On the desk there was a holodisplay with the time displayed. Six in the morning on the fifth. Well, at least the fourth was over, splendid day that it had been.

Pulling back the covers, Morgan noted she was still in the comical combination of hospital gown and the long coat the car man had lent her. Her arm was a tad itchy under the cast, but it would still be a few days before she could take that off. That was assuming whatever they used here wasn't more effective than the Quicknit she'd used in the past.

There were two doors on the wall past the foot of the bed. The left one was closed, but Morgan could see a bathroom through the open door to the right, reminding her of some pressing needs. As she hopped off the bed – feeling much steadier on her feet than she had before – she noticed a small pile of clothes on a fabric-padded chest pushed back against the wall between the two doors.

These weren't just any clothes either, but *her* clothes, her somewhat faded yellow dress on top. They'd been to her apartment? How had. . . oh, of course, Boris had retrieved her identification. That was all they'd need to get in, since Gertrude knew where it was. Morgan wasn't quite sure if she found it touching or an invasion of her privacy, but after a moment decided she wasn't going to worry about it, grabbing the dress and underwear from the pile. There was something else on the pile, causing her to pause before she headed into the bathroom.

It was a somewhat battered uplink unit, noticeably more rugged and durable than the ones commonly seen around Isa. Underneath was something even more unusual, a handwritten note.

"Not to be presumptuous," – Morgan wasn't sure what that word meant, but she continued reading – *"but I noted you do not own an uplink. This is one of my old units from my active military days, one I only kept because it was less of a hassle to keep than to dispose of it. I'll hear no objections, I insist on this small act of gratitude, especially since the act doesn't inconvenience me in the slightest."*

It certainly did look quite used, but slipping it on Morgan found it started up quite easily, confirming her identity before locking in her biometric information and locking to her possession. Morgan was tempted to check it out further, but she had headed towards the bathroom with some urgency, so she let it be for the moment.

Getting cleaned up and dressed took somewhat longer than normal, thanks to the awkward cast getting in the way, but it was still only seven when Morgan left the room, finding herself in the now familiar halls of Gertrude's home. The house was quiet, with neither Gertrude nor Haruhi visible or audible.

The kitchen looked quite different from Morgan's previous visit, a feat accomplished by the simple fact it was clean. Since it was also empty, Morgan moved on and headed towards the front of the house.

Through the small windows in the front door Morgan could see the back of someone, a man, dressed enough like Boris and the man at the car that she assumed he was another employee of Emily's. The only obvious explanation for him standing there was he was guarding the building, but that didn't make much sense either.

She finally found Gertrude, asleep on the very couch Morgan had spent a night on. Morgan didn't disturb her, instead wending her way back to the dining room and walking out to the patio. The tables and chairs from the breakfast gathering had been cleared away, and the patio was much more open. There were a few chairs scattered about, but long low ones designed for stretching out your legs. Morgan plopped down on one of the padded ones. She was still quite tired, so she dozed fitfully to the sounds of nearby birds chirping.

***

It might have been the sound of voices that woke her back up, or perhaps it was the smell of bacon. Either way she awoke to find the remaining table on the patio had been set with breakfast, three chairs set around it. Gertrude was putting down a plate of bacon next to the eggs and fruit.

It was, of course, nowhere near as large an affair as the last breakfast the space had seen, but Morgan's stomach growled appreciatively nonetheless.

"Ah, good, you're awake again. Just in time to eat," Gertrude said cheerily. "I have to say, that dress looks good. I almost didn't recognize you without a pair of coveralls on."

Morgan shrugged after she stood up.

"I have to have coveralls for school. Can't really afford to have two sets of clothes. Besides, I'm used to them. It's what I wore back home."

"Yes, I imagine mining encourages clothing that covers as much of the body as possible," Emily said from behind Morgan. Turning Morgan saw her exiting the dining room door, carrying a pitcher of juice. "There is much to talk about, but let us eat first."

The meal was good if. . . awkward. Morgan didn't know what to say to the other women, and they seemed content to eat in silence. Morgan finished first despite having eaten more than her companions, her hunger outweighing the need to savor the food.

Morgan waited until they finished before starting in on her manifold questions.

"How did you find me? For that matter how did you even know to look?"

"It wasn't that hard, never mind what we said to the doctor," Gertrude started, "Once we knew you'd been attacked, the hospitals were the obvious places to look. It would have been quicker if they hadn't assumed your ID was a fake."

"As for how we knew to look," Emily continued, "That was honestly partially a matter of luck. After our. . . disagreement the other morning I wished to speak with you again, to try and explain better what I was trying to say, as well as apologize for upsetting you. From Gertrude, I learned that you work at the school, and are there often studying. I am normally up quite early, so I went to see if I could talk with you, or at least arrange a time to speak when you weren't working. Your supervisor told me you had not come to work that day, and that such was unheard of for you. He gave me the name of your other employer, who obviously had also not heard from you. From there I got your address from Gertrude and called on you there."

"And I wasn't there either." Morgan supplied, wondering slightly if Emily was always this long-winded.

"Quite. I drew some unwanted attention myself in your neighborhood, which was fortunate in the end as it gave me people to inquire with. They were quite easy to bribe, which is how I learned of a girl matching your description – or rather, matching the description of your clothes at any rate – being attacked and carted off to the hospital."

"We tried calling around first," Gertrude interjected, "but we ran into problems because we didn't know anything more to tell them than your name was Morgan."

"I called on some friends at this point to look up some information on you to help us, including your refugee records. The rest you know."

"Not quite the rest, what is going to happen with me and the hospital?

The police? I don't even know if I still have a job at this point."

"The hospital has been dealt with. The details don't matter," Emily stated.

Morgan rather disagreed on that point, but those inquiries would have to wait.

"And I got your bosses' info from Lady Novan. I told them you'd been hurt and that you'd get in touch with them as soon as you were well enough," Gertrude added.

"The police might be able to track down the men who attacked you. Less likely things have happened, after all, but either way they won't continue to bother you about your age."

"Thank you," Morgan said after taking a moment just to take it all in, "I don't know what to say."

"'Thank you' is the customary response," Emily said. "Boris took the opportunity to gather your things from your apartment. Even if you do not take Gertrude up on her offer of renting here, it really isn't safe for you there anymore. If you want, I can help you find other arrangements."

"He emptied my apartment?"

"It. . . did not take him long."

"Which brings us to something a little more fun," Gertrude added with a smile, patting Morgan's hand where it rested on the table.

"I'm not following."

"The mugging and your attack have finally enabled me to convince Gertrude that she needs to have the means for self-defense. For Haruhi's sake, if nothing else. As it happens, I know a fine man a few cities over who sells such tools. It won't be much more expensive for us to buy two from him than one. That his store is nearby one of the best clothiers on the planet is a happy coincidence."

"I don't have money for this," Morgan protested. "I'm grateful for your offer, Gertrude, and it will save me money. That doesn't mean I have any right now."

Gertrude sighed.

"We know that. We're offering to help you."

"I don't *need* your help."

"We know that too," Emily said, matter-of-factly, "You were doing an admirable job of pulling yourself up by the proverbial bootstraps. If you hadn't of gotten involved with the men robbing Gertrude I've no doubt you'd be at work right now, or studying, or doing whatever else you needed to do. We're not offering because we think you can't make it on your own, we're offering because no one should *have* to make it on their own."

Morgan was unsure how to answer this. It was so hard to trust anyone, and yet. . . and yet she had to trust *someone*. She'd trusted her parents, implicitly, because they were her parents. She'd put her future in the hands in the crew of the *Pale Moonlight* because there was no alternative, but she hadn't trusted them. How could she? She didn't know them, and they didn't know her. She hadn't really even trusted her one and only friend Jane. She'd *liked* her, true, quite a lot, but trust? No, not if Morgan was being honest with herself.

She would never see Jane again. Or her parents, for that matter. How lonely would she end up if she never trusted *anyone*?

"Honey, you need to let people in. What do you think it is like, working on a freighter? Your life is in the hands of every single person there, and their lives are in yours."

Morgan slumped forward against the table, resting her head in her hands.

"I don't think I know how to trust," she said at last, without looking up.
"

"We can help with that too," Gertrude said, soothingly, standing up and putting her arms around Morgan. "Step one is even fun. You get to experience your first bona fide shopping trip!"

＊＊＊

Morgan couldn't say, afterwards, what she had expected clothes shopping to be like. Whatever she had expected, she had been utterly wrong.

In her admittedly short life, Morgan had only been shopping for clothing once. Once she was admitted to the school she had asked the recruiter about appropriate clothing for the work and where she could get it. She then went there and after holding a couple sizes up to herself to see what would fit bought as many as she could afford. It had taken her longer to get to the store than to buy what she came out with.

The stores Gertrude and Emily took her to – and she lost count of how many there were – were probably large enough to fit the entire population of Pari Passu in, assuming they were friendly.

But beyond the size of the stores it was the variety of clothes that was staggering. The other woman at times seemed to be speaking a different language than Morgan was familiar with. A-line, sheath, wrap – the names just kept coming and Morgan couldn't make sense of any of it. What made a dress a 'sun' dress anyway? The first one they showed her was yellow, so at first she thought it might mean sun-colored, but the second one had been purple, so clearly she was mistaken. It was just as well that they were focusing on dresses rather than blouses and pants, at Morgan's insistence, or they would have been at it forever.

Eventually Gertrude realized the terminology was getting them nowhere and started just asking what Morgan did and did not like as a means of narrowing it down.

Ankle length? No, too liable to trip.

Upper thigh length? Not simply no, but emphatically *no*. Morgan had to keep resisting the urge to tug it down every time her fingertips brushed up against her legs where they extended past the hem of the skirt.

Loose skirt or tight? Loose.

A dress over a blouse? No, too hot. Plus, why not just buy a blouse and a skirt in that case?

On and on it went. In the end they declared that Morgan had a preference for just above the knee length loose skirted dresses, either sundress or wrap style. Morgan was glad they felt better having defined her 'taste.'

Even when they had at last settled on Morgan's preferences there was still the matter of color, fabric, and then of course the *trying on*.

Gertrude certainly seemed to be enjoying herself, and Morgan had caught Emily cracking a smile a time or two. Stars above, the whole process was wearying.

This one was too tight in the shoulders, that one too tight in the waist, a third not cut to accommodate someone with as much arm muscle as Morgan.

The other women rejected far more dresses than Morgan would have. Even perfectly serviceable clothes that were only a little too loose were rejected alongside those that were liable to tear if she moved wrong.

The attendant in the dressing room had gently suggested Morgan try on some long sleeved dresses, but Emily had just laughed and said that there wasn't any need to cover up her scars. Doing so hadn't occurred to Morgan, but most of the people she'd interacted with hadn't commented on them either.

The attendant had apologized and been too embarrassed to offer more suggestions, until Emily broke the ice by talking about some of her scars picked up in the military. This had spiraled into a competition where Emily and Morgan compared scars. Morgan won for quantity. Emily won for method obtained.

Once they had four dresses worth buying Morgan had tried to get them to stop, but they insisted on getting at least twice that number.

Morgan had to admit, at least to herself, that the dresses were *cute*. Especially the one that had been declared the perfect 'little black dress.' This was apparently a description of function as well as how it looked, but never mind that, Morgan felt pretty wearing it.

"Does it always take this long?" Morgan asked them as they put the last dress back on its hanger and placed it with the others in the cart pushed around by another of Emily's employees, a woman who had only spoken a single word, and that to introduce herself as Kate.

"If you're lucky and have the time, yes," Gertrude said, laughing.

"Is our next stop this friend of Emily's then?"

"Oh, no," Gertrude said, quite seriously, "We're not done here yet. There are still odds and ends to get, like underwear – that shouldn't take as long – and then the really fun part. *Shoes!*"

Morgan managed to suppress the moan threatening to burst out, but only because it seemed rude to complain when the other women were picking up the cost.

"If it helps, I think you will enjoy shopping at Larry's plenty," Emily said, flashing her a lopsided smile.

***

At Gertrude's insistence Morgan had changed into one of her new dresses before they headed for their last stop, a pale pink wrap dress with sleeves that went down about a third of the way to her elbow and a deep pink sash holding it closed. The V-neck showed a little more of her upper chest than she was used to, but not greatly so.

She hadn't the courage to try the shoes with heels yet, so she was wearing the black flats, finding them still surprisingly comfortable. Not something she could work in, though.

When they slowed down and dropped to street level in front of the store Morgan almost mistook it for a warehouse. There were no windows and all four sides had massive black planters just past the sidewalk running all the way around the building. Morgan couldn't be sure, but they looked to be made of carbon nanotubes. It was an interesting choice for what was essentially a large plant pot. The guard stations in Pari Passu hadn't been this fortified. They were pretty plants at least, carefully sculpted bushes cheerfully offsetting the dour nature of the building. Some of the shapes she recognized, like the bushes shaped to look the roaring lion on Albion's seal or the dove clutching a sword and leafy branch in its talons that was Zion's symbol. The two on either side of the – clearly reinforced – metal door at one corner of the building Morgan did not recognize, and she almost wondered if it was even a real animal. It was very round, with a big flat tail and two broad flat flippers, and a large droopy almost doglike snout. Whatever it was they all certainly took a lot of time to craft. Morgan had no idea how the dove sculpture didn't break under its own weight in places, for instance. A sure sign the store was doing a good business, anyway.

The sign in the door's tiny window – not holographic but actual plastic hanging from some thin twine – said the store was closed, but Emily tapped the buzzer next to the doorknob anyway.

She waited for a full minute, and then rang the buzzer again.

It took a bit longer, but the speaker above the buzzer started up with a short burst of static, followed by someone speaking.

"Closed. Come back tomorrow."

"I know you are closed. Tell Larry that 'that damned taskmaster' is here to see him," Emily replied, completely ignoring the curtness of the stranger's statement.

"Seriously?"

"Those exact words."

The connection closed with another bit of static.

"A lot of this seems rather. . . old," Gertrude said, gesturing to the door.

"Larry is an interesting fellow. He hates to throw anything away simply because it's old. Some of the pieces he has in there in his private collection were made on Earth 800 years ago, and still work. The ones more than a millennia old don't function. At least I don't think they do. He probably has the best collection in the galaxy, at least without Earth to compete with."

"And what exactly does he sell here?" Morgan asked.

"As I said, the tools of self-defense," Emily replied, "which covers a fairly broad range of things."

"Guns, honey," Gertrude said, taking in Morgan's uncomprehending reaction to Emily's statement.

"They are more than simply 'guns,'" Emily said.

"Lady Novan, you know more about weapons than the two of us do about machines and repairs, combined. Probably twice over. If I were to try to explain the dozen tools I use to fix an antigravity engine to you, they might as well all be 'wrenches.' Gun is a good enough explanation."

Emily did not respond, due to the door opening just as Gertrude finished talking. A young man, perhaps even close to Morgan's age, was standing in the doorway with an awed look on his face. His name badge read 'Wendell.'

"Welcome, Colonel," he practically stammered. "Larry is straight back in the range. Would you like me to lead you?"

"No, thank you, I know the way," Emily said, "But perhaps you could do me a favor?"

Somehow the awed look on his face intensified, and Morgan wondered if he could even remember his own name at that point.

"Anything."

Emily pulled up a list on her uplink. She gestured to him and he primed his to receive information.

"I assume you know this establishment? It is not far distant. Get everything on that list, exactly as it is there, and pay them with this," she pushed a few more buttons, presumably authorizing temporary access to her accounts."

"I'll be back in twenty minutes." He assured them, moving to the side to allow the women to enter the store past him.

"Don't overexert yourself. Forty minutes is perfectly acceptable. We don't want it too early, after all."

"Why not just send your driver?" Morgan asked after the door had closed behind the young man.

"I could have, but this way he gets to feel useful and isn't hanging around here bothering us with his adoration."

"You've met him before?"

"No, actually," Emily answered, "but my reputation precedes me much more in a place like this."

The front end of the store was a narrow walkway leading to the other end of the store, a glass case separating the customer side from the staff, filled with small guns in a bewildering array of styles, though all sharing the same basic design, a horizontal grip with the switch below the barrel and the bits around it.

All of the walls to their left were covered with an even more varied assortment of accessories. Morgan hadn't ever seen a gun up close before. The Tinnys relied on brute force, short clubs, and the promise of retaliation rather than more advanced weapons. As such, the labels here helped her even less than the terms for dress types had. Magazines, holsters, barrels, triggers, and so forth.

The wall just a meter or so back from the glass cases held larger weapons, clearly meant to be carried and used with both hands. These were more varied than the smaller ones were, with one hand grip, two, or none, attachments for lights or none, round tube or not, and even some without an obvious barrel that could be seen from the side. Others had multiple barrels, including one that was probably almost as long as Morgan was tall with six barrels mounted in a ring configuration.

At the end of the store the walkway snaked back around the wall, presenting another aisle more or less the mirror image of the front of the store, only these guns were of a different type. All of these had a much broader barrel, at least twice the diameter of the ones in front. They also looked. . . newer somehow? Morgan couldn't quite put her finger on it, but the designs looked closer to the style and aesthetics she had seen elsewhere on Zion. The stuff in the first row almost reminded her of pictures she'd seen of Earth in the little time she'd had to study other topics like history since starting school.

The walkway looped back around again, though this time the aisle ended maybe a third the way across the length of the building, with a wall cutting off the rest, a heavyset door with no windows leading, presumably, to the rest of the building, a staircase next to it leading upstairs. It had no door, but did have a small sign held across its length with twine that read 'Employees Only.'

Again these guns were obviously of a different type. They had barrels that were narrower than even the ones nearest the entrance, looking too small for Morgan to even fit her pinkie finger in, were she to try such an unwise thing. These were almost entirely made of reflective metal, instead of the ceramics, common metals, and plastics of the first row, or the carbon of the second. Morgan had picked up something of an eye for metals even before escaping Hillman; if she had to guess these looked to be an alloy with at least some iridium. Why did such tiny guns need to be so durable?

She didn't have time to ponder this too long, Emily led them straight through the door into what was helpfully proclaimed the range by an overhead banner.

This portion of the building was two stories tall, mostly open, with a clear wall dividing the entryway from the rest of the room. Just past that there was a half wall divided into numbered lanes, each separated from the rest by two single-story walls perpendicular to the wall, as well as flat space on the top of the half wall, presumably to rest the guns on. Above each section there was a railing with a motorized clamp hanging down from it, extending all the way to the back of the range where the back wall was covered with some steeply angled piled of. . . something, Morgan couldn't figure out what it was made of, just that it was presumably meant to catch whatever the guns shot out.

Another helpful sign on the glass door read 'Eyes and ears on at all times beyond this point.'

Perhaps not so helpful, at least for someone like Morgan who was completely new to this.

The wall directly to their right as they walked onto the range was covered to a height of two meters or so with small cubbyholes, each labeled with a number. Emily reached into one, pulling out a pair of clear glasses and a pair of ear protection not unlike what they used at the school when working around some of the noisier equipment. Ah, *protection* for eyes and ears. That was reasonable enough.

"Do the numbers represent sizes?" Morgan asked, watching Gertrude pull out a set from another cubby.

"No, that's just so you know where to put them back," Gertrude said, showing Morgan the small number stamped on her ear protection, the same number as the hole. "They should fit just about anyone."

Shrugging Morgan pulled out the ones nearest to where she was standing. The glasses were a light yellow color rather than clear, but they fit fine. She settled the ear protection on, noting that these had the same technology in the others she had used, which allowed sounds like normal speech through fine, stopping only those sounds loud enough to be harmful.

There didn't seem to be any other obvious exits out of the range, so where was. . . Oh, there he was. On the far left end of the range there was a man leaning up against the divider sitting on a stool, leaning over the top of it fiddling with some fasteners on a remarkably large weapon. It looked a bit like the small telescopes the Tinnys used to watch workers from the top of their towers, so it was probably to help sighting at long distances.

Apparently satisfied with his work, he straightened up, raised the gun up to his shoulder, and pulled the trigger. Even through the glass wall – which was highly unlikely to be simple glass, now that Morgan thought of it – and despite her ear protection, it was *loud*. Loud to the point that the glass door shook slightly. He fired again and Morgan realized she wasn't hearing the sound of the gun firing, but of the bullet hitting the far wall – and exploding.

Morgan felt her eyebrows rise without any conscious thought on her part.

"What is *that*?" She asked.

"It *was* an NCR-7 standard issue battle rifle. Now it is a travesty of good taste and style," Emily replied over her shoulder, still looking at the rifle through the glass.

"Because of the exploding bullet?" Gertrude asked.

Emily laughed. "No, that's normal. He's replaced the stock, the sights, the grip, even the magazine well it looks like. What is that on the. . . did he attach an underslung *shotgun* on the thing? Is nothing sacred to this man?"

At this point Morgan started tuning her out. The words were gibberish to her, but the tone? That Morgan knew all too well. She'd used it herself a few times when discussing some ridiculous repair job one of the other tunnel rats had perpetrated on some poor machine that she then had to fix.

As she went on Morgan turned to Gertrude and shrugged, who in turn rolled her eyes and opened the glass door. This managed to get the attention of Larry, who had finished firing the gun for the moment.

"And what brings you here, oh harridan of my nightmares?" He said in a booming, but not unfriendly, voice, standing up. And up, and up some more. He was probably the tallest man Morgan had ever seen. He was also very broad, with a shaved or bald head and a bushy goatee, with skin somewhat between Morgan's and Gertrude's in color.

"Oh, nothing too unusual. Gertrude finally decided she needs something smaller than Gunny Suoh's hand cannon, and Morgan here is a babe in the woods who needs something to protect herself with."

"What, you think this is like the bad old days, that I'm just here to get whatever you need?"

"Of course not," Emily replied immediately, pausing for a moment before adding, "This is worse than the bad old days. Now I have to *pay* you."

Larry laughed. "True enough. It's good to see you, Colonel. You too, Gertrude. I wish I could have made it out the other day." He turned to Morgan, sizing her up. "A babe in the woods then? Have you ever even held a firearm?"

"Never."

"Well, at least you won't have any crap you need to unlearn. Come here," he added, beckoning her over. Once Morgan was standing next to him he pointed to a placard that was nailed to the divider wall beneath the other sign that said 'Lane 1.' "These are the basic rules of gun safety. They are not suggestions, they are not guidelines, they are rules. Tell me, do you work, are you in school?"

"School for starship mechanics," Morgan supplied. "Plus working as a janitor and ground car mechanic's assistant."

"Okay. This is just as important – more really – than the chemical and tool safety rules you have at school and work. You screw with this and if you're lucky you might end up dead. If you are unlucky someone else will end up dead. You understand me?"

Morgan nodded, looking at the sign. There were only four rules, written succinctly.

The gun is always loaded.

Never let the muzzle cover anything you are not willing to destroy.

Keep your finger off the trigger until your sights are on the target.

Be sure of your target and what is beyond it.

"Logical," Morgan said as she finished reading.

"Those rules have existed for hundreds of years because they work. Now, a gun is a tool like any spanner or bolt you work with, with many uses. Often times simply having a gun will be enough to get criminals to back off, but it isn't a magic button. It also isn't for everyone. There is no shame in being unable to try to kill another human being, even someone who is trying to hurt or kill you. Do you think you can do that, if it came down to it?"

Gertrude chuckled a bit, "I think she'll do just fine there."

"So does the Colonel, or you wouldn't be there," Larry agreed, "but I need to hear it from her."

Morgan thought about it before answering. She'd certainly been willing to attack the thieves to help Gertrude, but punching someone and shooting them were different things, emotionally. She knew she could still kill someone with just her fists, but knowing it and *feeling* it were different things. If she had had a gun when they'd attacked her again would she have used it?

Probably? It was hard to be sure, after the fact.

"I think so," Morgan said honestly.

"Good answer. It is not an easy question, and being too sure at this point generally means you haven't thought about it enough. Before we get into what kind of weapon is right for you let's have you start out on some of the classics to get a feel for shooting."

***

Morgan lost track of time as Larry explained the basics to her, how to stand, how to squeeze the trigger, how to use different kinds of sights. He stuck to handguns since the point was to get her something she could carry with her.

At some point Wendell returned with Emily's order, which turned out to be dinner ordered from one of her – and Larry's – favorite restaurants. As they ate Larry explained the three main types of guns to Morgan and Gertrude.

"Gunpowder has been used, little changed in formula, since many centuries before man left Earth. There isn't anything on Earth that works better to propel a projectile at high velocity at sizes small enough to be carried, at least not until we can figure out how to finally miniaturize rail guns."

"Rail guns?" Morgan asked.

"One of the main weapons on things like spaceships. We can explain those later. Anyway, there are in fact several designs of handgun that trace their roots all the way back to Earth, the most obvious of which is the 1911 design, which is still used with only slight modifications today."

Now it was *Emily* who interrupted him, "Oh of course, you can't pass up a chance to talk about your ancestor, can you?"

"Would you rather I hate the fact that my ancestors were technological geniuses? Can I continue?" He was smiling broadly, making Morgan think this was old joke between them.

"If you must."

"How gracious of you, your grace."

"Are you getting that wrong on purpose, or have you forgotten all the manners we beat into you?"

Instead of answering Larry continued on with where he had left off, though with a slight smirk. "The handguns and rifles from that long ago are still useful given how little more power can really be squeezed out of a gunpowder design. It also didn't matter much since there wasn't really any armor good enough to completely stop a bullet. Oh, they had vests that would keep it from punching a hole in you, but the impact was still generally enough to break ribs or knock someone out temporarily.

"This lasted until someone invented the first skinsuit. Are you familiar with those, Morgan?"

"Yeah, I learned about them on the way here from my homeworld."

Modern skinsuits – so named because they were skin tight and only a few centimeters thick over most of the suit – were designed to protect the wearer from vacuum, sudden pressure changes, and the extremely hot and cold extremes of temperature encountered on a space ship. They were nano-fabricated with some of the hardest materials available while still maintaining flexibility. Morgan had been told they were good protection even from fires or small explosions, so she could see how they would be useful against guns.

"Okay, I'll skip the explanation of those then. I will say it didn't take long at all for someone to adapt them for use as a more traditional armor. Against a skinsuit, even the most powerful rifle rounds will only leave a small bruise at best. Only a hit on the faceplate has any chance of penetration.

"To answer this problem, penetrator rounds were invented. You saw a few of them in the middle section of my store, as well as this," he patted the rifle next to him, "Penetrator rounds are a simple design, but brutally effective. There are two parts, the round and the penetrator. The larger part is the round, a shaped explosive that focuses all of its energy forward and wraps around the penetrator. The penetrator is a hardened hunk of metal, specially shaped, with an impact triggered detonator at its base. When the bullet strikes something the penetrator is pushed back into the round, triggering the detonator and propelling the penetrator forward with enough force to pierce even military grade suits, as long as you hit at the right angle."

"That may have been a bit too complicated for us," Gertrude said after a moment of working through all of the info.

"In basic terms PR weapons fire a big, slow bullet at something, which then explodes on contact pushing a small hard tip forward even harder."

"That sounds. . . painful," Morgan said, looking over at the rifle sitting on the ledge. With a barrel that wide there could be a lot of power behind a bullet shaped explosive.

"Well, yeah, that's the idea. They certainly are more dangerous than normal firearms, but most of human history can be summed up as 'got progressively more dangerous.' Against a skinsuited person though they aren't as dangerous as you would think. The explosion doesn't do much to the suit, and the penetrator is so small and so hard that it doesn't do much more than put a straight hole through someone."

"Are they legal to own?" Gertrude asked, clearly upset at the idea.

"They are. Of course the penalties for misusing one are really high, as are the consequences of mishandling one. Really though most people don't bother with them for self-defense as the instances of thieves, murderers, or rapists actually using a skinsuit to commit a crime is effectively zero planetside, and they are really hard to carry concealed."

"And there is the not so insignificant fact that they are really expensive to fire," Emily added.

"So what is the third kind? I assume those are the little shiny ones made with Iridium out there?" Morgan asked.

"You have a good eye. Those are something new, generally called 'Iridium Specials,'" Emily said.

"Are you doing the explaining or am I? Anyway, yes, those are Iridium Specials. There are very few places you can buy them, for the simple fact that it was my father who invented them 20 years ago."

"Joseph Browning was a genius. A pity such things tend to skip a generation," Emily said.

This just elicited a laugh from Larry. "As you say. Anyway, they're called Iridium Specials because of the bullet, not the gun itself. The frame does needs to be stronger than normal, but using Iridium there is more of a marketing gimmick than anything else. Not that we'd admit that out loud normally.

"Iridium Specials' took the same problem the PR rounds solved and came at it another way. Instead of going bigger in order to fit an explosive charge these are designed for speed. As I said before basic gunpowder hadn't changed in centuries, due to one iridium-clad limitation of physics. Put simply, the expanding gas would expand so fast, and no faster, no matter what was done to it. So after a certain point cramming in more powder or using a larger round wouldn't do any good.

"That's the 'special' part of the bullets. My father came up with a new propellant that had similar properties to gunpowder, but that expanded more than twice as fast. The hard part wasn't even the expansion speed, but stability. It was easy to get something much more volatile. Getting something that was stable at normal temperatures and expanded faster? That was his genius. Now I won't tell you what is in it or how we make it work – at least for the moment no one but the Browning Company can manufacture the stuff. That this also limits availability and raises prices didn't hurt our bottom line any either.

"The other half of the answer was new bullets, denser, shaped to pierce better. The final shape of the bullet he made has slowly ended up being incorporated into our penetrator rounds as well, but the exotic materials are simply too expensive for widespread use, especially for something as volume intensive as military applications.

"Iridium is the best answer, being the densest stable element naturally occurring in nature. Unfortunately, it is also one of the rarest elements in this part of the galaxy. Many planets don't have any at all. Asteroids can reliably be found with good deposits, but that's still fairly expensive.

"The most obvious added expense is the extra dangers of mining in space, and the isolation. And of course the gate system is useless for getting out to asteroid fields because there is no gravity well large enough to jump *to*, and right there the cost of shipping triples. Ships can jump back, but only if the ship is big enough to have an internal gate and the builders had been able to afford the hideously expensive system in the first place.

"After all of that we also have to compete with ship builders and mechanics for iridium supplies too, since so many systems in space ships need it also, thanks to its much higher heat tolerance than common metals and alloys."

"That was. . . informative," Gertrude said after he finally stopped talking.

"Don't mind him. He's proud of his family, after all," Emily said, smirking again, "Iridium specials use better propellant, and harder bullets, which lets them puncture suits, but also makes them expensive. Right now neither of you needs a PR *or* an IS gun."

"I guess I'd better start saving then," Morgan said at last.

"Oh?" Emily asked.

"I fully plan on working in space. That means skinsuits. I won't be helpless again if I can help it."

"Well, let's talk about that. They are expensive, but there isn't much point in you buying a gun you won't use or need. What about you, Gertrude? Do you want something you can take up into the black with you?"

"In theory yes, but I'm mostly doing this for Haruhi."

"Wouldn't she be hurt just as bad if something happened to you as if something happened to her?" Emily pointed out.

"True," Gertrude didn't sound happy at the thought.

"We can make this work. I loved Gunny, the magnificent bastard, and any friend of the Colonel's is a friend of mine. How about we set up a plan where you pay it off over the months between now and when you graduate? With whatever you can pay down now to start things off? I'm not even going to worry about interest."

"That's *very* generous," Gertrude said.

Larry shrugged. "We have a monopoly on the biggest innovation in firearms technology in the past two centuries. I can afford to be, especially to my friends. I will expect to see you out here twice a month for practice with them though; a gun you aren't familiar with is much less useful." He paused for a moment, thinking. "I'll have some normal gunpowder rounds made up for your weapons. Much cheaper to practice with. Normally we don't offer them, since the recoil is much less so it isn't quite as good for training *and* we can make more money that way. Of course usually anyone who buys one can afford it. Anyway, for you more practice will be better, even if it isn't quite what the real deal will be."

✳✳✳

With that settled, the visit devolved into something akin to the earlier clothes shopping. First it was picking out just the right weapon for each woman – Gertrude preferred something a bit larger for her larger hands, while the smallest one they offered was better for Morgan's smaller size. Thanks to her greater strength, Morgan could handle the added recoil just fine. Despite the small size of the pistol, the equally small size of the bullet and cartridge gave it a capacity of 30 rounds in a standard magazine, which was a nice plus. The pistol itself was slim enough that she could slide it into her coveralls pocket without it bulging out, and three slim magazines could fit in the opposite pocket easily.

Carrying it with a dress would be slightly more difficult, given most dresses lack of pockets, but they were able to find a thigh holster she liked with a little help from Emily.

Once they had settled on their personal choice of weapon, and fired an additional hundred rounds through it to be sure on the one hand and get pointers on form on the other. This went fine except for the one hot cartridge that flew straight back into the V-neck of her dress, causing Morgan to dance about a bit in pain, frantically loosening the tie a bit so it could fall the rest of the way through and land on the floor.

"In the future be mindful of what you're wearing for practice," Larry had said, "But also remember that you won't have the luxury of knowing ahead of time when you'll need to use the gun, so be ready to just grit your teeth and deal with it if one finds its way down your dress when you're fighting for your life. If your choices are a small burn or ending up dead, well, the choice is easy."

Larry then took them back out to the front to pick out holsters. Gertrude only wanted one she could use in either pocket or purse, but Morgan ended up selecting several, including one she could tuck into a boot top, one for pockets, and one she could strap to her thigh under a dress or skirt.

Throw in ammo, the extra magazines, and small handprint safes so the women could store the guns safely in Gertrude's home and the cost really added up.

They did run into one snag when they went to pay for the purchases. By Zion law anyone legally an adult could buy a weapon and carry it, concealed or not – though concealed was by far the more popular choice – although there were exceptions for this for criminals convicted of violent crimes and a few other cases. Gertrude's check in the system was over in less than a second, but the computer refused to process Morgan's without a last name entered.

"You seriously don't have a last name?"

"I really don't."

"Can you do it manually?" Emily asked.

"Yeah, give me a moment," Larry said, pulling out his uplink and looking up the code to connect to a real person at the records office.

"Honey, have you considered giving yourself a last name, just to make things easier?" Gertrude asked Morgan as they waited.

"Actually I hadn't," she replied.

"I wouldn't want to pressure you one way or the other, but given issues like this, or what happened at the hospital, you should at least consider it," Emily added.

"You're probably right," Morgan admitted.

"I can help you with the forms and hassle of getting it changed," Emily offered, "It wouldn't take more than a few hours with my people's help. Do you have anything in mind?"

Morgan thought about it, half-heartedly listening to Larry in the background arguing with the records worker. There wasn't anything tied to home she could use, except her parents' own names, but that didn't really seem like a good choice. Looking about the room her eyes caught on a small picture on the packaging for one of the brands of magazines. It was a simple starscape, a drawing of a bunch of stars with lines tying them together in a constellation, maybe the systems where they did business. She thought about how she'd felt on the trip to Zion, how anxious she was to get up there and make something of herself. 'The Long Black,' the freighter crew had called it, the emptiness between the 'Blue Isles' that were planets.

"How about Black?" Morgan said, turning back to face the women.

"Morgan Black? I like the sound of it. Why pick that one?" Gertrude asked.

Morgan shrugged, "What better name for a mechanic working the fright lines, up there?"

"It suits you," Emily said, nodding in agreement.

Somehow Morgan felt like this small decision was the start of something bigger, that she was starting to actually find a place of her own in the worlds and beyond. Or maybe she was just being silly, and it didn't mean much of anything at all.

CHAPTER 12

Hiring is a perennial headache for any competent boss, especially in the perpetually understaffed space sectors. They have to balance the dangers of unqualified candidates with the dangers of an overworked staff, on top of all the normal concerns of finding someone who will fit with the personalities of the rest of the team. Even minor conflicts can spin out of control after six months cooped up together in the same small starship.

- Lindsey Ballard, HR Director, Molon Shipyards

TWO ZION YEARS LATER / THREE EARTH YEARS

MORGAN WOKE as she did so many mornings, with Haruhi opening the door to her room as quietly as possible.

At some point this had become their game, Haruhi trying to wake Morgan up just before her alarm went off, and Morgan trying to pretend to be asleep until she could grab and tickle Haruhi as 'punishment.' At first, it had just been the weekend days Morgan didn't work early. But a year after moving in with Gertrude, Morgan had been able to find a regular position as a ground car mechanic, enabling her to leave her other two jobs and work a more normal schedule.

Even with two years of practice behind her Haruhi had still only managed to repeat her first performance some dozens of times, and most of those were mornings after Morgan had found herself staying up far too late studying or, as was becoming perhaps too common, mornings when Morgan had stayed up far too late reading a novel that could just as well have waited.

Still, the fact that she was now proficient enough at reading to enjoy such late nights was worth any sleepy days, and one of the most visible benefits to her friendship with Gertrude.

In either case what happened more often than not was that Haruhi either woke Morgan before she made it across the room to open the drapes around Morgan's small canopy bed, or Morgan was already awake and lying in wait for the rambunctious four-year-old.

As she waited Morgan realized that mentally she had automatically translated that figure from Zion years into Earth years, six in this case, but not into Hillman years. Taking a moment, she tried to do the conversion, but ended up having to guess, the fog of morning still slowing her thoughts. Nine? Ten? A couple short years before any Hillman child would have to start learning how to work the mines.

That pleasant thought distracted Morgan enough that she was still metaphorically shaking her head of the image when Haruhi enthusiastically tossed aside the curtain and yelled out.

"Wake up Aunt Morgan!"

And then Haruhi proceeded to jump onto Morgan's chest, practically bouncing up and down.

"Ooph. I'm up, I'm up." Morgan rolled over so Haruhi plopped off of her and onto the bed.

"I got you!"

"You did, Haru. Now go eat your breakfast and let me get ready. It's a big day, for your mom and for me."

"You don't have school anymore. Will you be here more?" Haruhi asked as she hopped off the bed.

"Maybe," Morgan said, trying to keep the sadness out of her voice. There weren't any freighter companies Morgan knew of that allowed parents to have their children on the freighters, it just cost too much, not to mention the dangers. Worst case Emily had offered to watch Haruhi, but even the best case she'd still be with the other employees' children on one of the big stations in orbit, watched over by the caretakers the companies hired.

As for Morgan herself, well, the odds of them both being hired by the same company were remote. Morgan knew that, and thought she had accepted it. But she found herself rather unhappy at the prospect of leaving her friends. No, she had to be honest with herself. She hated the thought of leaving her *family* again.

But there wasn't any way around it, and staying in bed would only end with her getting hired nowhere, so Morgan untangled her legs from the blankets and reached for her robe.

There were agents of a dozen freight lines and merchant houses in town to interview the fresh graduates from Isa Mechanical, and while there were probably more openings than there were graduates, the agents would still turn down bad candidates.

Morgan got ready more or less on autopilot, ate on autopilot. Simply too much on her mind. She didn't put her makeup on just as automatically because Gertrude stopped her and forced Morgan to let her help. . . after making her take it all off so they could start again.

Seemed silly anyway. It wasn't like she was going to wear makeup while working on a freighter, but if the last two years had taught Morgan anything it was that life rarely made sense. It made even less sense than Gertrude insisting Morgan wear her nicest dress with sleeves and a knee length skirt, instead of the more work-appropriate coveralls, but Morgan was willing to trust Gertrude knew what she was talking about.

"Are you ready for this, Morgan?" Gertrude asked, smoothing her own dress nervously.

"I think so. I mean, I had to do interviews to get my other jobs here. Well, besides the janitor position. That was part of my scholarship."

"Yes?" Gertrude turned the word into a question. "It is a bit different for professional jobs as opposed to those part-time gigs. The agents are looking for people to entrust with trillion dollar starships, at least potentially."

Morgan looked over at her friend. "Are *you* ready for this?"

"Okay, I am worried. I have so much riding on this and not just for me either."

"You'll do great. You had the best grades in our class."

Gertrude snorted. "Only because you struggled with the paper assignments. My resume is practically blank, while yours has, what, seven Earth years' worth of experience?"

"If you two are done psyching each other up, perhaps you could get a move on. Timeliness is not a factor to be ignored." How Emily had gotten inside, let alone all the way over to the main bathroom, without either of them noticing was not something Morgan bothered to wonder about. She just sort of *did* those kinds of things.

"We're ready here," Gertrude said, adding after a moment, "Almost." Grabbing a small tissue, she gently grabbed Morgan's chin, wiping a stray bit of lipstick off deftly. "Thank you for delaying your trip back to Albion to watch Haruhi for a few hours."

"Oh, that's a happy side effect, but it isn't why I stayed after the graduation ceremony."

"It isn't?" Morgan asked, raising one eyebrow.

"Indeed. I am here so we can celebrate the two of you getting good jobs tonight."

"The vote of confidence is appreciated," Gertrude added. "But we'd better get going or we will be late."

***

Morgan left her sixth and last interview nearly shaking from a mixture of exhaustion, nerves, and contained anger. Gertrude was waiting for her, having finished her seven interviews a full half hour before.

"That took a while. It went. . . well?" Gertrude asked. She looked over Morgan and tried not to frown.

"Not here," Morgan said in way of reply. "Let's get back to the house."

"We're not headed there just yet," Gertrude corrected, "Lady Novan wants to meet us at a new restaurant some acquaintance of hers opened up a few months back. Aloha Snacks I think she called it."

"She sure has a lot of acquaintances. What about Haruhi?"

"Haruhi's normal sitter got there," Gertrude checked the time on her uplink, "twenty minutes ago."

Morgan frowned and checked her own uplink's time display.

"That did take a long time. Well, let's get over there. I am rather hungry."

The pair said nothing as they signaled for a cab and waited for it to arrive. Once they were settled inside and the vehicles computer given the address Gertrude turned to Morgan.

"Okay, spill it. What has you so rattled?"

"I blew the interview with Takiyama. I'm sure of it."

"Oh, it can't be that bad. Tell me what happened."

"A lot of it was the normal stuff. What was your focus in school, what do you like and dislike in a supervisor, those kind of questions. Then they started asking about my years of experience, and I don't think they believed me at first." Morgan took a moment to blow out her breath hard before gulping in a quick breath of air. "I had to tell them about Hillman, but that just let them know I didn't go to school, and then it got weird."

"What do you mean, weird?"

"They started asking me all kinds of questions about the machines on Hillman, like how old they are, what kind of components, lots of questions. They've convinced themselves I only know how to work on old stuff."

"That is an odd assumption to make, especially since you just graduated from a school that teaches all the newest systems," Gertrude pointed out. "Are you sure they took it that way?"

"Mostly?" Morgan blew out another breath. "One of the three interviewers was really unsettling."

"Which one?"

"The tall lady with the white hair and icy blue eyes."

"White? You mean platinum blond?"

"Sure?"

"She was in my interview too. She's a bit intense, true, but that's not too unusual for a ship captain."

"You know who she is?"

"I've heard of her, that's all. Her name is Captain Karen Bogard, of the *Fate of Dawn*. It's one of the bigger ships Takiyama Merchant House has. It's less than twenty years old, though, so I don't get why she'd be curious about your knowledge of old ships, unless. . ." Gertrude trailed off.

"What?"

"You haven't looked into the ships of any of the companies, right?"

"I didn't see the point; I don't care where I end up as long as it is up there."

Morgan gestured inarticulately towards the heavens.

"For you that makes sense. Me, I worry about how long the ships' routes are, so I did some checking. TMH has one ship that is positively ancient, the *Shining Triumph of Earth*."

"*Of Earth*? That's an odd name for a ship out here. Don't they make their own ships at Takiyama Station?"

"There are several shipyards in orbit *now*, but that wasn't always the case. The thing is, this ship used to be part of Earth Fleet. Mr. Takiyama himself bought it when it was retired, the first ship he used for intersystem deliveries."

"But if he bought it from *Earth* it's. . . " Morgan trailed off.

"*Well* over a hundred years old, yeah," Gertrude finished.

They were interrupted by the computerized voice of the vehicle.

"We have arrived at your destination gentle beings," it said in its faintly feminine voice, "Which passenger's uplink account is to be charged?"

"Mine," Gertrude said quickly, before Morgan could volunteer. Morgan was doing a lot better for money now than she had when they first met, but it was still somewhat tight, something Gertrude knew, having helped

Morgan learn how to budget better.

They exited the vehicle quickly, stepping back so it could take off into the low altitude traffic patterns reserved for automated vehicles, then turned to walk inside.

"I'll bet that's what they want you for," Gertrude said.

"Well, at least if you're right I won't be working with Captain Creepy."

"That's the spirit, look on the bright side. Now, let's show the world how confident we are, and go celebrate."

***

Morgan's worries about the interviews slowly ebbed as the meal progressed.

This wasn't due to anything Gertrude and Emily did, though they did do their best to raise her spirits, along with sampling pretty much every food offered by the restaurant, but because as the afternoon wore into the evening the messages started coming into their uplinks, job offers.

The smaller companies were the first to message, probably hoping that the more promising candidates would jump at the first offer they received without waiting to see who else was offering, but slowly all of them sent offers to Morgan and Gertrude.

Except. . . they were nearly to the desserts, and nothing from Takiyama.

Morgan reminded herself they hadn't contacted Gertrude either, as she sampled a bit more of the brisket. Still, it was hard not to assume the worst.

As the first round of samples from the dessert menu arrived Emily caught Morgan fixating on her uplink again.

"I think that is enough of that. Hand me your device. Yours too Gertrude."

"What?" Morgan asked.

"Give me your uplinks. The chime is more than loud enough to be heard from inside my bag, and staring at them will not make the time go faster.

Morgan handed it over, but couldn't help looking at it forlornly as Emily put it in her bag. Gertrude had no such problems, but then again, she wasn't worried about the last one, being quite happy with two of the other offers.

"Why so worried about Takiyama, Morgan? You told me yourself you were fine with whatever offers you got. Valeyard Intergalactic has offered you a good salary on a good ship. Four month runs with two months off in-between is not bad at all."

"I. . ." Morgan started, but stopped when she realized she didn't know how to answer the question. Why was she so bothered by the Takiyama interview? Even if *had* gone badly, what of it? Morgan thought on this for a moment, absently chewing on some expensive cheese she barely tasted.

"Takiyama *is* a good outfit, to be sure, but there are others just as good," Emily opined, pausing to gesture the waiter forward with the first tray of tiny desserts. "If you would be so kind as to get the next set ready, I do believe we will be here for a while yet. If you would, also tell the chef that the Gouda will work best for this dish, in my opinion," she added for the waiter's benefit. Amongst the bits and pieces of their conversation Morgan had learned that the owner had traded Emily's experience with high cuisine in return for the free meal sampling everything on the initial menu.

"I suppose," Morgan started, taking a deep breath before continuing, "I don't like the way she looked down on me. She doesn't know me, or what I've been through."

"Condescension does rankle, especially when undeserved," Emily agreed. "Try this one, Morgan. It is a dark chocolate truffle with white chocolate and strawberries."

Morgan eagerly complied, immediately wishing the chocolate was more than a couple bites in size. Gertrude took the opportunity to speak while Morgan was savoring her food.

"I've got six offers to choose from, Lady Novan. What would your advice be?"

"In your case the pay is less a deciding factor than the child services, but you knew that. I had opportunities to work with Wallen and Sons in my military capacity. On paper they look good, but ever since the 'Sons' retired their management has suffered one mishap after another.

"Valeyard Intergalactic is a great company, but they're also a young company with young employees. Haruhi would not have many playmates on their small hub station.

"Garland Forks is a good choice, depending on which ship they would assign you to. The local runs only last weeks at a time, but their specialty shipping line might be gone more than an Earth year, since they go all the way out to the colonies closest to Sol."

Gertrude frowned in thought.

"I didn't know that about Valeyard. They offered me almost twice what Gailey Incorporated has, though Gailey's offer was insultingly low. It's even an officer slot, which makes more sense with what you said. They probably hope I'm mature enough to handle younger crewmen."

There was a quiet – but audible – chime from Emily's bag. All three women stopped and looked at it.

"And where was Takiyama on your list, Gertrude?" Emily asked.

"They talked up the schools on Takiyama Station, and its big enough and established enough that there are bound to be lots of kids."

Emily fished out the chiming uplink – it was Gertrude's, not Morgan's – and looked at the text scrolling across the physical screen.

"They're offering you a job as work crew leader on the *Daystar Fading*. The salary is. . ." Emily took a moment to reread the message, "Quite generous, especially since childcare while you are out is free."

"Does it say anything about the shipping route?" Gertrude asked, crossing her fingers.

"It doesn't, let me check with. . ." Emily trailed off, imputing some commands into her own uplink manually. "Ten months on, ten off, with a few weeks at the beginning and end in port. That's in Zion months. The salary is even better than I thought if you only work half the year."

Despite the longer year Zion's months were actually shorter than e-standard – they broke up the five hundred days of Zion's year into twenty months of twenty-five rather than try and stick to Earth's twelve months.

Gertrude's face fell, her brow knitting in a grimace. "That's a lot of time to be away from Haru," she said after a moment.

"It is, but she'll be with other children her age, and professionals," Emily said.

"It's a big chunk at once, yeah," Morgan added, thinking over the other offers, "But look at the others. Four months on, two off. Two weeks on, four days off. You won't be gone as long, but you will be gone more often."

"Morgan makes a good point," Emily added.

"Hand me the uplink," Gertrude said, her hands actually trembling with excitement and nervousness.

Once Emily had passed it over Gertrude pulled up all the offers with the holographic display. Two she eliminated immediately, leaving five. A third she swiped through with her hand after frowning over it for a moment, dismissing the message from Gailey.

"Wallen can go, based on what we know," Gertrude said, to herself as much as either of them, "And I don't want Haruhi to be lonely." Valeyard was removed as well. "Garland offered me the old colonies route, so that's out," another message dropped, "When you look at it like that, there isn't much choice, is there?"

Slowly, making sure everything was transcribing correctly, Gertrude spoke a quick note of acceptance into her Uplink, translated automatically into text. She didn't quite push the button to send the message.

"Am I doing the right thing? Ten months," She emphasized.

"Take a deep breath and relax," Morgan said.

Simultaneously Emily said, "You've thought this through. It is the best option."

Closing her eyes tight Gertrude mashed her thumb through the send button hovering at the bottom of the holodisplay. She didn't open her eyes until the 'message sent' alert had nearly faded, followed by the holodisplay shutting itself down.

"I feel a little funny," Gertrude said, slumping back in her plush chair.

Emily signaled the waiter over. "More of the dark chocolate strawberries. And a shot of whisky for my friend," she ordered, gesturing at Gertrude.

Gertrude drank it in a single gulp, coughing for a moment before taking in three long deep breaths.

"I'm okay, I'm better now. I can't change it now, and that makes it easier somehow. Whatever comes, I can deal with it."

"I think we should look at Morgan's options now. It doesn't appear that

Takiyama will be making you an offer after all. Still, twelve of thirteen between you is an amazing accomplishment. Even with the shortages of trained crewmen there are doubtless many of your classmates who are relieved tonight to find themselves with a single offer, and sadly others who got none at all."

"Yeah," Morgan said, more than a little dejected, and not just because the annoying interviewer had rejected her. Finding time to visit Gertrude and Haruhi in person wasn't going to be easy, whichever choice she went with.

"Five choices," Morgan said, gesturing for her own uplink. She put it on the table, pulling up the five options in the holodisplay like Gertrude had.

"You'd take the one from Wallen or Gailey?" Gertrude asked.

"Not really, no, so those two we can ignore. That still leaves Sutton Shipping, Rhoades Travelers, and Valeyard."

"Sutton," Emily said slowly, clearly not happy.

"What?" Gertrude and Morgan said at the same time.

"The military likes them," Emily started, but her tone clearly stated that they wouldn't like the reasons, "They'll ship to anyone and everyone, including many places the rest of the companies won't touch. It makes them a lot of money, but they travel through a lot of dangerous parts of the galaxy."

"Why would the military like them?" Gertrude asked.

"Because we can place spies among the crew that are allowed on a lot of planets we have no diplomatic ties with."

"You'd better not take that one," Gertrude said firmly.

"I guess that explains why they are offering triple the salary," Morgan said with a frown. "I had wondered why the recruiter mentioned that most of the staff was male, and that I'd be guaranteed a private room because of it."

"Okay, never setting foot near them," Gertrude said. "Who's next?"

"Rhoades and Valeyard."

"Your objections to Valeyard won't make a difference for me," Morgan said, looking at the two remaining offers side by side.

"You'd still be younger than any of them," Gertrude pointed out, "Even officially. That might make things a bit interesting."

"That will be true whoever I pick," Morgan countered.

"What is Rhoades offering?" Emily asked.

"Crewman second class, rotating position between radiator maintenance and hydroponics support."

Gertrude let out a small laugh.

"Oh my, they're offering you *that*?"

"What?"

"Half the time out on the hull of the ship fixing the radiator fins, or near it anyway, the other half making the crew's waste into fertilizer for the hydroponics bay? What a lovely job."

"Oh," was all Morgan had to say about that.

"They always try and disguise the crap jobs with fancier names. Well, out here anyway. Somewhere where all the jobs are bad I suppose you don't need to bother."

"It seems then the choice is obvious," Emily said.

"Yeah, I guess it is," Morgan said.

Gertrude apparently could hear the sadness in Morgan's voice, asking, "What's wrong then, honey?"

"I didn't want to say anything, but I had hoped to work *with* you, or at least for the same company."

"Why didn't you say anything before I decided?" Gertrude asked, putting one hand on Morgan's shoulder.

"I don't want you taking a worse job for me," Morgan replied, "And the only good one we had in common would be bad for Haru."

Gertrude hugged Morgan, "Oh you silly girl. Don't worry about it too much. We can still talk back and forth with video messages. Besides, with ten months off in a stretch I'm sure we'll get overlapping time off more often than you'd think."

"I hope so," Morgan said. "I guess I'd better accept the offer then."

"Valeyard is a good choice," Emily reiterated.

"Yeah, you're right," Morgan said, taking a moment to compose her own message accepting the offer.

"Here goes," she said, reaching out to push the send button, only to have the screen flash away to an incoming message just before she got there.

"Gah," she said, jerking back her hand.

"Who is it from?" Gertrude said as Emily picked up the uplink.

"Takiyama."

"I can't," Morgan said, meaning she couldn't look, but not quite being able to get it out. She covered her eyes with her hands, hyperventilating at the thought of what she had nearly done. Even a second later. . .

"I'll read it," Emily said.

Emily read it. Then again. For long seconds she said nothing.

"Well," Gertrude demanded, ignoring Morgan whose hands were still clasped over her eyes.

"It's a crewman first class slot, cargo loading and bay maintenance.

That's a lot of heavy work, but it isn't as bad as hydroponics or radiator duty. The pay is better than normal for the position too."

"Really?" Gertrude asked.

"Yes, it says something about unusual expertise on the ship's equipment."

"You mean?" Morgan said, peeking out between two of her fingers.

"They're offering you a job on the *Shining Triumph of Earth*. Takiyama's Flagship, and one of the last Earth built vessels in existence," Emily answered, sounding impressed.

"The name is a bit of a mouthful," Gertrude said, "But never mind that, congratulations Morgan!"

"Most of the crew calls the ship *Steve*, apparently," Emily said.

"Who names a starship *Steve*?" Morgan said, laughing.

PART 3:
THE LONG BLACK

CHAPTER 13

We spend so much of our lives looking forward. I'll do this when I grow up, we'll go there next year, once I get that raise we'll. . . the list is endless. How often does 'then' become 'now' and what we want doesn't happen, or it does and we find it isn't what was hoped for?

- Shelby Davron, from her seminar "How to Live in The Moment When You'll Live for Centuries."

YEP. MORGAN WAS LOST. Less than three hours on Takiyama Station – also known as TS1 or simply 'the station' – and she was completely lost.

It wasn't her fault, not really. The station was one of the oldest in orbit of Zion, and had a rather convoluted history. A history that naturally resulted in convoluted architecture.

That architecture, and the story behind it, was one of the more fascinating tidbits about the company Morgan and Gertrude had dug up after accepting their positions.

Originally TS1 had been known as 'Isa Shipyard' and had been one of the very first facilities outside Sol to build anything larger than a shuttle. Instead of dispersed 'dry' docks, as had been the norm in Sol and therefore the rest of the galaxy, TS1 had been built as a massive hollow sphere, honeycombed with docking slips that could actually be sealed off and pressurized to allow work without sealed skinsuits. The atmospheric requirements for this had been staggering, as well as the sheer tonnage of metal to build the exterior shell.

The sealed slips hadn't been used most of the time in practice, but for certain incredibly intricate installations and repairs it had been a noticeable time saver, giving them an edge over their competitors. The money had come rolling in, especially from the systems closer to Zion than Earth.

A hundred or so Earth years later the larger shipyard in orbit of Bountiful, Zion's largest moon, finished its first major expansion, allowing it to work on twice as many hulls at the same time as Isa Shipyard. The end result was a forgone conclusion. The station changed hands a few times in the intervening centuries, the longest stretch seeing the shipyard repurposed as producer of luxury yachts, but the infrastructure slowly became so old that the station simply couldn't fabricate the newest components and designs.

It was then that Takiyama had bought the station. It wasn't useful as a shipyard any longer, true, but the station was still large and made an excellent cargo depot. Several of the smaller docking slips had even been sealed permanently and converted into massive cargo storage areas and barracks for the crews to use in between their delivery routes. Parts of the fabrication areas were sectioned off and divided up into offices, officer apartments, and leisure facilities and the existing corridors were rerouted and modified as necessary.

In other words, any semblance of order and pattern to the station's layout was decades dead.

Morgan pulled up the map again on her uplink, the three dimensional hologram helpfully placing a blinking dot on the diagram to tell her where she was.

Another dot showed where she wanted to go – the block of offices assigned on the station to *Steve*'s officers and senior crew while in port.

What was missing was the route connecting the two. Despite being the finest and latest military tech (of ten years ago) the poor little computer intelligence of her uplink had tried for almost a minute to give her a route before glitching out in an error and giving Morgan the digital equivalent of a shrug.

Morgan's instincts for finding her way, honed over long years in the mines, had failed her just as thoroughly. Sighing she made a best guess and started out again. At least they would be expecting some amount of confusion, wouldn't they? She could hardly be the first person to get lost in the massive station.

A few turnings later found Morgan on the inside edge of the hollow sphere, looking through a transparent aluminum window opening onto the main hold. The row of windows ran the length of the corridor, giving a spectacular view of the mostly empty hold.

Off to one side Morgan could see the shuttle they'd come up in, just a few levels up and a few hundred meters off to one side. Seeing it was somewhat depressing, since she'd been wandering the station for at least an hour and was still within easy sight of where she had started.

Farther in were several of the company's freighters. They certainly looked impressive, not that Morgan had a lot of experience to judge them by. Not counting two shuttle rides she'd only ever been on one ship – the *Pale Moonlight* – and had never actually had the opportunity to see what it looked like from the outside, or even a picture of it. She'd studied ship design in school, but that was no substitute for personal experience.

Morgan leaned up to the window, trying to make out the name written on the freighters.

"The window can zoom," a rather gruff and slightly off sounding voice said from behind Morgan.

Turning around Morgan found herself facing a rather nondescript looking man, his coveralls' nameplate reading 'Brown.' Looking closer Morgan realized her first impression was in error – the man's neck was a mass of scars, and Morgan realized the odd note in his voice was because his voice was actually artificial, provided by a small cybernetic implant in his throat.

Realizing she'd been staring a bit too long Morgan cleared her throat.

"Could you show me?" She asked.

Instead of speaking the man gestured to the wall in between two of the panes of aluminum. There was a small control panel that Morgan had missed on her first glance at the wall.

It only took the work of a moment to pull up the display controls.

"The left one," the man said.

Seeing no reason not to, Morgan did as he suggested. The freighter seemed to leap forward until it filled the whole pane. Judging by the size of the cargo hatches it was a monster of a ship, certainly longer than five hundred meters, perhaps even closer to a thousand.

It was bulky, thick, and worn looking. The paint job was grey, but clearly redone many times over the years with slightly different shades of grey, giving it a very mottled appearance.

It was the prettiest ship Morgan had ever seen.

The design was different than the gate hoppers Morgan had studied. It was vaguely mushroom shaped, which was the biggest clue as to the ship's purpose. That type of design was only used on vessels designed to travel outside the gate system, most often to reach asteroid belts and other places without enough of a gravity well to allow a ship to leave subspace. It was also used in military vessels, especially the large carriers.

The head was one big mass of armor, designed to absorb impacts from stray particles and interstellar dust while traveling sixty kilometers per second, then filled with water to absorb incoming radiation. Particle impacts hadn't been as big a problem originally – Earth was inside the so called 'local bubble' with particle densities way down from the rest of the galaxy. None of the colonies shared the same favorable conditions, however. In fact many, including the Parlon system, were even higher than the galactic norm.

The back of the freighter flared back out again to fit stupendous fusion engines. Engines of that type were even rarer than deep space ships – they were powerful enough to accelerate the ship up to max cruising speed in mere minutes, but unlike the gradual acceleration of an EM drive it required fuel in addition to power. Morgan was surprised to see a civilian vessel with them – even the asteroid runners didn't *need* the high acceleration. Having the fusion engines meant the ship could also turn around and decelerate in a few minutes, minutes when the engines would not be protected from oncoming particles. It was an extravagant solution to the problem, modern design simply incorporated a double-ended approach with mushroom heads and EM drives at both ends, since even doubling the armor and engines needed was still cheaper than building even a single fusion engine. And that was *before* maintenance costs.

Between the armored head and the engines was the core of the ship, the long hull that held the crew spaces, engineering, the normal stuff any spaceship needed. Most of it wasn't visible, however, because of the cargo bays. It looked like the ship was completely encircled with modular cargo bays, a thin lattice framework extending out and around them on all sides to secure the bays and hold things like the ship's sensors and arrays. There were a number of heat radiators visible, fairly small fins that individually weren't very good at dissipating waste heat. What they lacked in size they made up for in numbers, as well as the many other spots that looked like they held retracted radiators.

Having retractable radiators in a civilian design was also unusual. The retractable radiators themselves were easier to repair and maintain, but the machinery to extend and retract them were *harder* to maintain and repair. Most vessels had between two and four massive and intricate radiators, since many small ones also increased the amount of maintenance required.

There were a few other hatches dotting the sides of the freighter, too small to be cargo hatches even if they had been on the modular bays rather than the lattice framework surrounding them. They were also too large to be a crew airlock, they almost looked like. . .

"Is that a military ship?" Morgan said, turning to the laconic newcomer. There wasn't much doubt, not with that many odd design choices.

"Formerly. The name?"

Morgan hadn't looked at the name closely yet. She'd been too busy taking in the design.

It was a little hard to read, since the lettering wasn't all in the same shade of black any more than the hull had been grey, but after a moment she made it out.

Shining Triumph of Earth, Vessel 5.

"That's *Steve*?" Morgan said, almost not daring to believe her luck. This beautiful, powerful ship was going to be her new home, her new job.

"Yep. Welcome aboard."

"You know who I am?"

"Only new hire up today for *Steve*. Easy."

Morgan tried to compose herself as best as she could.

"Thank you," she paused for a moment, then added, "Sir?"

"Second Lieutenant." A shrug. "Call me Jacob. Offices are this way."

Morgan followed him, sparing a moment to glance back at the enlarged picture of the ship. It was a majestic sight all on its own, but it was also the first time Morgan had ever seen something actually made at Earth before. She wasn't quite sure what to think of that. Gratitude that mankind had spread to the stars, surviving whatever unknown catastrophe that had struck Earth? Sadness at its loss?

She had actually almost made it to the offices without the help – it was only three or four turns and a pair of ladders away – but Morgan was still grateful for the escort. He didn't say anything as they walked, which was fine too. There were so many conflicting thoughts and emotions running through Morgan that she wasn't sure she could manage even light small talk at the moment.

They were just outside a hatch prominently labeled 'S.T.E.V.5' when her uplink chimed that she had an incoming call. Not just an incoming call, but an urgent one.

The moment she accepted the connection Gertrude started talking, her voice raised and agitated.

"Morgan, please, I need your help."

The call was audio only, but Morgan could still tell how upset Gertrude was. She glanced at Jacob.

"This might take a bit."

"S'okay." He pointed at the clock above the door. "Still have time." He leaned against the wall, twisting his neck left and right, accompanied by startlingly loud popping noises.

"What happened, Gertrude?"

"I won't let these people take care of Haru. Morgan I won't. I *can't.* I'll quit first."

When they'd left the shuttle Gertrude had gone first to the daycare facilities for the crew of the *Daystar Fading* instead of meeting her captain. It was an easy guess that was what had her upset, but why?

"G, you need to give me details. Is it the facilities? The employees?"

"Yes!" Gertrude said, her voice rising. Morgan knew that Gertrude wasn't cryptic on purpose, but at least long exposure had helped her puzzle out the other woman's meaning.

"Both. Right. Can you make a complaint? Ask to put Haruhi in a different ship's childcare? They won't be all the same, right?"

A bit of movement drew Morgan's attention. Looking up she saw Jacob was shaking his head, a sad smile briefly on his lips.

Gertrude was talking again, so Morgan looked away.

"Oh, they aren't. Of course the manager of the facility here is *married* to my captain, and anything I say about her will of course get back to the captain, and *she's* not likely to take my side against her spouse. Besides, the childcare is structured around the ship's schedules, so the round the clock care is only available while the ship is out."

"Could we talk with them? Maybe the problem is something we can work through?"

"Morgan, I almost slapped that woman after less than a half hour. She sucks the joy out of everything around her. She stopped my tour five times to punish children for the tiniest of things, things that are *normal* for children. And the punishments! She raps them on the hand for minor things. She has this ancient bit of wood called a ruler she uses, and I heard her order one child to bed without dinner."

That didn't actually sound all that bad to Morgan, depending on what the punishments were for. However, she also realized her childhood interactions with adults on Hillman were considered child abuse elsewhere in the galaxy, so she didn't point that out.

"What can we do then?"

"I don't know. There have to be other members of the crew who take turns watching their kids rather than put them in the facilities here, but I don't know any of them, and they don't know me. I also don't have anything to offer them – I don't have a spouse who can take a turn wrangling kids."

"You have me," Morgan said, quietly. It was hard to say, but she meant it. "I can help."

"Morgan, you can't do that. I won't let you give up your career – on your first day no less – for me."

"Why not? You'd do the same for me if I was in your position."

"It's not fair to you. Besides, how would it work? You'd be without an income, and while childcare is included in my pay, food and everything else isn't. Even with the renters in my house covering most of the bills for the house, I won't be making enough to support all three of us."

"Is there something the company can do? Something like this has to have happened before?"

Jacob cleared his throat, a rather jarring noise with the added electronic distortion.

Morgan turned to look, one of her eyebrows raised in a quizzical expression.

Jacob stepped closer so the uplink would pick up his words.

"Sorry. I try not to eaves. Heard anyway. It isn't hard to guess the details. Single mother, new job."

"And you have a suggestion?" Gertrude asked. Morgan could hear her annoyance, understandable given that she couldn't know who was talking.

"Plenty of couples who both work for the Company. Easy enough to put them on ship's with opposite schedules."

"And you'd help us?" Morgan asked. "You'll likely lose me from your crew."

Jacob shrugged.

"Better to lose you for a bit than forever. You know old equipment. You'll be back to *Steve* eventually. Let's do talk to the captain." Jacob turned and opened the hatch. He beckoned for Morgan to enter before adding for Gertrude. "She'll call you back. Wait. Captain's a reasonable sort."

"I think we should listen to him, G. He's the second lieutenant of my ship."

"Okay." Gertrude didn't sound happy about it, but at least the tension in her voice had lessened. "I'll take Haruhi up to our quarters and get some stuff settled in."

The Captain's office was just past the main hatch, the door open and inviting, a placard above the door reading simply Captain Harold Rain. Jacob strode right in, not even pausing to see if Morgan was following him.

As she entered the room she was surprised to see it sparse and utilitarian, one chair behind the smooth desk and three in front, a dedicated computer uplink on its uncluttered surface. There were no decorations in the room. Perhaps because it was his office on the station rather than the actual ship?

Morgan left off wondering as she realized Jacob had already launched into an explanation for the captain.

"Morgan's friend is a mom. Assigned to *Daystar*. Either she or Morgan here will quit before they put the girl in care there. Which ship is opposite *Daystar*?"

He didn't respond at once, giving Morgan a moment to at least look at her captain, however temporary the arrangement turned out to be. He was seated, so she couldn't be sure, but he looked to be fairly short, at least by Zion standards. He would still have a number of centimeters on Morgan, of course. Bald with wisps of white hair on the sides and back of his head, his face seemed wrinkled into a perpetual smile around his eyes. When he did talk it was directed at her, not Jacob.

"So. You must be out new crewman, Morgan Black."

"Yes, sir." Morgan fixed her gaze on the desk rather than the man, an old reflex to dealing with people in authority. Maybe he was a nice man, but then again, maybe he wasn't. Potentially antagonizing him wasn't of any benefit.

"And you would really quit in order to help out your friend?"

"Yes. She's the only family I have left."

"What's her position with the *Daystar Fading*?"

"Work Crew Leader."

"Your accent. Hillman?"

Startled Morgan looked up before answering.

"How did you know?"

He waved a hand dismissively.

"I've been working freight lines for, well, longer than you've been alive anyway. You pick things up, including an ear for accents. It's a useful skill, especially for anyone interested in being an officer. Are you?" He paused for a moment, considering her. "Interested in being an officer, that is?"

Morgan wasn't sure how to respond. One moment he was asking if she'd quit to help Gertrude, the next if she want to be an officer?

"If I can. I want to work in space."

"Felt the call of the long black, did you? Good." The captain gestured to Jacob, a subtle signal Morgan didn't understand, but Jacob just nodded and closed the door. "I don't talk about the other ships or their captains, and I suggest you don't either. Gossip is always rampant on any ship, but it shouldn't be encouraged. Still, that doesn't mean we can ignore problems when they come up. Kindly keep quiet unless asked a question, Crewman Morgan."

The captain pushed a few buttons on his desk, activating a large screen behind the desk. He turned about so he could see it. After a moment an icon appeared on the screen, the stylized freighter on a red circle that was the sign of the merchant house.

"Who can I connect you with?" It was a female computer voice, but not the standard uplink voices Morgan had heard before. It spoke English with a slight accent, not unlike the one of Morgan's neighbors whose first language was Japanese. Why they had programed a computer to have the accent she couldn't imagine.

"The AIC, plus the Captain of the *Fate of Dawn*."

"Priority of call?"

"Medium."

"Please hold."

The screen's hidden speakers actually started playing music as they waited. It wasn't the normal bland nothing Morgan was used to hearing as hold music, rather a soothing piece with some kind of flute Morgan wasn't used to and some drum like instruments that sounded a bit like bits of hollow wood knocked together.

Morgan stood there, fidgeting nervously. She had been tense enough to meet her captain, and here she was about to be faced with a second captain plus whatever the 'AIC' was, presumably someone in charge.

After a minute or so of waiting the captain turned back to Morgan and Jacob.

"This might take a bit. Jacob, go ahead and let her crew chief know that he might be short-staffed. See if you can work with him on adjusting the schedule to cover the absence. This close to our departure date we're not likely to get a replacement, unless it's from the other ship."

Jacob snorted.

"Not likely."

"I know. Stranger things have happened though. Off you go then. Crewman, you can take a seat if you'd like."

Morgan settled down into one of the chairs in front of the desk. It didn't do anything to ease her nerves, but it at least it stopped her shifting her weight back and forth from foot to foot as part of her subconscious thought about bolting.

The captain was quiet, spending the time waiting by looking at a few documents on his other screen. Morgan couldn't read them from her seated position, but there were little pictures of people at the top, so probably personnel files.

The large screen split into two halves, the left still showing the sign of the house, the right fading to black with a single line of text saying the captain of the *Fate of Dawn* was standing by.

The Fate of Dawn.

Morgan had heard that ship name before.

Where. . .

. . .It hit her after a moment. The woman in the interview. Captain B-something. Emily had said the *Fate of Dawn* was her ship. Inwardly Morgan groaned. Why was that woman, out of all the ship captains being included?

The left side of the screen changed abruptly, now showing an office that looked similar to the one Morgan sat in, only much more lavishly decorated and appointed. The woman looking out at them was older, her hair steel grey and her face lined. The right side of the screen changed as well, and it was the woman who had interviewed Morgan.

"Problems, Captain?" the woman on the left said without waiting for any introduction or explanation.

"You could say that. One of our new hires finds our childcare facilities wholly inadequate, and is considering quitting for the good of her child."

"This woman here? She hardly seems old enough."

The other captain narrowed her eyes, looking to the right a bit. Telling where someone was looking in these split calls was never easy, but Morgan was pretty sure she was looking at Morgan on her own split screen. It wasn't a friendly gaze.

"I remember you," she said, clearly to Morgan. She then turned, looking to the left. "Administrator Amori, this crewman did not mention any child during the interview process, nor in her paperwork."

"No, she didn't," Morgan's captain said, not *quite* cutting off his peer.

"Her friend is the one with the daughter, her friend for whom she'd give up her career to watch the child if it came down to it. I can't speak for you, Administrator, but I'd rather not lose a new young crewman and the decades of service she potentially represents, not when it can be avoided. Especially someone who will be easier to train on the old systems I have on my ship."

"If not your ship. . ." the other captain started saying, pausing for a moment as her brows knit in concentration. "You want to dump her off on me? The woman's the new hire for the *Daystar*, isn't she?"

"Yes, Captain Bogard, that's exactly what I'm suggesting."

Bogard was about to reply, but stopped the moment the administrator made a move to speak.

"Not unheard of, but this is rather short notice to be changing crew manifests around," Administrator Amori said, holding up a palm to quiet the captains while she thought. "Why not just change the other woman to work the ship opposite yours, Captain Rain?"

"It's easier to move a crewman first class than a crew chief. Also, I won't oppose the transfer. I can be patient." Left unsaid was the clear implication that the captain of the *Daystar* might object.

Captain Bogard was muttering under her breath, clearly not meant for anyone to hear, though Morgan thought she heard something about *'never should have hired the wife in the first place.'*

"I don't need her on my ship, and I don't have anyone I can spare for yours. Not with the skill set you need, anyway. To be frank I don't really want her, either," She added for everyone to hear.

"I appreciate your candor, Captain, but there are the needs of the house as a whole to consider. You've only just got back from your last run. By the time you return from the next, it will be easy enough to arrange things for the crewman here to return to Captain Rain's crew, and for the new chief to take up duties on one of the ships on the opposite rotation. We do such transfers all the time."

"Very well, but I can't take her on as a first class. Fourth class is the most I could offer for what duties I have to be done. Otherwise I'm risking jealousy and damaged morale from the people who'd be doing more and getting paid less."

Morgan wanted to protest. Crewman fourth class was usually reserved for trainees with no practical training or job experience. It was also a lot less pay. She clenched her jaw to keep from saying anything, and from the look on his face Captain Rain wasn't too pleased either.

"You know your crew better than I do, of course," the administrator allowed, speaking slowly, before adding, "Though I would *recommend* you work on their work ethic and morale to lessen this tendency in the future. Disaffected crewmen can cause a lot of damage on long voyages with their petty grievances."

Captain Rain nodded in agreement, and then added a few words of his own.

"I'd like it in writing that she'll be bumped back up to first class at the end of her cruise on the *Fate of Dawn*. Loyalty is to be rewarded, even if it is loyalty to something besides the company."

"Easily done. Is there anything else that needs to be addressed?"

"I don't think so, administrator," Captain Rain said.

"Just one thing on my end," Captain Bogard said, once Rain was finished. "My crew spaces are fairly full already. Perhaps it would be prudent for the crewman to share quarters with her friend in *Daystar*'s section? Especially since she'll be caring for the child the next ten months anyway?"

"That seems prudent," the administrator agreed, "I'll let the *Daystar*'s captain know to move the chief over to quarters with three bedrooms. It is just the one child, correct?"

Captain Rain turned to look at Morgan and gave a very tiny nod.

"Yes. Chief Suoh and her child, Haruhi," Morgan said succinctly.

"Thank you. I expect to hear good things about you. Welcome to Takiyama."

The left side of the screen went black as the administrator ended the call.

"My third lieutenant will get you your job assignment and any relevant details. Right now we're just doing systems checks and maintenance, routine after returning from our last voyage. Port work schedule is designed to be compatible with school hours," Captain Bogard said, her screen going black just as abruptly.

Captain Rain swiveled his chair back around, a slight frown on his face.

"This doesn't leave this room, but I do believe that captain dislikes you."

Morgan couldn't help but let out a small laugh at this completely unnecessary observation.

"Yes, it was quite obvious, wasn't it? Her reasons for demoting you made her crew look bad in front of the administrator in charge, which no captain likes. Have you met her before? This is your first job, correct?"

"She interviewed me. She didn't seem to like me then either."

"Unfortunately, there is nothing for it. I only bring this up because I want you back after this is all sorted out. That won't happen if you give her reason to fire you. Do your job well, and be polite, always. Putting you in *Daystar*'s section means you'll be at least twenty minutes' walk from the *Fate of Dawn*. Leave early each morning, do not be late. It will also make it harder for you to get to know your shipmates, and for them to get to know you. Do what you can to earn their trust. I'm sorry this has happened, but life seems to trend towards maximum perversity."

"I don't know what you mean by that, sir." Morgan said after a moment trying to work through his meaning.

"Old saying from my home planet. In part it means that life isn't fair, but also that life seems to like going with chaos and the absurd more than not."

"That I can agree with. If I can leave, sir, I need to go talk with Gertrude."

"Yes, of course. If you're lucky she won't have unpacked too much yet. I'll see that your things get moved over to your new quarters today by one of my crew. I imagine you'll be busy enough as it is."

"Thank you, sir. I look forward to being able to serve under you."

CHAPTER 14

It's simple really. The single biggest factor in people quitting their jobs isn't the pay, nor the benefits. It's their boss. If you see a department losing people left and right, look to the management.

- Lisa Brilhead, Nova Shipyards HR Director

THREE WEEKS LATER

MORGAN WAS SURE she'd been more tired than this back on Hillman at the end of her shifts. She was positive she had been. It just didn't *feel* like it after the relatively pampered years she'd spent in school.

She staggered through the hatch to their quarters and through the door just to the left leading to her cozy bedroom. Her bed was a simple low ceilinged bunk set into the wall with a retractable privacy screen. Not even bothering to take off her skinsuit Morgan sprawled onto the mattress, one leg dangling off, the heel resting on the floor below.

If this was only the lighter work load for a ship in port, Morgan wasn't sure she'd survive a month of the full time cruise, let alone ten.

Even her heavy-worlder strength had turned out to be a hindrance more than an asset. Once her crew chief found out she was from a High-G world, he'd simply given her more and more of the heavy lifting to do.

Morgan finally was forced to point out that she'd been living in lower gravity for several years and had lost some strength. Plus, despite some growth over the last few years, was still under a hundred and fifty centimeters tall. This had only caused him to agree with her, and then arrange for time for Morgan to spend in the gym with the gravity cranked up to *more* than twice Earth standard for her to work off her 'baby fat.'

Privately Morgan was actually glad of the gym time, in theory. It had bothered her to watch her strength slowly ebbing away, but there hadn't been any easy – or rather, any cheap – way to counteract it while living on the ground. The problem came in that her choices were a grueling workout before her daily shift, making her tired before she even started, or at the end when she was already tired. She had chosen the latter. Work was the more obvious priority, after all.

The first couple weeks hadn't been so bad. Without a skinsuit of her own she'd been limited to assisting with minor maintenance, the kinds of things she'd learned in the first months in school. Like her or not, the captain hadn't been lying about the kind of jobs Morgan would be doing. It was hard work but not mentally challenging.

The appointment to get fitted for her skinsuit, on the other hand, had been one of the most profoundly uncomfortable events of her life. There was an understandable urgency to get all the new hires fitted, though Morgan was towards the bottom of the list because her ship wasn't due to leave port for months yet. This still only pushed her back to her third day of work.

She'd had the process explained to her a couple times in school, but the explanation hadn't quite done it justice. The suit had to be skintight and individually fitted, nanofabricated to order. A quick virtual scan wasn't good enough because of the elasticity of flesh as the suit was donned, and the better hyper-accurate scanners took far too long to be used on a living subject, even if simply breathing wasn't enough to foul it up.

Needing to do the fitting naked, Morgan had expected. The room was private and operated by machines, so it wasn't embarrassing or anything.

Having to shave off every bit of hair below her neck had not been mentioned in class, however. Once she had been told, she understood why. Not that it helped her dislike it any less. The pattern for the suit was made by standing in a narrow tank and the liquid mold material added until the person was submerged up to mid-neck. With the final suit, hair (or lack thereof) wouldn't matter. For the fitting it would make the mold less perfect.

Moving was also a potential problem, both while the liquid was poured in and while it hardened. While it was possible for some medical procedures to give the patient something to temporarily induce paralysis, the mold process had to be done standing. It was simply up to the person being fitted to keep still. Most were highly motivated to do so, since messing it up just meant doing it all over again.

Morgan was used to tight places, but standing there, holding as still as she could, as the lukewarm liquid slowly poured in around her. . . well, it wasn't something she wanted to dwell on.

So much so that Morgan found herself rather uncomfortable now lying on her bunk with her skinsuit still on. Groaning she swung herself upright, leaning forward to keep from banging her head on the ceiling of the bunk.

She'd been out on the exterior hull again today, inspecting the port radiator sail of the ship, so she had the bulkier magnetized boots on over the skinsuit's softer booties.

Wearily she pulled them off, dumping them unceremoniously to one side.

Her uplink followed, though it was placed carefully on the small table attached to the wall just above the head of the bunk. The sturdy military unit would likely survive being dumped on the floor, but Morgan had never been one to abuse her tools.

Next she carefully pulled her pistol out of the right hip pocket of the suit, followed by the magazines in the left. Even with the tiny Iridium Special weapon it was a tight fit. Getting it out in an emergency would be a bit tricky, but it still beat being unarmed.

Checking the magazines over Morgan set them aside, then pulled the trigger guard off the pistol, checked that everything was still clear, then put it back before putting the pistol on her bedside table. Before she left her room she'd need to put it in the more secure drawer, but that meant standing up, which she wasn't quite ready to do. Though she could at least secure the room.

"Hey, room," she called out, her voice sounding even more exhausted than she felt.

"Receiving," the room's automated systems replied, in the same accented voice as the station's main computer.

"Lock the door to my room."

"As you wish," it replied.

Getting off the suit was a somewhat involved process. The front of the suit overlapped, closing across the left breast with some heavy duty closures. Once the front was open it was just loose enough to get it past her shoulders, then it was just a matter of slowly peeling it down her arms and body. Once her arms were out getting it down the rest of her torso and legs was easier.

She had already been sweaty before the session in the gym, so lying back down with her skin directly on the sheets was unappealing, especially with her spare bedding already in the bin to be washed.

With another groan Morgan forced herself to her feet, staggering over to the tiny bathroom attached to her bedroom.

The room was slightly more than a meter wide and long, twice that tall. Shower, toilet, sink with a mirror. That was it, but it was private. Morgan had taken a few minutes one day to check in on her room onboard the *Fate of Dawn*. Six bunks in a small room with drawers built beneath each, a bit of desk space with a screen and keyboard for each. There was a room across the hall with machines to clean normal clothes as well as skinsuits, and bathroom, both of which were shared with another six bunk room.

The bathroom had four toilets with some semblance of privacy, four sinks, and in two corners a pole with four shower heads attached. *Everyone* stayed on station while in port.

A quick shower got the worst of the grime off, followed by an even quicker toweling off. Morgan crashed back onto the bed, a slip thrown on almost as an afterthought.

Her damp hair was getting the pillow wet, but she didn't care. She had let it grow longer than she had growing up. Even so it was still short, not even reaching her chin. The pillow would dry out before she got back to bed that night, to be sure.

Morgan dozed for a bit. By design, the workday ended three hours before the school day ended. In Haruhi's case it wasn't quite formal schooling as of yet, getting out an hour earlier, which left Morgan maybe a half hour for a nap before the little girl got back, thanks to Morgan's gym time.

It felt like her eyes had barely closed when the uplink chimed; ten minutes to Haruhi's return.

Morgan grumbled, turned over, and ignored it.

The uplink was unperturbed by being ignored. It simply waited the requisite five minutes, and then blasted the chime at three-fold volume.

This did the trick, waking Morgan up forcefully, followed by her jerking upright to stop the offending noise. Her head bounced off the roof of her bunk. Thankfully it had clearly been designed by a genius, since the ceiling at the head of the bunk was just as padded as the mattress was.

Morgan rubbed her forehead and wondered when she'd gotten out of the habit of lying still when she woke up long enough to figure out where she was. She'd have to get the habit back – her bunk on the *Fate of Dawn* had no padding besides the mattress, and even that wasn't all that much.

Rubbing her eyes Morgan quickly threw on a dress she'd rummaged from the drawer under the bunk. It hardly mattered which one she'd grabbed. Gathering up her boots and discarded skin suit she walked to the door, only to remember that she had locked it. Dumping the skinsuit at her feet she walked the few paces back to the bunk, grabbing the pistol from the table and depositing it in the other drawer under the bunk, the one that locked.

"Room, unlock the door," she said, giving the computer only the time it took for her to walk back to the door and grab the suit to comply.

The suit washer took up its own room, sandwiched between Morgan's room and Gertrude's. Its door didn't open automatically, due to the potentially dangerous nature of the machine to wandering children.

"Washroom door, open up." Almost by default, Morgan spoke politely to the various computers she interacted with on a daily basis. Except this one. This one had some kind of fault in the programing, or sensors or something, the end result of which was it didn't recognize Morgan as authorized for entry. Maybe she wasn't tall enough for the parameters, or her voice was too high pitched, she wasn't sure. She'd put in a request to get it fixed, but the request had been routed to the *Daystar Fading*'s maintenance list, and well, they weren't around to do anything about it.

She'd considered fixing it herself, but most of her training in was in physical systems, not computer programing.

"Access denied."

"This is Crewman Morgan. You know blasted well I'm allowed in."

"Invalid biometrics. Access denied."

Morgan tossed one of her boots at the door's speaker. It bounced off with a satisfying thud. It didn't help, of course, except in that it freed up her right hand to activate the door's thumbprint scanner.

"Do you recognize that?"

"User Black recognized. Access granted."

Morgan knew her next request wouldn't do any good, she'd tried it four times already, but the slim chance something would happen made her persist.

"Add the person standing in front of you to the authorized list."

"This door is unable to do so. You do not have the proper permissions."

"Tell me who does."

"Authorized maintenance technicians, Chief Gertrude Suoh, and Crewman Morgan Black."

"I'm Crewman Morgan Black. You're scanning my thumb right now."

"Unable to verify."

"One day, door, I am going to dismantle you."

The door didn't respond. Pity. Telling her that would be wrong or that it would void a warranty or *something* would have made her feel a bit less stupid for being at war with a freaking door.

Shaking her head Morgan went in, dumping the suit in the waiting washer. If Gertrude had still been in port she'd have needed to wait for hers. The cycle took long enough that you couldn't run it twice in the same night. Gertrude had departed with her ship a week previously, so there was no need to wait.

Honestly Morgan thought she'd taken her departure worse than Haruhi had, at least so far. Morgan was bracing herself for the inevitable tears as the little girl figured out just how long her mom was going to be gone.

As if summoned by thinking of her, Haruhi burst through the quarter's main hatch, a miniature whirlwind of papers trailing glitter and sparkles. She barely paused long enough to take her shoes off and put them on the rack next to the door. Was it craft day again already? Morgan tried not to wince, thinking of all the floating glitter getting pulled into the air systems, all over the furniture, their clothes. She wished the teacher would tone it down, just a little, but that wasn't much more likely than her wish to own her own starship.

"Welcome home, Haru," Morgan said, bending down to scoop the girl up in a hug. "Ooph. You get much bigger you'll need to pick *me* up."

Haruhi giggled, hugging Morgan back. She held up the solitary paper that hadn't slipped from her grasp onto the floor.

"We drew the sky today, Aunt Morgan!"

Morgan looked at the drawing, nodding appreciatively. It was just a black piece of paper with glittery stars added, but for a four-year-old it was hard work.

"Oh, that looks wonderful. Should we put it up with the others?"

Haruhi nodded vigorously, so Morgan walked over to the blank wall they'd dedicated to Haruhi's exploits. At the moment it only held a few drawings and paintings secured to the wall with simple magnets, but Haruhi still had most of ten months to fill the rest up. The starscape got a good spot along the top edge, next to a drawing of their house on Zion. At least, that is what Haruhi said it was. It was house-shaped, at least.

"There. We'll leave that for your mom to see when she gets back. Can you go wash your hands? I'll have dinner ready soon."

"Okay," Haruhi said as Morgan let her slip down to the floor. She padded off to the other side of the quarters that held the open kitchen, the main bathroom, and Haruhi's bedroom.

Morgan took a moment to straighten one of the drawings that had slipped a bit, and then followed after Haruhi, headed towards the kitchen. By the standards of space the quarters were really quite large, though still small compared to Gertrude's house planetside. The main room acted as study, living room, and dining room, with the wash and two main bedrooms on the left, the aforementioned bath, kitchen, and child's room on the right. Behind the bathroom, accessible through the kitchen, was the storage area, mostly for food, but with some other things thrown in. That front wall opened onto the corridor, of course, and the back wall had no adjoining rooms, just some more storage spaces recessed into it.

The kitchen capacities, small as they were, far outstripped Morgan's abilities. Gertrude had taught her a few things over the past few years, but boiling noodles and opening pre-canned sauce was about the most complicated thing Morgan was confident enough to try.

This wouldn't have been a problem if it was just Morgan. She was perfectly fine repeating the same three or four dishes pretty much forever. Haruhi, however, was rather pickier than Morgan was.

Fresh foods were also harder to get on the station, the proximity to Zion notwithstanding. Things like fruits and vegetables were simply too bulky to bring up in quantity and spoiled too quickly once there.

Heavy use of hydroponics was the obvious solution, and each ship had its own bay large enough to support the crew while on their routes. For a station as big as Takiyama, however, the capacities of hydroponic bays were pressed to their limits.

The long and short of it was that even with one of the largest hydroponics bays in the system, or even the nearby systems, roughly half their meals came from dehydrated or frozen sources.

Tonight it was to be dehydrated. This suited Morgan's exhausted state just fine. Open the package, pull out the dish, put it in the machine, wait. That was it.

The food was blander than fresh, some of the flavor was inevitably lost in the process to remove all the water, but at least chicken nuggets were one of the options. Haruhi liked those.

While the machine worked Morgan pulled out plates and such, putting them on the small table bolted to the wall just outside the kitchen.

"Haruhi, it's just about done. You finished washing your hands yet?"

"Yep," Haruhi said. She had made a detour into her room, and had grabbed her kid-proofed tablet uplink, already loaded up with one of the educational games she liked.

"Haruhi," Morgan said, stressing the syllables.

Haruhi tried to look innocent, sitting at the table, the tablet placed on the plate.

"Come on now. You know the rules."

Haruhi continued to feign ignorance, though she did subtly turn the audio off.

"If I have to take it, you won't get it back until tomorrow."

Sighing dramatically Haruhi hopped off the chair, dragging the tablet off the table loudly.

"Be nice," Morgan admonished, shaking her head slightly once the little girl had disappeared into her room. If her mother had been here, Haruhi wouldn't have dreamed of trying to bring her game to the dinner table. It wasn't surprising that she was pushing boundaries, but Morgan hoped she could get things worked out before they got out of hand.

As Haruhi clambered back up her chair the machine beeped. Food ready. Morgan grabbed the mitten and pulled out the hot plate.

Sliding it onto a cooler plate Morgan got it onto the table. There wasn't much room on the table left, but she managed to fit a pitcher of juice on there in the space Gertrude's plate would normally take up.

"Okay Haruhi. Do you want to pray?"

"No." Haruhi was pouting, her arms crossed over her chest.

"Come on Haruhi. You know your mom wants you pray at each meal." Morgan wasn't sure what to do if Haruhi kept up with her pouting. Morgan knew the form the prayer should take, but she didn't think she should offer it if Haruhi refused – she'd never gone to church with Gertrude and Haruhi on Zion, mostly because of work but also because she didn't feel comfortable attending for something she didn't know or believe in. It was important to Gertrude, though she hadn't talked about it much with Morgan. She supposed she'd be learning a bit more now; she'd be taking

Haruhi herself to church the next Sunday.

"Not gonna."

"Don't you want to say thank you for the food?"

Haruhi just grunted.

"Okay then. I guess I'd better put the food away."

"Humph."

Morgan slowly picked up the plate of food, standing up in an exaggerated fashion.

"No. . ." Haruhi said, reaching out for the plate.

"You sure? If you aren't hungry. . .?"

"No. I wanna pray."

"Good." Morgan put the plate back down and then bowed her head.

Haruhi's prayer was basically unintelligible, but sincere.

The meal was eaten mostly in silence, but not an uncompanionable one. Haruhi was mostly just interested in getting her food eaten and back to playing her game, and Morgan was enjoying the quiet and chance to relax.

Haruhi dashed off for the couch as soon as she had finished her food, leaving the cleanup for Morgan. Well, she was a bit young to be helping with that yet.

Morgan had the plates in the sink, the water running, when Haruhi looked up and glanced at Morgan's bedroom door.

"Your uplink," she said, looking at Morgan and pointing back to her room.

Turning off the water Morgan could hear it chiming too. Grabbing a towel, she quickly headed over, drying her soapy hands.

"Uplink, answer incoming call," she said as she walked in the room, waiting a few seconds before continuing, "This is Morgan Black."

"Chief Nakamura here. We've had a breakdown in the hydroponics bay on the *Fate of Dawn*. The irrigation lines are all non-functional. They have to be repaired before morning or some of the seedlings will start to die. You've drawn the short straw."

"Sir, I've got a young child here. There isn't anyone to watch her."

"Leave her with the neighbors. Every other person in our crew has pulled emergency duty already in the last few months. Except you. Get it done."

The line cut off before Morgan could so much as ask "what neighbors?"

Technically there were some people still in her block of quarters, spouses of the *Daystar*'s crew. Morgan knew none of them enough to trust Haruhi to their care.

Though. . . the water lines. That would be a long involved process, to be sure, but a lot of it would be on the external pipes, in the hydroponics bay itself. It would only be a few hours until Haruhi would need to go down for the night. If Morgan took her along and let her bring the tablet to help keep her occupied, she could do the stuff there until Haruhi got sleepy. Then Morgan could return to the task once Haruhi had fallen deeply enough asleep. Haruhi had always been a good sleeper, and her waking up in the night was quite rare.

She could even tie her uplink into the system in Haruhi's room, keep an ear on her at least.

Not ideal, but until she actually got to know her coworkers – and Gertrude's for that matter – there were only so many options.

At least it wasn't a job that would require her skinsuit. She could end the wash cycle early if she had to, but putting on a wet and slightly slimy skinsuit was *gross*.

Quickly Morgan went and changed into one of her sturdier pairs of coveralls, though not the nice ones. Anything involving hydroponics invariably ended up with fertilizer *somewhere* on her. No such option with her boots; she only had two pairs of those. At least she could seal the cuffs around the tops of the boots and keep the laces clean.

"Haruhi, we're going to go for a little walk. That sounds like fun, doesn't it?"

"Where are we going?"

"It's sort of a park. It will be nice and quiet, and you can play your game until you get tired. Do you have your socks?"

"Yes," Haruhi answered, then looked down. "No."

It took a few minutes to find the one missing sock, followed by Haruhi needing to use the restroom, a few minutes convincing her to wash her hands. The usual. All told it was closer to an hour later than not when they got to the ship's docking ring, Morgan having carried the already slightly tired girl about halfway.

Compared to *Steve,* the *Fate of Dawn* didn't look like much from the outside. It had no mushroom head, nor massive engines. It was still more or less a cylinder, with cargo spaces on the outside and the crew areas in the core. Smaller EM engines were placed at strategic spots around the hull, making the ship more agile, but slower to speed up and slow down. It was not a ship that could venture beyond a planet's orbit, or go much farther than from one gate to another at a time. It would look somewhat like a giant butterfly in flight, thanks to the two large radiator wings extending from the midpoint of the cylinder. The wings were swept back to keep the ship's profile smaller and help it fit more easily in docking slips. This was also to allow stations to pack in ships more tightly, without the massive wasted space that perpendicular radiator wings would cause.

It was newer, for what that was worth. Every ship Morgan had ever seen was newer, so it wasn't exactly a large point in the ship's favor.

The dockmaster raised an eyebrow as she caught sight of Haruhi. Morgan just shrugged as best as she could.

"What else do they expect me to do, ordering me to fix the hydroponics bay after school gets out?"

The dockmaster gave Morgan a rueful smile, but didn't say anything. She did wave them onboard, and then turned back to the novel she had on her screen.

The nature of the problem was, sadly, obvious once Morgan got into the bay. One of the primary pipes had burst, perhaps from a section freezing. It would be a simple fix.

It would also be a grueling, long fix.

"Haruhi, come sit over her by this tree. Isn't it a pretty tree?"

"Yeah."

"Okay. Now Aunt Morgan has to do some work in here. Can you promise me to be good and sit here and play your game?"

"Okay. I will."

"Ship's Computer, lock the doors to the hydroponics bay, except for authorized personnel."

"Confirmed," the computer responded. *The Fate of Dawn*'s computer had a strong masculine voice, a deep tenor.

"With the doors locked like this the other person currently in the room cannot leave, correct?"

"Correct."

"Thank you, computer."

Morgan got to work. All the tools she could possibly need were right here in the room, so leaving wasn't going to be an issue. She tried to keep an eye on Haruhi as much as she could. Every minute or so at first, then every couple minutes. Gradually her work started demanding more attention, and the time between glances grew.

Morgan felt bad about it, but what else could she do? There wasn't anything dangerous in the room besides the tools, and those were right at Morgan's side. She supposed Haruhi could eat some dirt, but children had been doing that for centuries, usually with no ill effects. Besides, Haruhi was a bit old for that.

Morgan wasn't quite done with the external work when she glanced over and saw that Haruhi was laying on the floor, asleep, her face lightly lit by the screen of her tablet.

Perfect. Now to get her back to her bed. It was too bad it was so far. . .

A thought hit Morgan. She had a bunk on *this* ship. She hadn't used it yet, but it was there, and it was hers. It was also far closer. The room would be unfamiliar to Haruhi, but the bunk itself was pretty much the same.

Morgan finished anything that wouldn't keep until she got back, then cleaned up as best she could.

Haruhi didn't stir when Morgan picked her up. Her bunk wasn't too far from hydroponics – truthfully nothing in the crew sections was terribly far from hydroponics, since it was part of the core of the crew sections.

Morgan got the girl situated on her bunk, closed the privacy screen, then secured the room so that Haruhi couldn't go wandering about if she did wake up. The last thing she did was call her uplink from the room's system so she could listen in, muting her own end so that her banging away wouldn't disturb Haruhi.

Suppressing a yawn Morgan got back to work. There was still at least four hours work ahead of her. The station kept Zion time, with its longer day, but it was still doubtful she'd get much sleep herself that night.

***

Morgan was mostly finished, putting the finishing touches on a new valve in the crawlspaces behind the wall when a cry pierced her concentration. It was Haruhi, whimpering in the throes or a bad dream.

Cursing her bad luck – or perhaps just the laziness that had let Morgan think that putting the girl in an unfamiliar bed wouldn't have consequences – Morgan started working faster. She couldn't leave the valve half-done, but if Haruhi woke the rest of the way before she finished. . .

. . .so of course Haruhi woke up completely a few moments later, a pitiable little cry as she jerked herself awake, as best Morgan could tell from the audio.

"Momma?" Haruhi asked on reflex, adding after a moment, "Aunt Morgan?"

Quickly unmuting her uplink Morgan called out to her.

"Did you have a bad dream, Haruhi? Don't worry, it's over now."

"Where are you?"

"I'm still working on the plants, sweetie. You're in my room on the ship. It's still pretty late. Do you want to try to go back to sleep?"

"It's scary here." Morgan could hear the bunk's privacy screen being retracted. "It's too dark."

Morgan groaned inwardly. She'd forgotten to turn one of the small lights on. How good were the voice controls in the bunk?

"Sweetie, say, 'Room, turn one desk light on.'"

Haruhi did, and Morgan could hear the room respond to her

commands. Luckily the lights weren't user restricted like the doors were.

"Is that better, Haru?"

"Yeah. Where are you? Can you come here?"

Morgan was still working on the valve as they talked, and she was nearly done, but it would be at least another ten minutes.

"I'll be there as soon as I can. Would you like me to tell you a story while I finish?"

"Yeah."

"What story would you like?"

"Princess Story?"

Morgan smiled. The old tale Haruhi had dubbed 'Princess Story' was one of her favorites. The little girl had it memorized far better than Morgan did.

"Of course sweetie. Let's see. How does it start? Oh yes, once there was a brave little princess. . ."

✳✳✳

Haruhi fell back asleep before Morgan had finished the story. Morgan's repair job hit the requisite spanner in the works an hour or so later. It was nearly time for Haruhi to go off to school by the time Morgan finished.

Caked in sweat and dirt, oil and, yes, fertilizer, Morgan carried the sleeping Haruhi towards the docking port. She had wrapped the girl in the sheet off her bunk to keep her clean. It would come out in the wash. And if not, well, it wasn't like a mechanic's sheets didn't invariably end up stained by such things eventually anyway.

The same dockmaster was still on duty at the airlock. She looked tired too; her shift had to be just about over as well.

"Finally finished?" she whispered as they passed, taking in the sleeping

Haruhi.

"Finally. I'm still reading through the employee manual. Do they expect me to be back to work in an hour?" Morgan asked, not sure if she wanted the answer.

Before the dockmaster could answer, an unfortunately loud voice rang out from the other side of the docking tube.

"Crewman Black, are you early, or did that simple repair take you all night?" It was Chief Nakamura, and he didn't look pleased. Of course he knew she was just finished, one glance at her coveralls would tell him that.

"Please, sir, keep it down. Haruhi is still asleep. I'd rather she stays that way until I get back to my quarters."

The chief grunted, but he did keep it down.

"You'd better hurry if you're going to be back for your shift."

Morgan closed her eyes, willing down her exhaustion alongside her urge to yell.

"Sir," Morgan began, her voice faltering. "Sir," she said more forcefully, "If I come back in today, after working for, what, sixteen hours straight? I will be a danger to myself and others."

The chief grunted. "Good. You pass."

"I. . . what?"

"It is important that you recognized that you shouldn't be working. You stood up to me.

"This. Was a test?" Morgan asked, barely remembering to keep her voice quiet.

"Yes. You could also think of it as a rite of passage, if you'd like."

"It is a good thing my arms are full, or I might do something neither of us would like."

"You're tired. I'll pretend I didn't hear that threat and you can go sleep it off."

"Next time do your blasted tests when I'm not taking care of a young child."

"I suggested you leave her with your neighbors."

"The neighbors I don't know? That I haven't even had time to know? Do you have kids?"

"No."

"Yeah."

Morgan turned and left, abruptly, which was by far the better option, rude or no.

CHAPTER 15

Teaching is a wonderful way for not only the student to learn, but the teacher as well. By going over the core elements of the subject, the basics, the pupil is taught and the instructor reminded. Putting it into words helps us understand what we have learned, but may have forgotten.
- Professor Laura Anderson, University of Ein, planet Zion

TEN ZION MONTHS LATER / NINE EARTH MONTHS

"COME ON HARUHI, you're going to make us late." There were times Morgan wondered if she said these words more than anything else, but right now, she was more concerned with the reality behind them. It was Sunday; their one day off from work and school, and Haruhi had misplaced her sock. It would have been easier if it had been *both* socks, since Morgan could then have convinced her to simply get another pair out, but no. It was *one* sock, and it was her favorite pair of socks, so they looked.

Morgan wished she could just get Haruhi to wear her shoes in their quarters, but the custom of leaving shoes at the door was reinforced by the general culture of the company and her own background, at least on Haruhi's father's side.

Besides, they'd probably just end up looking for socks *and* shoes in that case.

Even after ten months, Morgan still felt a little uneasy taking Haruhi to church. She was the only person there not already a member of the congregation, besides the children, of course.

The bishop hadn't pushed beyond a few gentle inquiries and suggestions, and those had all been in the first few weeks. Morgan would show up, Haruhi in tow, sit quietly – well, as quietly as an active child would permit – and try to keep said child paying attention. Then Haruhi would go off with the children for Sunday School and Morgan would stay in the main chapel not really paying attention. Throw in encouraging Haruhi to pray at mealtimes and before bed and keeping some religious stories in the rotation at bedtime and that was the extent of Morgan's involvement.

It wasn't that she disbelieved what the bishop was saying, but she didn't *believe* either. The whole concept of a deity was something she just couldn't seem to wrap her head around.

"Did you check under your blankets?" Morgan was looking in most of the common places herself, but the uncommon places weren't as uncommon as they should be. How that little girl managed to lose a sock on top of the rehydration machine Morgan would never know.

"I found it!" Haruhi shouted from the other room.

"Where was it?"

"In the sock drawer."

Haruhi had been *wearing* it an hour before. Morgan had put them on her feet herself.

Never mind, they'd found it. Morgan ran down the 'before you leave checklist' in her head.

Tablet, with the books, songs, and such for Haruhi, uplink for Morgan?

Yes.

Shoes and socks? Yes.

Dresses clean and presentable? Yes. No, wait. *Morgan's* dress had a bit of oil on the hem, probably transferred from one of her coveralls.

Grumbling Morgan quickly threw on another dress. Luckily, her shoes were black so it still worked with the yellow floral pattern instead of the light grey she'd been wearing.

"Come on then, Haru. If we hurry, we can still get some of the padded seats."

***

Morgan heard even less of what the speaker was saying than normal.

Each week different members of the congregation took a turn giving a lesson on some topic or other, with differing levels of success. Morgan knew very few of them, though that was mostly due to her own indifference.

Who was present changed week to week as well, of course. Most of the churches paid their ministers. They rented space among the non-crew spaces of the station alongside the shop owners and other people living on the station not directly working for Takiyama. The one Gertrude belonged to wasn't one of them, instead filling their needs by drawing upon the members already on station for their services. Morgan wasn't sure if that was how it was everywhere or if they just did it in isolated placed like the Station. Either way, given the rotating nature of the ship's routes, who did what changed regularly.

One of the bishop's assistants was an officer on *Steve*, or at least Morgan thought so. She had only seen him the once, in passing, during the brief time she'd been part of the *Steve*'s crew, and since the ship had left around the same time Gertrude's had she hadn't seen him until *Steve* came back six months later. Besides him Morgan had seen a couple of the regulars around the *Fate of Dawn* or by her quarters in the *Daystar Fading*'s area, but the rest were from the other ships, or their families, and Morgan didn't really bother going to their social events, except to drop Haruhi off for the ones the children did.

At least today's topic wasn't as esoteric as many of them ended up being. Talking about their deity dying and coming back to life was much harder to follow than the simple stuff like being kind to one another – today's topic – or other lessons on good things to do or bad things not to do. The ones based on history were even worse. Morgan barely knew anything of her own home planet's history, and while she'd learned a bit about Zion over the years her knowledge of Earth was almost nonexistent. After ten months of infrequently hearing about it all she could say for sure was that the ancestors of this particular group seemed to attract enemies.

Morgan normally was content to sit quietly through the service. It was a chance to relax, after all, and she didn't have to wrangle Haruhi the whole time. Today though she was anxious, because it was a big day for the pair of them, although Haruhi didn't know it yet.

Today the *Daystar Fading* was returning.

Ten months without her mom had been hard on both of them. After the third month Haruhi had stopped asking when momma was coming home and Morgan had stopped mentioning the time left, or Gertrude at all really. Haruhi was clearly still missing her. She wasn't sad, exactly, but noticeably less exuberant, and prone to falling quiet at times.

They got video messages somewhat regularly, of course, whenever a courier vessel that had passed Gertrude's ship came through Parlon. Even when the messages arrived out of order Haruhi didn't care, watching them over and over. Three times the messages were duplicates arriving weeks apart, which happened when more than one ship had copies of the messages. Those times were hard on Haruhi, because they wouldn't know it was one they'd already seen until they were actually watching it.

Getting messages back to Gertrude was spottier, but messages took up so little space that the carry fees on the couriers were negligible. A shotgun approach of copying each message to a dozen different couriers was usually necessary.

Which made Morgan think. As hard as it was for them to get the few duplicate messages, how would it be for the person on the freighter? Some messages would likely never arrive, and probably none of them in order, with many more duplicates.

Gertrude only mentioned receiving messages a few times, though she was always happier in those messages. She was careful not to mention how long until she was returning, Morgan noticed, though she might have been omitting it only because of the time delay.

In any case, it was finally over. They should be – Morgan checked her uplink surreptitiously – yes, the *Daystar Fading* had reached the outer doors of the station just as they were sitting down in the chapel. After the services ended, they would be able to leisurely stroll over to the ship's dock and meet the crew disembarking after finishing locking everything down.

In just a few days, Haruhi would be turning seven Earth years old, and she'd grown five centimeters while Gertrude had been gone. Morgan idly wondered how Gertrude had changed over the months. It had been years since Gertrude had had a fulltime job, either a real fulltime job like this one, or even the 40-hour workweek kind.

Morgan supposed she'd changed as well, though it was gradual enough that she couldn't be sure what had changed. At least work had settled down into a manageable routine, both because they'd stopped hassling her quite so much and because she'd found her footing.

The woman seated a few chairs down from Morgan got her attention with a quick wave of a hand down by her knees, so as not to disturb others. She had some papers on a clipboard, announcements and the like, along with the sheet to track attendance. Why they were actual paper rather than electronic. . . well, Morgan had long ago assumed was due to traditions and stubbornness. They certainly didn't seem to mind that the language of their books was antiquated long before Man had left Earth. The odd construction and words like 'thee' and 'thou' were still hard for Morgan to parse.

They also seemed to like to have little flyers with quotes and inspirational messages, sometimes artwork, reminders to put physically on the wall or some such. Today it was a stylized quote, presumably tied into the lesson Morgan wasn't really paying attention to. The artistry of the quote was actually quite well done, with some flourishes that made it stand out, if also slightly harder to read.

"And behold, I tell you these things that ye may learn wisdom; that ye may learn that when ye are in the service of your fellow beings ye are only in the service of your God."

Morgan glanced at the other papers, passing them up to the man in the row in front of her, and then sat back, trying to work out what that even meant. Did that also mean anything bad anyone did to each other was the same as doing it to their deity? What about something like the fight Morgan had gotten into with the muggers who had attacked Gertrude back on Zion? Was that good because she was helping this hypothetical deity, or bad because she was attacking him?

It was all very confusing.

Morgan gave up trying to work her way through the implications, as Haruhi was tugging on the skirt of her dress.

"What is it, Haru?" she whispered.

"I need to go potty," was the whispered reply.

"Okay. Do you need me to come with?"

Haruhi shook her head, hopping off her chair and scooting past as Morgan turned to the side to give her room.

Haruhi returned a few minutes later, and Morgan fixed her with a steady gaze.

"Hands?"

"I forgot."

Haruhi hurried back out of the room, her shoes clacking in the fake wood of the floor. She made it back, hands still damp, just as the last song was starting. After finishing with a prayer, the group started getting up and heading to the next part of the services. Morgan held out her hand for Haruhi, and the pair followed the crowd out of the chapel and into the second largest room assigned to the church, where the children were taught lessons at their level.

Haruhi safely seated among the other kids her age Morgan returned to the chapel, grabbing a seat at the back near the door this time.

Truth be told she dozed a bit, without Haruhi to keep an eye on or any desire to listen to the teacher.

She was only dimly aware as the second part ended and the men left for their smaller room. Given the gender realities of starship work the largest single group present each week was the adult women, so they got to stay in the chapel. Thankfully, the song at the end woke her up, and even did so gradually enough that she didn't jerk awake and draw attention to herself.

Collecting Haruhi took some minutes, most of the people present were all too happy to visit and chat amongst themselves, while the children generally ran about and had fun.

Usually Morgan let Haruhi mingle until the parents started leaving with their children, but today they had somewhere to be. Morgan did a quick check to make sure Haruhi hadn't gotten her dress dirty somehow – unlikely at church, but Haruhi had once managed to come home from school muddy once. On a space station.

Haruhi was fine, so off they went with a wave to her friends.

As they got back onto the main network of corridors, Haruhi started skipping ahead, now knowing the complicated path back to their quarters by heart.

"Come back, Haruhi. We need to go somewhere else before we go home."

The little girl complied, hopping back, her hand slipping into Morgan's.

"Did you have fun at church?" Morgan asked as they walked.

"Yep! We learned about Daniel and the lions." Haruhi paused for a moment, then added, "Aunt Morgan, what are lions?"

Morgan chuckled. Hopefully, the lesson's main point had been conveyed better than information about the animals involved. Granted, Morgan only knew what a lion was because it was the symbol of their neighboring planet of Albion. Many species had been transplanted all over the galaxy from Earth, being useful or pretty, or even a few that had been able to sneak aboard ships and survive the journey. Lions were not any of those things, and only existed on Earth – maybe. Morgan had spent an afternoon learning about the animals, curious after encountering the seal of

Albion, and learned about their habitats on Earth. They had been doing quite well after a long time at risk of extinction when contact was lost with Sol.

"Lions are like a very big cat. They aren't nice like cats though. They hunt other animals for food."

"Oh."

They walked quietly for a bit, Haruhi clearly thinking about big mean cats.

"Would the lion have eaten Daniel?"

Morgan hesitated in answering. The last time she'd truthfully answered a question like this Gertrude had a very long night as a terrified Haruhi kept waking up from nightmares. That had been near the beginning of Morgan's stay with Gertrude, though, and Haruhi had grown quite a bit since then. It was also apparently important to the religious story, and the teachers had felt it appropriate to talk about in the first place. . .

"Lions didn't normally hurt people, but yes, the lion could have."

"Daniel was brave."

"I'm sure he was," Morgan agreed, though she didn't actually know the story she was talking about.

Morgan paused a moment to check her uplink map and make sure they were still going the right way. She'd only been to the *Daystar Fading*'s docking slip twice, and both of those times she'd started at their quarters, not the chapel. She was getting better at navigating the confusing space station, but better and good weren't the same thing in this case. At least she'd been able to get a supplemental program for her uplink allowing it to make sense of the map and give proper directions.

"Where are we going?"

"Well. It's sort of a surprise."

Morgan closed down her uplink holo-map. There were actually making good time, and it was only a few turns more. They should be able to see the ship soon. If Haruhi recognized the ship that would be the end of the surprise, but given how far away it would be Morgan thought it unlikely.

"We're not going to go shopping." It wasn't a question, not really. Haruhi had balked the first time Morgan had tried to use her day off for shopping – most things they could get delivered, but Haruhi had grown so much that she needed a whole new wardrobe, and that meant fittings.

"No, we're not going shopping. Do you want this to be a surprise or not?"

"Nope. Are we going to see someone?"

"It's a surprise!"

"Uh-huh. Who?"

"I didn't say it was a person."

"Didn't say no."

The pair came around a bend, entering the observation ring that ran nearly the whole exterior of the main hold of the station. They actually weren't far from the *Fate of Dawn*, just ahead of them on their right. Its rounded cylindrical shape was a comfort in its own way, because all the hull plating and external hatches were closed – there would be no more maintenance and repair work on the ship's exterior before they left on their delivery route.

"There's your ship, Aunt Morgan. Are we going there?"

"That is my ship, but no, not today. No work on my day off."

"Then where?" Haruhi dragged out the second word, acting a bit more exasperated than Morgan suspected she really was.

"You'll see."

The next slip, the largest in the whole bay, was *Steve*'s. They were still working on maintenance, and several of the cargo bays had been pulled out. They were balanced at the bottom of the slip, separated by a few meters of empty space in the zero gravity of the bay, to allow easier access to the framework.

They stopped for a moment to look at it.

"Which ship is that, Aunt Morgan?"

Morgan felt a pang of regret as she looked at the scarred bulk. Such a beautiful machine. The moment passed and she turned to Haruhi.

"That's *Steve*. It's the biggest ship here."

"It looks different."

"It is. It's a very old ship."

"Are we going there?"

Morgan chuckled. "You don't give up, huh? No, we aren't. Come on then."

They walked on, Morgan giving Haruhi's hand a quick squeeze.

As they passed the side passage that led back to the crew area for the *Daystar Fading* the previously empty corridor rapidly gave way to a small throng of people headed towards the docking slip. Most of them Morgan at least recognized by sight, if not by name. Haruhi looked around, taking in the cheerful faces about them, the children bouncing up and down, and then looked back to Morgan.

"Momma?" she whispered, halting in her tracks.

Morgan gave her a big smile of her own.

"So much for the surprise, then."

Haruhi didn't bother responding, instead tugging at Morgan's hand as she surged forwards, using her small size to squeeze between the adults around them. Morgan kept up, barely, her tight grip on Haruhi's hand keeping her from going too fast.

The lobby outside each docking slip was intentionally large for occasions such as this. It was quite full apart from the roped off section in the middle to give the crew room to disembark. The large airlock doors were still closed, so they hadn't arrived late.

They managed to squeeze close to the front, but not all the way, so after a few moments of Haruhi jumping up and down trying to see Morgan grabbed her under the arms and lifted her up onto her shoulders. Even with their combined heights, Haruhi could only see over some of the crowd, but it was still better than nothing.

They stood there for long minutes, but nobody seemed to mind. There was a definite festive feel to the air, and everyone was happy the long months were over, making minutes seem like nothing and an eternity at the same time.

The announcement system crackled to life in the lobby at last.

"This is *Daystar Fading* Actual. We are moored." The next bit Morgan couldn't understand because of a quick cheer from most of the people present. "All crew except designated watch standers are released for two days R&R. Be sure to be back promptly after that. We still have a lot of work to do."

The line clicked off, accompanied by a somewhat quieter cheer.

"She talks funny," Haruhi said, leaning down to whisper in Morgan's ear.

"A lot of the officers talk like that. I thought it was funny too. I asked someone about it, and they said that it's the way the military talks."

"Why?"

"I'm not sure they even know. Because they've done it that way for hundreds of years."

"She's that old?"

Morgan laughed.

"No, the military, not her personally."

"Oh."

The seals on the airlock hissed, releasing air to equalize pressure inside and out. Once that was done the two halves of the door groaned slightly as they started pulling apart, sliding into the floor and ceiling slowly.

There was no rush forward by the waiting crowd, most of them had done this enough that they knew better, and the few that hadn't – like Morgan – were held in place either by their fellows or common sense.

It was still a minute or two before the first of the crew emerged into the lobby. Waves and shouted greetings flew back and forth, and people flowed towards the back end of the room to meet their loved ones.

Haruhi was bouncing up and down enough that Morgan was having trouble keeping her balance.

"Calm down , Haru. It won't be long now."

Haruhi stopped fidgeting, for a minute anyway.

It was easy to forget how large a crew a modern freighter had, given how compartmentalized the crew was. Cooks and pilots, mechanics and nurses, officers, mercenaries who acted as security, engineers, a couple botanists for the hydroponics bay, even counselors and barbers.

Given that Gertrude was the chief for one of the engine maintenance crews, Morgan wasn't surprised that the crowd leaving the ship had thinned considerably – accompanied by a similar thinning of the waiting family as they slowly made their way back towards their quarters – with no sign of Gertrude. It was a long way from the airlock to the engine spaces and their quarters, since the *Daystar* was laid out to have crew quarters near their workspaces, rather than centralized in designs like the *Fate of Dawn* or *Steve*.

At last, Morgan caught a glimpse of wavy brown hair, shorter than she remembered perhaps, but still familiar.

"Down," Haruhi ordered, impatiently, almost toppling them over as she tried to help Morgan put her down. Haruhi rushed forward, a shouted "Momma," as she flung herself at the skinsuited figure. Gertrude barely had time to move her duffel bag to the side in order to catch the flying little girl.

"Oh my, little one," Gertrude said, her face positively beaming, "You're not so little anymore."

Gertrude kept walking, hugging Haruhi tightly, and meeting up with Morgan at the end of the lobby. Morgan hugged the pair of them tightly.

"Welcome home, G," Morgan said simply.

"It feels good to be home," Gertrude whispered.

Shifting Haruhi in closer Gertrude managed to get the strap of the duffel bag off, so Morgan take it. The trio started back towards their quarters, Gertrude letting Morgan take the lead. Morgan briefly wondered if Gertrude remembered how to get there after all this time. She hadn't exactly had a lot of time to learn the layout before leaving, after all.

"You're looking pretty today, Haru. Did you have fun at church?"

"Yes, Momma. I missed you."

"I missed you too, honey. But I'm home now, and I won't need to go away for quite a while. I hope you were good for Aunt Morgan?"

Haruhi nodded briefly before snuggling in closer, burying her head in

Gertrude's shoulder.

Haruhi babbled to Gertrude the whole way back to their quarters, about nothing really, day-to-day things, the other kids in her class, a veritable flood of the tiny details of life. Gertrude listened in rapt attention, of course, sighing every occasionally in contentment.

Once they were home, Morgan made dinner while Haruhi showed Gertrude all the things she learned and made over the preceding months. Even as Gertrude put Haruhi to bed, Morgan still hadn't had a chance to talk with her friend.

Morgan didn't mind though. She understood a little bit what Haruhi was feeling. She had missed Gertrude herself, after all, and she still sometimes thought about what she'd say to her parents if she ever had the chance to talk to them.

"I've made it, Daddy, Momma," she murmured to the walls as Gertrude told Haruhi a bedtime story. "I've made a life for myself."

Once Gertrude had safely seen Haruhi to sleep, she sat down next to Morgan on the couch.

Gertrude let out a big breath, sagging a bit as she finally let her weariness show.

"Were the months as long for you as they were for us?" Morgan asked.

"Longer, I imagine. It's going to be hard to leave again, even if I get ten months here first."

"Yeah."

"You'll have to do it soon, you know. How long until you ship out?"

"A few weeks. I'll be here for Haru's birthday, at least."

"That's something. Look, Morgan. . ." Gertrude started to say.

"You don't owe me a thing, G. Watching over Haruhi for you was worth

273

every moment."

"And your work? I've heard the stories about the *Fate of Dawn*. The hazing disguised as extra duties or emergency repairs?"

"Survivable."

"It can't be easy, having a captain who doesn't like you."

"I doubt it helps, but really it isn't that bad. I don't think I've seen her more than a handful of times across ten months."

Gertrude narrowed her eyes, looking at Morgan.

"What is it?"

"What?"

"You seem, distant somehow."

"Oh. Just. . . thinking about my parents, I guess."

"I guess it isn't easy watching Haru and me, knowing you won't see your parents ever again."

"I'm used to that. It helps, reminding myself that they gave me up so I'd have a better life."

"Thinking about where you'd be if you hadn't left?"

"Not really. It isn't hard to imagine. By now I'd probably have three kids and a husband I might like, if I was lucky. Or not, if he'd died in the mines."

"What a terrible way to live."

"For most. Some of the people there were still happy. They made themselves find the little scraps of happiness they could. Their kids, their spouse. Stories told around the fires where the Tinnys couldn't hear."

"Doesn't sound like a life you'd like much?"

"No. I think by now I'd even miss the mines, the chance to fix things."

Gertrude chuckled.

"Born mechanic."

"I take after my dad."

"You've mentioned before that he was an engineer."

"A good one. I've spent some time here and there looking at his research. I still can't quite grasp all of it, and there isn't anything like it out here. Though there isn't much need given the gravity levels of most settled planets."

"You'll get there."

They sat in companionable silence for several minutes before Gertrude asked another question.

"Are you going to be okay?"

"Of course, G."

"It's hard, being alone on a ship for that long. I know I missed you as much as I did Haruhi."

"I doubt that."

"Well, okay. *Almost* as much. You'll miss us too."

"Why did we choose this life again?"

"I think the standard answer from my coworkers is 'adventure and babes.'"

Morgan laughed.

"That's it. Definitely."

Gertrude smiled.

"I should get some sleep. It was a long day."

"Goodnight, G. It's good to have you back."

"Goodnight, Morgan. Don't stay up too late."

Morgan sat there for twenty minutes or so, not really regretting her choice to be a mechanic but regretting the sacrifices that went along with it.

It was still worth it. She believed that. She'd get to see more of the galaxy than the vast majority of people ever did. For a girl who'd grown up not even seeing her own sun that was a pretty good deal, if a bit lonely.

She thought of Haruhi, and whether she'd ever get a chance to have kids of her own, and how that would affect her career.

Well, no sense worrying about that yet. She wasn't even eighteen Earth years old yet, plenty of times for everything, especially since she could look forward to a few hundred years at least.

CHAPTER 16

Everyone knows that piracy is dead. That it is nothing more than an abandoned barbarism of a forgotten age when the inhabited worlds were far apart and help even farther. Everyone knows that with gates guarded and governments strong piracy can never happen again. They're mostly right. Privateering, on the other hand. . .

- Captain Charles Talmadge the Third, Unified Defense Fleet, Holdor System

SIX ZION MONTHS LATER / FIVE AND A HALF EARTH MONTHS

MORGAN WEARILY SLUNK through the *Fate of Dawn*'s dimly lit corridors, making her way towards her bunk. The ship was five hundred meters long and nearly half that wide, and a three meter by five meter room was all that was hers. Well, hers and the other five girls who shared the cramped room, anyway.

Her uplink had notified her that a letter had come for her from Gertrude with the last courier boat that had transited the system. If she hurried she could watch it alone while the rest of them were getting dinner.

Most people would have just listened to it direct on the uplink, but Morgan wanted to use the screen at her desk. Bigger picture and clearer than the holodisplay.

It wasn't that living with the five other techs had also made Morgan a little self-conscious about her relative clumsiness with the uplink. No, not at all.

To be fair to herself, there was the added fact that while most people thought nothing of others overhearing their messages Morgan hated eavesdropping and eavesdroppers. Unfortunately, privacy in general was at best a polite fiction in a technological society. Gertrude, and Haruhi of course, were family. These five near strangers were not.

This was the first message she'd received since she'd left on her first delivery run, though Morgan had sent a dozen or two and undoubtedly Gertrude had sent many to her.

She had expected it after the troubles they'd gone through to send messages to Gertrude while she'd been out of the system, but it was subtly different being on the receiving end, especially since Gertrude had at least received a couple of the messages within three months.

It was almost worse because there wasn't even anyone to blame for the delay. Catching a freighter that made stops in more than a dozen systems was both hard and expensive. Instead of trying, courier boats just transited system to system, stopping only long enough to deliver whatever they could at each stop and pass along the non-sensitive messages to the other couriers. That way whoever ran into the freighter in question first delivered it, and then flagged the message for deletion from the other couriers as they met back up again.

That it worked was a testament to the dedication and professionalism of the courier companies, as well as their standing policy that any party trying to interfere with the mail would be denied any use of the system in perpetuity *and* that courier boats were under the protection of all navies equally. There had actually even been a couple instances where two ships from nations at war had been required to work together to rescue a waylaid courier. Those incidents were famous for their oddity, not to mention the fact that it had actually ended without any violence. Generally speaking, no one messed with the couriers.

That information, delivered in a briefing for the new crew as they transited out towards Parlon's system gate, had made Morgan feel a little better at least. Looking back there had been a few times she'd left something out of her messages to Gertrude because she was afraid who else might end up seeing it.

The galactic power plays of the courier companies were not on Morgan's mind at the moment, of course. She was much more curious to hear how Gertrude and Haruhi were doing. She had gotten used to Gertrude's absence to an extent while she was away, but this trip was her first time away from Haruhi in years. The first week she'd had a terrible time just getting out of bed without Haruhi there trying to surprise her awake.

Morgan yawned. It had been a long shift, but satisfying. The entire time had been spent fixing the massive cargo hatch that had become stuck when the automated crane had malfunctioned and shoved a cargo container squarely into it – while still closed. The container had proved to be the weaker sword to the door's shield and the container had shattered, scattering fluffy toy animals everywhere. Since the gravity had been turned off to facilitate cargo transfer, the toys had actually scattered quite far and wide. Just one of the joys of delivering to a backwater planet without proper cargo receiving systems.

Well, the crew called it backwater. It wasn't as bad off as Hillman, by a long shot. The notable difference was that the rulers of the planet were just as bad off as the people, while Hillman's comrade managers would be considered wealthy almost anywhere in the known galaxy.

Morgan had asked her crew chief what a planet skirting the raw edge of poverty needed with a bunch of sappy toy caricatures of the animals of Earth, but he had just laughed and said that they were popular across the whole quadrant, and that even people with very little needed things to make them happy.

As to why they didn't make them themselves, well, the only answer she'd gotten was some nonsense about that particular kind being the best. Apparently they were made the 'old fashioned' way and not nano-fabricated.

Whatever people wanted to buy, let them buy, Morgan supposed. More freight going around was only a good thing, after all.

Besides, one container of lightweight toys hardly caused a blip on the cost of delivery.

Of course Crewman Fourth Class Black was given the task of retrieving all of the errant toys, as well as the innards of the ones torn open during the collision. The hazing had stopped, but giving her the worst jobs hadn't.

With that much time to examine them, she had been forced to admit they were cute. On a whim, Morgan had stuffed the bits of a couple ruined penguins into her skinsuit's pouches. Perhaps she'd see if she could find some thread later (black and white were common enough, after all) and get a whole one out of the pieces.

They were a lot smaller than the one she had won for Haruhi back when they first met, but the reminder would be welcome. She might even be able to get two whole penguins out of the bits and pieces, so she could give one to Haruhi as the twin of hers.

The best part of the shift had been that she'd been allowed to actually help with the main parts of the repairs once she had finished her original task. Granted, they'd only pulled her in because her small hands made getting to a couple of the release catches easier than it would have been for the other techs, but she wasn't about to complain about the whys. It was beyond frustrating to not be allowed to help with a lot of things because she was only a fourth class, and then watch them struggle to do things she'd been capable of back on Hillman.

As she walked Morgan wondered if the problem with the hatch would delay their return to Parlon any. If they couldn't get it fixed they'd have to reroute all that cargo through the other bays, which would slow them down. She had signed up for an advanced course on some of the trickier routine maintenance fusion reactors needed, and she'd hate to miss it. For one thing she'd paid in advance, and for another the other time it would be offered would be a week after Gertrude departed again, so she wouldn't be able to attend then.

Without any warning the deck beneath her rumbled. It felt like it was coming from the port side. The first few months Morgan had panicked at each little tremor the ship made while underway, but now she had a feel for it, and the normal rumbles were simply background noise. Whatever that was, however, it wasn't normal. It was too localized, and the ship was still physically docked with the station. She supposed it could have been something that had happened on the station that had transferred through the dock onto the *Fate of Dawn*, but she couldn't think of anything obvious that it could have been.

Best to hurry back to her bunk. If it was something they needed her for they'd call, and if not she'd do the crew a favor by not being in the way and do herself one by getting some sleep.

If she got to sleep soon enough she might be able to squeeze some time in the gym before her next shift started, and if she was really lucky it would be empty enough for her to be able to crank up the gravity to Hillman's level. She could only manage that a few times a week with the more crowded facilities onboard, and it was starting to show.

There was an odd popping noise from the speaker system, then a strange somewhat garbled voice said, "All crewmembers, return to your berths." Instead of cutting off clean the message had a few further seconds of odd popping noise.

That was odd. It hadn't sounded like any of the officers, but it wasn't like Morgan had actually talked to more than a couple of them, or even heard a couple of the others speak. If there was a problem, why order them *all* to quarters? For that matter, berth was an odd choice of words. Morgan knew what it meant, but had never heard that particular word used by anyone from Zion or Albion.

Old instincts whispered to her that something was wrong. Morgan pushed them aside and started heading back to her cabin. She had been heading there anyway, after all, but she also slid her hand in the pouch of her skinsuit just above her right hip.

Tapping her uplink, she pulled up a link to her immediate supervisor, Chief Nakamura. It was possible, probable really, that he knew more than Morgan did about what was going on. If he got on Morgan's case for bugging him she could just blame it on the poor quality of the transmission. There really had been parts she couldn't understand. She just didn't need to tell her that those parts weren't really part of the main message.

"What is it, Black? Aren't you off shift?"

"I was hoping you knew what that last ship-wide was about. It was rather garbled over where I am."

"What was there to misunderstand? I swear, you'd lose your head if it wasn't attached. Just get to your bunk and stay. . ." Chen stopped talking, and for a moment Morgan thought she'd lost the connection. Looking down at her uplink she could see that it was still transmitting clearly. Then the link started picking up sounds again, only they weren't words. It was the unmistakable sound of gunfire. In fact, they sounded like gas-powered high velocity dart guns. She had once seen them used, back on Hillman, when a crowd had gotten too rowdy. They were useful because they wouldn't ignite any flammable gasses in the air around the mine, while still effective against unarmored targets.

They would be even better on a spaceship, Morgan realized, since they weren't likely to damage fragile stuff like the computer consoles or other equipment.

Part of Morgan froze, completely stupefied that someone was attacking her ship, her crew. Where had they come from? What did they want? Was it a member of the crew? The other part of her didn't freeze, however. Without conscious input she opened up a channel to the bridge, but only got a message from the uplink that there was local interference and that the network was not functioning. Hustling down the corridor she found a wall mounted com unit, which thankfully worked.

"Bridge, com tech Nancy here."

Not even bothering to identify herself Morgan just blurted out, "I just heard gunfire coming from Damage Control Central."

For one second, two, Nancy just stared at her. "What, you have to be pranking me. Who are you?"

"Just listen!" Morgan put as much steel in her voice as she could, forcing herself to forget for the moment that the woman on the bridge was probably twice her age and a lot more experienced. "It sounded like a gas rifle, probably more than one of them given how many shots I heard." Morgan hadn't realized she'd realized that, but thinking back she was right. "There was an odd vibration just a few minutes ago, plus that strange message about all crew returning to their bunks."

"There wasn't any communication. . ." Nancy started to say, but Morgan cut her off.

"Then you didn't hear it on the bridge. Get ahold of yourself, I think we've been boarded." Morgan was almost yelling now, which was a bad idea on several fronts. If anyone was nearby they've be sure to hear her, and it made Nancy the com tech less likely to listen to her.

Finally, Nancy ducked out of the screen's pickup range and the officer of the watch appeared. Normally Morgan would have felt intimidated just by seeing him, let alone having his undivided attention, but right now that was far from her mind.

"What's going on?" He said bluntly.

"I heard gunfire from DCC. Probably more than one weapon, gas-rifles. The uplink network is being jammed, and there was a weird vibration a few minutes ago, right direction to be coming from the docking port."

"You mean like a breaching charge?"

"Could be. It felt a bit like the stuff we used back home to blast new tunnels in the mines. There was also a strange voice ordering all crewmembers back to their quarters. I think they hacked in."

"Find somewh. . ." He cut off in mid-word as the screen went blank. It took Morgan a few moments to realize that the terminal was completely offline.

"Find somewhere, somewhere what? Safe?" Morgan muttered to herself. Finally, the emergency alarm started up, the high-pitched whine that she had only heard in drills once before. "Ship has been boarded by hostiles," it meant. Well, at least everyone knew. So where was safe while the ship was being boarded? Obviously not her bunk – they wanted everyone there. Oh, of course. The answer was obvious. Head for the mercenaries' office.

As she got closer she heard gunfire again, only this time not through her uplink. It was sporadic at first, then more frequently. They weren't all gas rifles either. At least a third of the shots were the unmistakable crack boom of suit penetrator rounds.

It dawned on Morgan that she had probably made a mistake. Of course the ship's defenders would be a primary target too. She was stuck now, though. The only things to her left and right within quick reach were cargo bays. They were both currently empty as they had already passed the midpoint of their delivery route, and wouldn't pick up their return cargo of raw materials for a couple stops yet. Not the worst place to hunker down and hide, but nearly.

Behind her there were more options, true, but they included both the docking port, DCC, and the barracks, all of which she was certain held boarders.

She rounded the last corner to the merc's barracks and armory only to flinch back as several bullets whizzed around her. They smashed the lighting unit on the far wall, sparks flying as small bits of the composite cover splintered. With her heart pounding almost out of her chest it took a few moments to realize that it had been a regular bullet, not a penetrator or HV dart.

"Are you a pirate or one of the Aegis Mercs?" she shouted, pressing herself up against the wall for at least an illusion of cover.

Whoever was around the corner actually laughed. "Wouldn't I say I am either way? Pirates aren't exactly known for truthfulness."

Right. That wasn't the stupidest thing she'd done that day, or even in the last hour. The trend was troubling.

"Fine. What's the name of the ship's doctor?" Morgan figured the pirates might know the captain's name, but the doctor was less likely.

"Uh, isn't her name Carson?"

Okay. He was a merc. Something else occurred to her, "So why'd you shoot at me? I'm wearing a TMH skinsuit."

"I couldn't see you very well, I shot above your head to force you back while I figured out which side you're on."

Morgan walked around the corner, hands on her hips. "Well that was irresponsible of you, wasn't it?"

"I'm not the one wandering around the corridors when we're under attack. Now get behind me."

The armory was a chokepoint by design, sitting at the top of a T intersection that led to most off the rest of the ship, and holding almost all the weapons on board. At some point, probably all the way back when the room was made into an armory, they had put up barricades in all three branches with a fourth curved one just in front of the door. The merc, who Morgan had not seen before, was the only person in view. His brown mottled skinsuit helpfully indicated his name was Hudson. His helmet was down, showing a young face, maybe early twenties, tan, with dark fuzz for hair and deep brown eyes.

He was rather cute, actually.

"Where are the rest of you?"

"Out securing the ship." He rolled his eyes.

"And they left you here alone?"

"They're sweeping out from this position. I'm just here as backup. We're a little shorthanded here on account of so many of the guys helping with the unloading. Plus, the other marines who were supposed to be here are cut off right now, blasted shift change. I'm it for now. Now please stop talking and get behind me."

Morgan complied, huffing sullenly. "Can I have a rifle?"

"Darlin', even if I had the codes for the armory that is about the last thing I would do."

Morgan harrumphed. "Fine. I'll just use mine." And she pulled the compact pistol out from her hip pouch, a pair of spare magazines from the left.

She could practically hear his eyebrow go up. "What's a brand new tech doing carrying that around?"

"Seems to me that I have it *for situations just like this.*"

"Fair enough. You shoot me in the back I will haunt you."

"Fair enough," Morgan echoed, not quite keeping the disdain out of her voice. Who was he to question her competence? Sure, she was a mechanic and not a shooter like he was, but she'd practiced as often as time (and money) allowed. What use was the thing if she wasn't ready to use it?

"Leave the spares in your suit, if you need to move you won't have time to grab them off of the barricade."

"Oh, yeah," Morgan said, scooping them up sheepishly.

"Just make sure you aim for the head – the faceplate if they have helmets up – or guys not in suits. That little thing won't do anything to a skinsuit."

Morgan actually managed a short laugh. "You sure about that?" She put the pistol carefully down on top of the barricade, the barrel pointed at the wall, then thumbed the top bullet out of a spare magazine. "These will do the job." She held it out for him to look at.

He took the bullet from her, glanced it over, then handed it back with a whistle.

"Girl, where did you get the money for Iridium Specials?"

"I will *not* be defenseless. There weren't many other options."

"Nah, I suppose not. You're so tiny trying to hide a PR pistol is just silly. What are you, twelve?"

"Twenty-one, Earth years." Morgan replaced the bullet in the magazine, then picked the pistol back up. Was he trying to insult her, saying he thought she was that young? Sure, she wasn't twenty-one, but she *was* seventeen, close enough to a legal adult as to make no difference.

Five minutes went by with no one else coming their way. Then ten. She could still hear gunshots coming from all around them, but they were coming in controlled bursts rather than continuous hails.

Morgan was finding it harder and harder to just sit there, not knowing what was happening. She had started to ask a question several times, but Hudson had shushed her immediately. Finally, she couldn't take it anymore and blurted out, "What's going on? Are we winning, are we losing?"

"If I answer will you keep quiet?"

"Sure."

"From what I can hear of the com chatter through the jamming we've secured half of the ship. It looks like they hold half of the station right now though, and we're badly outnumbered. . . " A shot rang out from all the way down the hall, and Hudson ducked, one arm pushing her down with him.

"Pirates," he mouthed to her, then shifted about to get a better firing angle."

Clutching her pistol tightly Morgan moved to get her whole body behind the barrier on that side of the intersection, careful to keep her finger off of the trigger. She hadn't been able to practice as much on the station, since she'd had to keep an eye on Haruhi. On board the *Fate of Dawn*, though, it had been easy to get time in at the small range they maintained, mostly for the mercs' use. Despite that, she was finding it hard to remember the training and advice through the adrenaline and the rapid fluttering of her heart.

A head appeared around the corner at the far end of the corridor, pulled back quickly as Hudson let of a single shot from his rifle. This time it was a PR round, the charge blowing a ragged hole in the bulkhead at the corner. Morgan winced. There were going to be so many things to fix tomorrow.

A few moments passed, then several rifles stuck out awkwardly into the corridor, literally firing blind at the lone merc. Hudson seemed to be content to let them waste their shots and he motioned again for Morgan to stay low. The barricade shuddered under the impacts, but it was designed with explosive rounds in mind, and it held.

The sheer noise level was something Morgan hadn't counted on, however. Within moments all she could hear was the ringing in her ears. With her free hand she awkwardly hit the buttons to manually deploy suit's helmet.

Silently, the folded collar of her suit slid upwards hood-like as it deployed into the flexible yet tough helmet. The segmented clear faceplate slid down and snapped into place with a hiss as the suit's oxygen systems came online.

During a pause in the fire, Hudson cupped his mic in one hand and said, "I've got a couple tangos poking their noses around the armory, approaching from the starboard. I'm fine for the moment, but if they try and flank me. . ." He paused, listening to someone on the other end. "Roger that, dispatch. Five minutes. Be advised, I have one crewwoman here with me, and she is armed." Another pause. "No of course I didn't give her a weapon. Crazy little thing brought her own."

"Hey!" Morgan cried out, ducking involuntarily as a dart pinged off the top of the barrier.

"I copy. Backup will approach from the stern. Hudson, clear."

"They're sending more people?" Morgan asked, trying her uplink com into his headset.

"Yeah. Keep your head down. We'll be fine." He returned fire at them, either to keep them from trying to peer around and aim, or try and hit the ends of the guns, Morgan wasn't sure.

Morgan put her back to the barrier, pulling her legs up to her chest, resting the gun on her knees carefully pointed away from Hudson. There was a bit of movement down the hall in front of her. Wait, he had said they would be coming from the stern, not port. . .

"Behind you!" Morgan yelled, throwing herself back towards the final barrier in front of the door where she could get at least some protection from both sides. She wanted to just shoot at them, but she wasn't sure which side they were on.

Apparently Hudson didn't have that problem. He only took a single look before sending a full-auto burst whizzing down the hallway with the newcomers. Instead of pulling back this new group just kept coming forward, even as the group to starboard intensified their fire. Morgan didn't dare move to get a better look, but there were at least four or five of them, large imposing shapes in red colored skinsuits. No helmets though. She wondered why they weren't wearing them, and why Hudson wasn't either.

Morgan hadn't handled anything like his rifle before, but she definitely wanted a look after this. She hadn't seen him change magazines yet but he was easily switching between normal and PR rounds and single fire, burst, and fully automatic.

"Ah, crap." Hudson said, putting down his rifle for a moment to pull something off his belt.

"Is that a grenade? Are you insane?" Morgan asked, leaning to one side to shoot two rounds towards the starboard group now that he had stopped keeping their heads down.

She hadn't actually fired any of the IS rounds before. The recoil was noticeably greater than with the practice rounds, enough that the second round put a neat hole into the ceiling rather than the end of the corridor. The sound was drastically different too. Much more high pitched for one thing.

"You have a better idea?" He said, poking a couple buttons on the grenade before pulling the pin. . .

. . .And promptly getting shot in the shoulder, a lucky ricochet from who-knows-where. It didn't look like it had breached his armor, but the force and surprise were enough to knock him about a bit. The grenade dropped from his hand bouncing a foot or so away as he stumbled. Oh, she was going to die, she was going to die and she didn't even know why the pirates were here.

That was the loudest voice in Morgan's head. It wasn't the calmest though. Her eyes firmly on the grenade Morgan lunged forward, her fingers missing it as she fell almost onto it. Shaking she scooped it up, standing up fully as she flung it towards the bow as hard as she could.

Time seemed to slow, the grenade tumbling end over end from her clumsy throw. Somehow it flew straight enough, actually hitting the lead pirate right in his mustachioed mouth. His face erupted in blood as it dropped to the floor at his feet. "Oh sh. . ." was all he got out before the grenade detonated, Morgan only thinking to drop down to the ground at the last instant. She had expected a fireball, a huge sound, something flashy, but apparently it wasn't like in the vids.

There was a single thud, loud to be sure, but only a bit louder through her helmet's noise reduction than the shots had been. The walls and ground shook, just a little bit, she probably wouldn't have noticed at all if she hadn't been hugging the ground with all her might. The fire from the other corridor stopped. They probably were pulling back in case he had another grenade ready. Morgan grabbed the rifle, moving to cover the starboard corridor, then realized that she didn't know the first thing about it. She put it back down and trained her pistol around the edge of the barrier instead.

"You okay?" she whispered, not daring to look, at least not yet.

"Armor stopped it," he said, and she could hear him start to get up off the floor. "Nice work with the grenade, I could kiss you."

"Yeah. You got this?" Morgan asked, not daring to comment about the offered kiss one way or another.

"We're in trouble if they decide to come at us from both angles again."

"Can I hope that you have more of those grenades?"

"You can hope, Darlin', but that won't add to my empty belt. All the rest are in the armory."

"How are you for ammo?"

"Well, that depends on how many targets show up."

"That low?"

"It's not as much as I could wish for, no."

"We'd have better cover inside the armory. Ammo too."

Hudson shook his head. "I wasn't kidding when I said I don't have the codes. They won't transmit them to me with the enemy close enough to intercept it either. We only need to hold out a few minutes more. We'll be fine."

The universe being what it was, that was the precise moment five more pirates showed up.

Morgan squeezed off the rest of the magazine towards the newcomers. Slow, aimed shots that failed to do more than force them back around the corner. Hudson fired at the other three. She couldn't spare the second to look, but it sounded like he hit at least one of them. Surprisingly, the pirate's scream was audible over the gunfire. That woman sure had a loud voice.

"Can you cover me?" Morgan asked, stuffing the empty magazine in her suit before sliding a new one in.

"Not for long, especially if you're doing something stupid."

"We need to get in there. I'm going to persuade the door."

"I'm sorry, I heard you say you're going to 'persuade the door.'"

"That's right, can you cover me?"

He shook his head, "You'll never be able to hack the door. We used military grade encryption. Even if you could, I don't think I could hold back both groups at once."

"Well, let's fix that second problem then," Morgan said with much more confidence than she felt, "And I'm not going to hack the computer system."

Shots were still pinging off of the barricade steadily, as well as more than a few thumps from the explosive rounds. Pieces of the barricade started breaking off, chips and splinters bounced off of everything, including their suits. One collided with Hudson's cheek, leaving a small cut. He grimaced, but otherwise ignored it.

Morgan took in a deep breath, trying to calm herself. She needed steady hands for this, both for aiming and what came after. Five, maybe four, to port. Probably only two to starboard.

She waited for Hudson to fire, then glanced around the corner and took the time to look. One pirate was lying in the hallway, unmoving. Judging by figure it was the woman she'd heard scream earlier.

Morgan crouched down farther, propping her elbow on her knee to steady her hands even further.

"I'm going to let up, get them to think I'm reloading. Wait for them to come more into view before firing."

"And what will you be doing?"

"Reloading."

Morgan focused intently on the corner they were hiding behind. She tuned out the sounds of gunfire from behind then, edging closer. She ignored her sweaty palms in her suit gloves, her ragged breathing, even the pounding of her pulse in her ears. All that mattered was that corner.

Hudson pulled back, the empty magazine clattering to the ground at their feet. No wonder he'd lasted so long on a single magazine; it alone was far larger than her whole gun. Morgan could see him tugging a fresh one out of his boot, but still she focused on the corner.

First a barrel appeared, firing a couple shots blindly. No reply. A head popped out. Morgan leaned to the side, getting as much of her small frame behind the barricade as possible, but gave no reply.

She waited agonizing seconds as the two pirates cautiously came out into the corridor. The fire from the port slackened. Morgan figured they were being careful not to run afoul of friendly fire. When they were ten meters forward of the corner Morgan fired.

The first shot struck the closer pirate squarely in the chest. He screamed and fell to one knee, but didn't fall.

If there was one major drawback to the Iridium Specials, besides the small bullet size, it was the fact that so much was focused on penetrating the armor the bullet didn't deform at all once it did.

Even now, centuries upon centuries later, standard bullets were made primarily out of lead. Sure, it was cheap and easy to work with, but mostly it was because lead flattened and spread out when it hit someone, causing more damage. Either way all a bullet really did was poke a hole in someone. If you didn't hit any organs or cause enough shock damage, the wound was only fatal quickly through blood loss.

Given the choices of bouncing rounds uselessly off of the armor and making smaller holes the choice was obvious.

The solution to the problem was also obvious. More holes. So Morgan shot him again. It wasn't hard, in that he was now that much closer and no longer moving, but at the same time it was one of the hardest things Morgan had done.

When she had thrown the grenade at the pirates it had been instinctual, more reflex than anything else. Now she was coolly and coldly shooting someone whose face she could see, whose eyes she could look into.

Sure, he was trying to hurt or kill her, but he was still a person.

All of this ran through her head in less than a second. The second bullet hit him a bit higher than the first, and a bit to the right. His cry cut off into a ragged gasp. Maybe she hit a lung or something. He fell, still writhing and moaning, but clearly not an immediate threat.

Meanwhile Hudson had gotten his rifle reloaded, and his first shot hit the last pirate to starboard just above the collar of her suit.

It had been a penetrator round. The suit wasn't effected much by the explosion, though the penetrator did punch through. Her faceplate, on the other hand?

Morgan closed her eyes to the sight, but not fast enough.

Later. She could deal with that later. For the moment they were clear to starboard and within seconds Hudson had reengaged the pirates to port. Right now she had to deal with the door.

Hands shaking, she put the safety back on her pistol and slid it into the holster in her suit pocket. From a thin pouch on her thigh she pulled out her lucky spanner and went to work on the panel beneath the armory's sophisticated lock.

"You'll never get it open," Hudson said over his shoulder as the last bolt fell and she yanked the panel free. He was taking more risks now, standing next to the barricade, his rifle braced along the top of it. He had forced the pirates back around the corner, but it also left a lot more of him exposed to their fire. He barked a command and his helmet deployed itself. It was slightly different from hers, with a much smaller viewport in the faceplate.

Maybe that was why he hadn't deployed it before? Because it interfered with vision and hearing? Morgan idly thought to herself that she'd have to rig her suit to give her voice control over the helmet.

"Stop worrying about me and start worrying about them."

Really, the task before her was quite straightforward. The question wasn't 'how do you defeat the security lock' but the much simpler, 'under what circumstances would the door open anyway?'

The most obvious was an emergency situation, something requiring evacuation of the ship.

It wasn't as simple as that, of course. If the computer thought the room was empty it wouldn't open up even in an emergency, and it was also designed to double check any sensor triggering said emergency with the rest of the ship.

So straightforward, but not easy.

The first thing to do was to convince the computer that the room was occupied. Morgan dug around in the wiring and encased nano-circuit boards, more by feel than sight, until she found the heat sensors. She couldn't do anything to the system directly, unfortunately. It was notoriously hard to manipulate molecule thick boards at the best of times, after all.

The normal cables linking systems together though? Those were designed to be user friendly.

Morgan pulled out a small knife and began cutting and splicing the wires. It was trickier with her gloves on, but there was too much active current in there to risk taking them off.

A few judicious changes later and the computer was convinced that the armory was occupied by two people, and the corridor empty. Amazing what you could do simply by swapping inputs.

Disabling the damage control system in such a way that it thought it was still working was distressingly easy. Morgan supposed they had put all their effort into protecting against the ways it could become damaged and non-responsive rather than worrying about how it could be intentionally circumvented. Something else to look into later, it seemed.

The last step, triggering the emergency, could have been as simple as triggering an alarm. That was a bad plan, however, since it would be ship-wide, and any areas the pirates were locked out of would suddenly become vulnerable, including the bridge.

Morgan certainly wanted to live, but not if it meant putting everyone else at risk to do it. Besides, it wouldn't do her any good if she got this door open and the rest of the pirates captured the ship anyway. So, she had to sever the local alarm system from the main hub. She was up to her elbows in the wall, making a fine mess of the cables and various circuit board boxes. Finding the armory's hub took her a bit, her own fault really since she'd been shoving things out of place.

Then she just had to follow the cables back to the relay hub. . .

. . .and her hands ran smack into the wall where the cable disappeared into the space running under the door.

Well, things had been going her way so well, it was certainly time for something to go wrong. She yanked the alarm box forward until it was at the front, then scrambled over to the other side of the door, right where Hudson was standing.

"Coming through," she said, crawling between his legs so she could get to the bolts holding the paneling in place.

"What in the galaxy are you doin', Darlin'?"

"Working," Morgan grunted. "Just be glad the armory wasn't part of the original ship design. I doubt this would work otherwise."

A dart ricocheted off the floor next to Morgan's knee, causing Morgan to flinch back instinctively. It was amazing how quickly she'd been able to tune out the sounds of gunfire. Adrenaline sure had some funny effects on the body.

Why were they even bothering with the gas rifles? They were both in skinsuits, after all.

Pushing that random thought aside Morgan got back to work on the panel. Once off she started in on the bundle of cables. They were labeled, but reading them under present conditions wasn't a quick process.

Yellow, yellow, yellow, why were so many of the cables yellow? Did the designers have something against red or blue? Ah. There is was, the orange of the emergency system. Morgan reached for her knife, realizing she'd left it on the other side.

Grumbling under her breath she slid out from under Hudson and scooted over to grab it. He had started saying something, but she couldn't make out the words. She was almost afraid to ask, and she definitely was afraid to look over to see where the pirates were.

"What are you saying?" She asked as she got back into position.

"What?" He said, almost absently, momentarily ducking down as he reloaded.

"What are you saying?"

"Sorry, wasn't talking to you. Don't worry about it."

"You're not cracking are you?"

"No I was just. . . I was just praying."

"What?" Morgan had gotten the first couple cables bypassed, only three more to go. She was slowing down, too many things to align, too many different feeds, power lines to leave intact.

"You know, praying?"

"Is now really the time to talk to someone you can't even see?" Morgan asked, not looking up from the cables.

"Yes, it is," Hudson said while firing a couple shots down the hallway. Morgan heard the end of a scream at the tail end of the boom of a penetrator. "This is my last magazine. If I run out you need to be ready to cover us as we pull back to the other end of the hall."

"Never mind that," Morgan grunted. "Last cable."

"And what, the door just opens?"

"No, then I go back over to the alarm and trip it manually. *Then* the door opens."

The incoming fire intensified, enough so that even Morgan noticed lying on the corridor floor with her head and shoulders shoved into the wall. More bits and pieces were coming off of the barricade as well.

Morgan slid out, remembering to shove the knife hastily in a pocket this time.

"Right, now I just need to. . ." she said as a chunk of barricade was blown off of the top edge, violently slamming into the alarm's box. The jagged chunk of reinforced ceramic armor buried itself at least halfway into the box. Morgan supposed it sparked and crackled as the boards fried, but she couldn't hear it over everything else.

She slumped back against the barricade, half standing, staring at it dumbly.

"What happened?" Hudson called over his shoulder. He only fired his rifle once, and not even a penetrator as far as Morgan could tell. He had to be getting low on ammo.

"Shrapnel. Took out the system."

"So fix it. We're in a spot of trouble here if you can't."

"I can't fix it. Even if I had a machine shop it'd be faster to just build a new one. I can't get the door open."

"Think, girl. You came this far, there has to be a way."

Morgan thought, frantically tearing through her brain for a way to trigger the alarm. She could probably get the next alarm panel triggered, but that would just set off the whole system. There was no way she could repeat the modification, not out in the open in the corridor. If she had time, time when she wasn't being shot at, she could yank the system out entirely down the line and replace the box here, but she might as well wish her uplink could turn its hologram display into an x-ray laser.

Uplink. There was something there, but Morgan couldn't quite grasp it. Her mind was muddled, flooded with fear and the ringing of her ears, adrenalin and the panic that was threatening to overwhelm her.

So much hardware in there, and she couldn't change any of it. . .

. . .but she could change her uplink.

Tearing it off her wrist so she could use both hands Morgan pulled up the holo display, the full controls. There was already a program built in to warn of emergencies, designed to tie in to a city's automatic network. It wasn't used much on a ship, but the program was still there.

"Darlin', you got something?" Hudson hunched back down, leaning his rifle against the wall.

"Almost," Morgan answered automatically.

Hudson yanked off his glove and roughly shoved his large hand into her suit's pockets, grabbing first her pistol, then the remaining full spare magazines.

"Whoa," Morgan said, dropping the uplink.

"Sorry, but I need these more than you at the moment. I also didn't want to interrupt you."

"Ask. Ask next time. You did just fine interrupting me as it is."

"Be quick," he said, standing back up and firing at the pirates. "I'm not so good with pistols I've never fired before."

Morgan didn't bother picking up the uplink; the holo-keys had helpfully adjusted to stay in easy reach. Her fingers flew across the air, only the dull flashing of the keys letting her know what buttons she was pushing. She was risking making a mistake, going so fast, but there just wasn't time.

Falling to her knees Morgan shoved the uplink onto the shrapnel jutting out of the box, a most inconvenient-yet-convenient hook. The cables she'd already spliced came free with a simple hard yank, and she roughly shoved the appropriate bits into the inputs of the uplink.

"If this doesn't work now it never will," she called out to Hudson.

"Just do it."

Mashing the physical button just below the screen Morgan wondered if it was comforting to have something to pray to. She was trusting in nothing beyond her own skills and luck. Quite a sick feeling, knowing that live or die was all down to her actions of the last few minutes.

The speakers above the door tried to come on, blaring their siren, but it just sparked and died. It had taken too many bits of shrapnel, too many bullets, even for something that sturdy by design.

No matter though, the door opened. Morgan dived forward, rolling around and grabbing the rifle from where it leaned next to the door.

"Hudson, get in here!" She shouted.

He stumbled back, catching himself on the rack of shelves that was just inside the door to one side.

"Close it," he said. He tossed Morgan her pistol, the slide locked open on an empty magazine. He snatched up the rifle, grabbing one of the full magazines off of the rack.

"I can't. It will take hours to fix all the things I broke to get it open in the first place."

Hudson grunted. "I was afraid you'd say that. Plan B then."

He grabbed two small spherical grenades from the different rows of the rack opposite the rifles and magazines. His visor turned opaque, and he activated the first grenade.

"You'd better polarize your visor. They'll be trying to box us in quick. I'm going to have to just roll the flashbang out the door, then jump out and throw the frag while they're disoriented."

"Just do it."

"Visor," he repeated, then gently rolled the first grenade out so it was between the doorway and the barricade. Instantly gunfire erupted from down the hallway, the pirates either firing at the movement or actually attempting to hit the grenade, Morgan couldn't tell.

She looked away and got her visor polarized just before the grenade detonated, but for a moment she wasn't sure she had. The flash was still bright enough that her eyes hurt, and it sounded like the noise had actually blown out the pickups of her suit, that or it did just sound like an overwhelming screech of static and electronic noise.

Shaking her head for several seconds in a futile attempt to clear her head she finally she just retracted her helmet. Nope. Speakers were working fine. Her ears on the other hand. . .

When she looked back around Hudson had already picked back up his rifle, though she hadn't heard the second grenade go off, let alone notice him throw it.

"I need to go check. I can't risk them getting all the way up to the door."

"I should. . . "

"No, you should stay here."

"I'm not waiting around doing nothing but be helpless."

"Fine. Stay close, and don't shoot unless I do. Backup should have been here already. Hopefully they aren't far away."

"Did you at least leave me any of my ammo?"

Hudson's head twitched. She couldn't tell with the visor darkened, but it looked like he'd rolled his eyes. He shifted his rifle into a one handed grip and fished a magazine out of a pouch.

"Last one, I'm afraid." He glanced down at Morgan's face and added with a chuckle, "Feel free to bill Aegis later."

Hudson leaned up against the doorway, tapping a few holographic buttons on his uplink. Now that she could see it more closely, it looked like it was a military model, though newer than hers was.

"Too many heat sources out there. I can't get a good reading." He stuck the arm with the uplink out the door, out and then back in.

"Ugh. I don't think we need to worry, at least for the moment. We're clear. You. . . you probably should just wait here for a bit. It's not a pretty sight."

Hudson cocked his head, clearly listening to a com line Morgan wasn't included in.

"This part of the ship is secure. Friendlies will be here in fifteen seconds."

Morgan plopped down against a bare patch of wall. "Oh, sure. Now they hurry."

"Don't go looking for dark clouds to that silver lining."

"I have no idea what that means."

"It means you're safe. Celebrate rather than complain," a woman said from the doorway. In her merc skinsuit, helmet deployed and visor darkened, all Morgan could tell about her was that she was large, easily twice Morgan's mass. Her nameplate read 'Marigold.'

"Lieutenant," Hudson said, shouldering his rifle on his left side while saluting with his right hand. "Armory is secure, ma'am."

"I can see that corporal. I'm sure the explanation as to why the wall is opened up and strewn about will be amazing. Not to mention the uplink that is warning me that there is a hull breech in here and that I should evacuate.

Right. Morgan couldn't hear the alarm since she no longer had an uplink to hear it with. She probably should get it pulled out of the systems, but suddenly she was feeling quite queasy.

"Is it all over then?" Morgan asked.

"Station security is done with the fighting on their side, but the ship is only *mostly* clear," the lieutenant answered, shaking her head slightly. Morgan was sure she'd have more than a few uncomfortable questions to answer herself, not to mention a massive amount of repair work, but later would have to take care of itself. Right now she felt like she needed to sleep for a day or three.

"Good." Morgan hunched over more, pulling her knees up to her chest. She leaned to one side and threw up noisily, more than once. "You still want that kiss, Hudson?"

CHAPTER 17

Hiring mercenaries is either a wise decision or a suicidally stupid one. Trouble is, there is no way to tell the difference until after you're committed. Will the company fold under pressure? Will they stay fast as long as the money lasts? What happens after?

- Exchequer Milton Tannenbaum, Third Baron of the Kaldon, Her Majesty's Government of Holding

HUDSON DIDN'T, though not for the reason Morgan would have assumed. If Morgan had been a guy, well, that would have been a different story.

There wasn't any time to relax though. They weren't out of danger just yet.

While the mercenaries present gathered the weapons – and covered the bodies – of the dead pirates, Morgan got her uplink back and got it set back to normal.

"Can I get tied into your communication network, just for the time being?"

"'Fraid not, Darlin'," Hudson said, shaking his head, "Non-military uplinks don't have the encryption capability we use for the network."

"My uplink is military. A bit older, but military."

"Let me see that," the lieutenant cut in, holding out her hand for the uplink, her helmet retracting as she did so. The face behind the helmet was worn and lined, both by age and by scars. Her hair was barely more than stubble, dark brown liberally mixed with grey.

Morgan handed it over, watching the woman turn it over. Her reactions were impossible to read.

"And where does a young mechanic such as yourself come across an Albion Special Forces issue uplink?" the lieutenant asked, inputting some commands Morgan couldn't follow in both Morgan's and her own uplinks.

"A gift from a friend."

"You have some very good, very interesting friends. Their name?"

"Lady Novan."

"Indeed?" Marigold's voice didn't waver one bit, but one eyebrow crept upward ever so slightly.

"And here I thought describing women as a mystery was mostly exaggeration," Hudson said with a low whistle. "Or is it just you, Darlin'?"

The lieutenant handed back the uplink.

"I've tied you in to our network. Don't speak unless it is absolutely necessary."

Morgan reconnected the uplink to her suit, then deployed her helmet so she could hear the mercenaries' communications, as at some point her ear piece had gone missing.

It was quieter than she would have imagined, with only brief bursts of chatter as one group or another reported in. Much of it she didn't understand, references to tangos and numbers, along with what sounded like shorthand for the different parts of the ship. Judging by their tone of voice a couple of the people talking were actively firing at someone, but all she could hear was their voice, none of the gunfire or other noises of battle were carried over the line.

Then the captain's voice came on over the system, jarring in its difference from the disciplined mercenaries.

"You need to get your troops up to the bridge *now*. We just had a bunch of these blasted pirates get past your oh–so-effective barricade. If I had sealed the bridge even a moment later they would have taken control of the ship."

"And my men?" another voice asked. It wasn't one Morgan recognized, presumably the commander of the mercenary forces.

"I don't know. Only one of them was on the bridge proper."

There was a long moment of silence.

"I see," the commander said.

"Clear the channels, everyone. You too, Captain."

This was done in moments.

"Lieutenant Marigold, leave one person to guard the armory, and bring everyone else you can to the bridge. Lieutenant Jacobs, Lieutenant Kaldrin, leave a three-man team at your checkpoints and do likewise with the remainder of your combat capables. Everyone else push hard to get the rest of them accounted for."

Five quick affirmatives and the com line went quiet again.

Morgan looked up to see the lieutenant looking at her.

"Have you fired rifles before?"

"Not nearly as much as my pistol, but I do have experience with the NCR-7."

"The NCR? Not a shotgun, or a hunting rifle, but the standard infantry rifle?"

"Yeah. Larry liked them, let me borrow his from time to time. Is that a problem?"

"No, just another oddity about you. Never mind. It doesn't matter. Hudson, get her a rifle."

"Right." He walked over to the rack, picking up a slimmer rifle than the one he carried. "This isn't as advanced as what you've used, or even our normal gear for that matter, but we don't have time to familiarize you with that. But it isn't *too* different from the NCR."

Hudson made a big show of taking the safety off, reengaging it, then handing the rifle to Morgan, the barrel pointed straight up.

"It is semi-automatic, with penetrator rounds." He handed her a thin, long magazine to Morgan, showing her how to seat it. "You'll need to reload often since the magazine is a single stack. As big as it is, it still only holds fifteen rounds."

"I'd need spare magazines for that," Morgan pointed out.

"Yeah, yeah, keep your skirt on, Darlin'." Hudson next grabbed a belt with three magazines stuck into slots on each side. He deftly slung it around Morgan's middle, the belt's magnetic clasp automatically latching closed on contact.

"Just remember, don't point it at anything you like, and don't fire if your target is too close to a friendly."

"Right." Morgan didn't feel like telling him she knew all of this. Safety was important, even when doing things that were decidedly unsafe. Given how many grenades the mercenaries were adding to their belts Morgan hoped they believed in safety too.

"Crewman Black, your job will be watching our backs. We should be clear from here to the bridge, but I never much cared for should. We'll need to move quickly. If you see anyone coming up on our flanks or rear, tell us before engaging. Do not fire at any hostiles in front of us unless I tell you to."

"Wouldn't it be better to leave me here? You could bring another trained mercenary with you."

Marigold shook her head.

"Better to have the weak link with the larger group. As it is I'm only bringing you at all because I need to leave two people here. The commander doesn't know the door is non-operable and now isn't the time to tell him." Marigold turned to the other mercenaries with her. "Numen, Ortiz, you're staying here. Check your targets, but don't be afraid to use grenades. The armory is vulnerable. Act accordingly."

Nodding, the two mercenaries took up positions on either side of the room, crouching behind the weapon racks that looked like they could easily double as barricades. Ortiz got his rifle ready while Numen carefully pulled the last few grenades off the rack she was behind, placing them on another rack farther back in the room.

"Let's move out. If they manage to take the bridge we're in trouble."

"I'm sure we can take it back before they figure out the codes, sir," one of the mercs said.

"Possibly, Private, but more importantly if they take the bridge we're likely to lose our contract when the dust settles. Little things like letting officers get captured or killed tends to spook companies."

Morgan suppressed the desire to snort in amusement, but only just. Somehow she doubted the lieutenant would have been quite so blunt if any of the merchant officers had been present. For her part, Morgan had no interest in repeating what she'd said to anyone later. She appreciated the confidence that they'd live to worry about such things, and it wasn't like she was wrong anyway.

With that Marigold, Hudson, and the other three mercenaries started out, Morgan trailing behind a few paces.

✱✱✱

The quick march to the bridge – or rather the corridor a hundred meters away from it – went fast and without incident, leaving Morgan wondering why they'd even bothered to bring her along. From the chatter she could hear through the merc's communication's net it was clear they had a good idea where all the remaining pirates were onboard, and most of the crew too.

Morgan could hear the pirates ahead of them from quite a long way back. It sounded like they were hitting the bulkhead leading into the bridge with everything they could in an attempt to breach it. Even with her helmet's noise cancellation turned all the way up Morgan could still hear very little other than the repeated explosions and concussions against the metal.

"Do we give them a chance to surrender?" Hudson asked on their subgroup of the com system as they reached the last turn in the corridor before they would be visible to the attackers.

This actually elicited a couple laughs from the other nearby mercenaries.

"Cute, Hudson. Perhaps we should invite them to tea while we're at it?"

Morgan didn't know who had said it, not that it mattered.

"Cut the chatter," Marigold said. "Game faces on. If they drop their weapons quick enough, great. We're not going to give them a chance to turn on fire on us first. If we can get the element of surprise, we take it." The lieutenant switched from their group channel to the main one. "Marigold here, we're in position."

"Jacobs here, we're pinned down at juncture A-3."

"Kaldrin, we're clear, but something caused hydroponics to seal itself off. We'll have to work our way around, maybe five minutes."

The commander was the next person to address them.

"Marigold, do you have enough with you to take the bridge on your own?"

"I only have five of our people, along with an armed crewman. Do we have any intel on the numbers we'll be facing?"

"They took out the cameras pretty quick, but it looks to be fifteen to twenty tangos." It wasn't the commander, but another female voice Morgan didn't recognize. Presumably whoever they had managing the surveillance on the ship.

"That's pretty steep odds, even with the element of surprise."

"Steep odds or not, can you do it?"

"Weapons-free?"

"Affirmative."

Marigold was quiet for a moment as she thought about it.

"We can do it, or at least buy the captain enough time for someone else to get here and finish up."

As scary as that statement was for Morgan – the willingness to go out there and pick a fight while outnumbered – it was the way she said it, completely without emotion, that was even more chilling.

Morgan toggled to a private channel so only Marigold would hear.

"You want to go out there and attack, three of them for each of us, without any cover?"

"What I want is irrelevant. It is what we *must* do."

"And you expect me to do the same?"

"Yes," was her blunt reply. "Without you the odds are even worse. If we fail, what is likely to happen to you and the rest of the crew?"

"Didn't you just say the others would get here in time?"

"I lied. If we fail, the pirates can likely take the grenades off of us and breach the bridge."

Morgan felt another deep chill at this simple statement.

"You're no coward, Crewman Black. Your actions at the armory show that. You can do this. You can help save the ship."

Morgan swallowed hard. The deep chill coiled around her stomach making her wish she could throw up again.

"I. . ." she paused. Could she do it? Should she do it? "Okay. What do you need from me?"

Instead of responding directly Marigold switched channels so the group could hear her.

"There isn't time for anything elegant. We toss flashbangs, then a mix of concussion and frag grenades. Two seconds after we rush the corridor and shoot everything."

Marigold let the murmurs die down before she continued.

"For the newbie's benefit I'll spell out how we're going to do that. We're coming at the corridor from the side, and don't want to mess up each other's field of fire. The first three out will turn, step forward a pace, and crouch down to fire, the first turning immediately, the second after two meters, and the third after four. The three after that will take up position two meters behind the first three, offset by a meter. Crewman Black, you'll be the last out, meaning you will be standing a meter to the side of the last crouching shooter."

The explanation was followed by a series of hand gestures that the other mercenaries clearly understood perfectly well, as they nodded and started preparing. Two started pulling grenades from their belts while a third edged towards the corner, extending a small sensor out to get a better idea where the pirates were. He activated a holodisplay that showed the pirates clustered in the middle of the corridor, enough so that, with the addition of a fair bit of haze and smoke from the explosions and so forth, it was hard to tell exactly how many there were.

It did seem to Morgan that fifteen was on the low side of likely, but the mercenaries didn't seem bothered by the numbers. They just started lining up a bit back from the turn in the corridor in two rows, the front two the mercenaries with the grenades.

Morgan took her place at the back of the second row, her rifle carefully pointed down at the ground and not at the two people in front of her.

They waited.

Nervously Morgan checked the magazines on each side of the belt, making sure they were loose enough to be grabbed easily, but not so loose that they risked falling out. Next, Morgan checked her pistol in her pocket, still in easy reach with her last magazine loaded and ready to go. Finally she thumbed off the safety on the rifle, only taking a moment longer because of the unfamiliarity of the weapon.

Marigold tapped the lead mercenary of the right row on the shoulder. He nodded and held up a hand, counting down from five. Suddenly Morgan realized that she'd already tuned out the loud noises of the explosions and gunfire from the pirates attempting to breach the bulkhead.

If only it were as easy to ignore the pounding of her heart.

The count reached zero.

The grenades were softly tossed around the corner, rolling forward until they exploded. As before the sound was much less than Morgan had expected, barely noticeable over the racket the pirates were putting up.

The same mercenary held up two fingers, then one, and then surged forward with a closed fist held up.

Morgan was so focused on following the back in front of her and not tripping over her own feet that she didn't see anything that was happening. The mercenary in front of her turned and stepped forward, so abruptly – from her point of view – that she almost collided with him.

She managed to catch herself, as well as complete her own turn a few steps farther on.

The scene she was presented with was chaotic. There were too many pirates still standing for a quick count, along with a jumble of shapes on the floor. The smoke hanging in the air seemed to be tinged red, though Morgan convinced herself it was her imagination.

Morgan brought her rifle up sighting through its simple iron sights at the nearest moving shape in front of her. She tried to squeeze the trigger, but hesitation stayed her hand just long enough that one of the other mercenaries fired first, sending the pirate sprawling with an ugly ragged hole in her back. Morgan fought the urge to close her eyes.

The pirates weren't surprised anymore. They were turning around, their weapons coming up.

Morgan aimed at another pirate, her hesitation slightly more pronounced this time as she looked into the face – or at least the visor – of the pirate. He was bringing his rifle around, his first shot going short into the floor in front of the mercenaries. A small piece of the flooring bounced off Morgan's ankle, the blow enough to startle Morgan out of her shock.

Again resisting the urge to close her eyes, Morgan squeezed off one round, her aim with the unfamiliar weapon slightly off, her shot going high over the pirate's shoulder.

Everyone was firing now, mercenaries and pirates. Morgan fired again at the pirate she was aiming at, missing by less this time. Before she could correct her aim and fire again someone else hit that pirate, so Morgan moved onto another target.

A bullet struck her in the knee. Luckily it wasn't a penetrator round, so it only stung slightly, barely noticeable amongst the pumping adrenaline, the pit in her stomach, and terror in her breast. Morgan wasn't even really aware of the mercenaries or any of the sounds around her. There were the pirates, her, and her rifle.

The next thing Morgan was consciously aware of was her rifle clicking on an empty chamber, her magazine empty.

Morgan fumbled at the magazine release, actually dropping the first magazine she pulled. It was quicker to just pull a second one.

It took two tries to slap it in hard enough that the mechanism engaged. Once that was done, Morgan was back to shooting in moments.

There was. . . almost a calmness that came over Morgan. Turn, aim, fire. Wait a moment, then fire again if needed, or turn anew.

A bullet smashed into her chest, driving the breath out of her lungs, but as before it wasn't a penetrator round. All it managed to do was stun her for a moment.

Morgan reached for another magazine, only to come up empty. Grunting she reached down, hunting among the empty magazines and bits of shrapnel and debris for the full one. She found it and slapped it into the well before she realized the sounds had stopped.

Glancing up, Morgan immediately wished she hadn't. The scene of carnage in front of her was beyond description. But she was also relieved – there weren't any pirates standing. Looking around her she saw three of the mercenaries were also down, though two of them looked like they were still alive.

Her hands now shaking, Morgan moved over to the wall, carefully set the rifle down, then slumped down next to it.

She didn't throw up, though she wished she could.

After a minute Marigold came over to her.

"You did well."

"I feel terrible."

"Now, sure. There's nothing wrong with that. In fact it's a good response to a life and death tussle like this one. You acted decisively when it was needed. Most pros freeze up, at least the first time or two."

"If you say so."

"I do. Come on, we'll talk more later, if you'd like. Right now let's go tell your captain that the ship is saved."

"I'd rather just stay here, if I could."

"If you really want to stay here, fine. But I'd like to tell the captain how you helped, and it would be nice if you're there for that."

Morgan thought about telling Marigold that it wouldn't have the effect she expected. It was a nice gesture, though, so Morgan just rose to her feet.

"All right."

The hatch to the bridge had to be pried open manually, only possible once the captain released the locks on her side.

"What did they do to my ship?" the captain demanded once they were inside. She looked quite harried, and Morgan would have sworn there were new lines on her face.

"They took DCC and the secondary environmental plant, as well as most of the quarters. We've reclaimed the first two without serious losses, but the quarters were a delicate situation."

Marigold was quiet for a moment, obviously listening to someone on her suit's com.

"We've confirmed, the ship is now clear. It will take us a while to compile a list of casualties, or for engineering to get a damage report."

"They didn't take the armory? I'm getting all kinds of bizarre messages from that area. At least from the equipment that is still working."

"They tried. They did not get in, thanks in large part to the crewman here."

The captain turned to regard Morgan coolly.

"What are *you* doing here? We don't need a cargo hauler at the moment."

"The lieutenant asked me along."

"Why?"

"Because without her fast action we *would* have lost the armory, and likely would not have stopped them from taking the bridge," Marigold interjected quickly.

"Somehow, I imagine you overstate the case."

"Not at all, ma'am," Hudson spoke up; his voice more respectful than it had been when talking with either Morgan or Marigold. "I was attacked by nearly a dozen pirates at the armory. Without Morgan helping me they would have taken the armory, at least temporarily. If they had the lieutenant would have been hard pressed to stop them. Even if she had stopped them, there would have been casualties."

"We had six people against nearly twenty pirates here. Without Crewman Black that would have been more like three or two, in which case we would have had to wait for the other groups," Marigold gestured to the hallway, "who still haven't arrived."

Morgan considered pointing out that they hadn't arrived because once they'd been told the bridge was secure they had diverted to other areas of the ship, but only for a moment.

"Whatever," the captain said at last, dismissing both of them, turning back to the display in front of her.

Morgan hadn't expected much from the captain, she knew the woman disliked her deeply, even if she didn't know why.

Shaking her head Marigold pointed out to the corridor, turning and walking out followed by Morgan and Hudson.

"Can you come with us back to the armory, Darlin'?" Hudson said quietly, once they were out of earshot of the captain.

"Why?"

"The armory is still open. We need to get that fixed more than just about anything else. You know what you did to the systems, so fixing them will be easier," Marigold clarified.

"I'd like to sleep for a week, but, as you said, what I want is irrelevant."

"Well said."

They were quiet the rest of the way back to the armory, but once they were there the lieutenant pulled Morgan aside.

"I have a proposition for you. You're clearly being wasted as what? A conduit scrubber?"

"Cargo hauling."

"Like I said, a waste. You've shown ingenuity, tenacity, and a cool-head under fire. You also seem to be a good shot. With those you'd do well as a mercenary. Even at your young age you could make officer quickly."

"Ah, sir, you don't ever say such nice things to me," Hudson commented.

A couple of the other mercenaries busy carting off the bodies laughed.

"That's because you're a born corporal, Hudson. Just enough smarts to get yourself in trouble," one of them said.

"Stow the chatter. This is a private conversation."

"What do you say? The pay is good – better than you get now. Better than even what the crew chiefs get, and most of the time it isn't hard. Stuff like today isn't common, not at all. Something like half the mercenaries I know retired without ever firing their weapon outside the range."

"Let me think on it," Morgan said, bending down to pick up one of the empty magazines for her pistol that had been forgotten the first time around.

Chapter 18

Never give up what you want most for what you want right now.
- Fleet Admiral Maxwell, Zion Navy, quoting his ancestor

Gertrude
Four Zion Months Later / Three and a Half Earth Months

Gertrude waited at the dock, without Haruhi. News had been infuriatingly spotty about whatever had happened on the *Fate of Dawn*, but enough had leaked to know that many of the crew had been injured or killed.

That they hadn't called off the rest of the route was almost certainly due to the fact that, given where they had been attacked, it would only have saved a few days anyway, just that needed for loading and unloading cargo. The quickest path back to Parlon was through the very same systems they were delivering to anyway.

Looking about Gertrude saw very few children waiting. The mood was decidedly more somber than it had been when Gertrude's ship had returned, that was sure.

The crowd was also a bit smaller than Gertrude had expected, but she supposed not every family had the strength to come and meet a casket in place of a loved one. No one but family had been told who had died. The ship's captain had forbidden any letters from the crew to keep gossip down. The bitch.

Gertrude could see the others glancing about, and frowning. Unlike her they knew each other, and could see by the absences who some of the casualties must be.

The ship arrived, without fanfare.

"Ship docking complete," the captain said over the intercom. "We will unload as efficiently as we're able." There was a long pause, "We'll unload the caskets first. Please be respectful."

The request was hardly necessary. The lobby was dead silent while the caskets were unloaded, save for someone on the intercom reading off the names.

There were so many, more than even the absences had suggested. Part of Gertrude was amazed the ship had managed to survive with that many dead. Not to mention an untold number of injured. The larger part of her, though? That part was remembering a far smaller gathering, with four sealed coffins draped in flags.

And all of her didn't know what state Morgan was in.

At last the caskets ended, followed by the wounded, walking or otherwise. Gertrude wasn't the only one breathing a quiet sigh of relief. She immediately felt bad about it, given how many others were quietly – and not so quietly – crying, but she pushed through the guilt. She couldn't change what had happened. Not now, and not then.

The rest of the crew started trickling out finally, and to a man they looked exhausted. Given what they'd had to endure to get everyone else back home safely, plus fixing whatever damage there had been and caring for the injured, it was no wonder.

Morgan looked like death warmed over as she staggered out of the airlock tube. Gertrude had seen Morgan after a compound fracture and nearly bleeding to death, and she hadn't looked quite so bad then. She didn't care.

Only respect for the dead kept Gertrude from rushing over to embrace Morgan. She waited until Morgan was a few paces away.

Gertrude lifted Morgan in a tight embrace, which the younger woman returned, albeit not as enthusiastically.

"I'm all right, G, I'm all right."

"What happened? Were you hurt?"

"It's a long story, but part of it is a job offer."

"A job offer? For what?"

"The Aegis Mercenary Company," a voice said from behind them.

"Captain Rain?" Morgan said, incredulously, "News travels fast, then."

"When not blocked by the captain's order, yes, it does," he said. Gertrude put Morgan down and turned to face him. She recognized the captain of *Steve*, but hadn't talked with him herself.

"You didn't take it, did you?" Gertrude asked Morgan. A year ago she would have been sure the answer was no, but she also knew that she hadn't had the easiest time among Captain Bogard's crew, even before a third the crew had ended up injured or dead.

"My info doesn't say. Apparently the captain was less concerned with that than getting you off her crew." Captain Rain was whispering, but even so it was clear there were things he was pointedly not saying.

"I. . . did not," Morgan said. "It was tempting, sure. They get a lot more respect than I did. A lot more money too."

"Indeed. More danger, as well, but given what I've heard I suppose that wouldn't deter you."

"Okay, what happened?" Gertrude demanded, of both of them.

"Pirates, Chief, pirates," Captain Rain answered. "And a bit of crazy quick thinking on our friend's part that very well may have saved the day. It definitely saved some lives, at the very least."

Morgan was blushing so hard that Gertrude could see it, dark skin or no.

"It was nothing."

"It was enough to drive your captain into fits with the aftermath. That alone would have endeared you to me, if I wasn't already so inclined."

"Excuse me, Captain, but why are you here?" Gertrude asked, looking back and forth between the two of them.

"Is it not normal for a captain to welcome back one of his officers, after distinguishing herself so nobly?"

"His what?" Gertrude and Morgan said at the same time.

"Officer. Fourth Lieutenant, to be precise."

"Wait," Morgan said, "*Fourth* Lieutenant? Did you invent a new position while we were out? Our ships only have three."

"Normally, yes," Captain Rain said, nodding, "The Fourth Lieutenant is a training position, there to help the other three with their duties to give them enough extra time to train the new lieutenant on what the job requires. This also lets us be sure the new officer can do the job before putting them actually in charge."

"Isn't that a little too big a jump?" Morgan asked.

"If you think you can't handle it. . ."

"No, no, I'll take it," Morgan quickly said. "What about Gertrude? She still needs my help, and she'll be departing with the *Daystar Fading* in just a few weeks."

Captain Rain waved his hand dismissively.

"We've got that all figured out. We knew this was coming, remember? In four months the *Beacon of Twilight* will be back from its run, a few weeks before *Steve* leaves next. Until then the Chief here will help us get ready and help out while we get you trained on your new duties. I assure you, having the wee one in *Steve*'s daycare a few hours each day will go much better than your other options. If there are any problems we'll deal with them."

"What do you think, G?" Morgan asked.

Gertrude found herself smiling quite widely.

"I think it sounds excellent," she paused for just a moment, winking briefly, "sir."

THE END

ABOUT THE AUTHOR

J. M. Anjewierden spends his days hawking others' books in his job for the Salt Lake County Library System. It's a job he loves, and being able to recommend good books is a big part of that. He has a degree in English from the University of Utah, and nearly a Masters of Library Science from the University of North Texas.

He presently lives in Sandy, Utah with his wife, who is expecting their first child.

The Long Black was his first novel.

Made in the USA
San Bernardino, CA
08 September 2017